IDOL

PAINTED BLIND
PUBLISHING
LITERARY ALCHEMY

PAINTED BLIND
PUBLISHING
LITERARY ALCHEMY

Idol
© 2022 Regina Watts
ISBN: 978-1-957469-02-7

Text: Regina Watts
Book Design: M. F. Sullivan
Cover Art: Dusty Ray

Regina Watts Online: hrhdegenetrix.com
Painted Blind Publishing: paintedblindpublishing.com
Join Regina's mailing list for three free stories!

*For the Divine Master
of all space and time.*

ONE

THE TATTOO TOUCH-UP was just an alibi for obtaining the Rohypnol, but she was still damn proud of how it looked. Rexie had brought her the image in a year-old dream, and a tattoo artist at an expo had brought it to life.

She'd tried to draw it herself, of course, but the results were predictable. It pained Mel to look at her efforts; as if looking at them would erase from her mind the image that had been, in the dream, tattooed over the side of her calf. Thankfully, no matter how bad her drawings were, when she closed her eyes it was still clear.

Time ticking on, Mel was hopeless with frustration until one day, while driving Becky June to work, they saw a billboard printed with the big, bold words: TATTOO EXPO. Talk about signs! Of course, despite her seventeen tattoos of various types and themes, she'd never been to a tattoo expo and had no idea how one worked. Frankly, the idea seemed kind of stupid to her…but how stupid could it really be if she was thinking about going?

The stupid thing wasn't going, it would turn out. The stupid thing was going without trying to book a spot with one of the artists…but, if she had done things properly, she wouldn't have ended up with her tattoo looking as good as it did: and if her tattoo hadn't come out looking so good, well—maybe it was a little far-fetched to say that Melba wouldn't have gone through with the whole operation to get Rexie. But that was how strongly she felt about making the tattoo live up to what she saw in her mind. She was therefore crushed when she got to the expo and realized near all the artists were booked completely, and those that weren't…suffice it to say that they weren't exactly what she was looking for in an artist.

After wandering for a couple of fruitless hours, on the verge of tears for how annoyed she was, she stepped outside to smoke a Kool and toy with the idea of texting Junie to come back and pick her up. Her task was interrupted by the stubbornly impotent clicks of an empty lighter. To her right, there'd been this guy: so tatted he could only be an artist, and so thin he could only be a junkie, recovering or otherwise. But his tattoos looked good, and as she lit his cigarette for him and he graciously thanked her with a doff of his snapback, she said, "I like your ink. You an artist?"

"How'd you guess?"

She smiled a little, crooked like always.

"Probably busy as shit, huh?"

"You don't even know," lamented the man, managing a shake of his head amid the plume of his smoke. "This is the first cigarette break I've had since I got set up."

"Damn, dude." Her phone read noon thirty or so. She puffed her menthol in a second of reflection. "Kinda sucks. A liberating job like a tattoo artist, but no time to smoke."

"Ah, if I really wanted to, I'd take a break. I don't, because I love working. Don't want to interrupt the flow."

"Can I see some of your work?"

She'd expected him to pull out his phone. Instead, he bent at the waist and untucked his cargo pants from his boot. This, he rolled up to reveal, in a miraculous synchronicity, a tattoo placed upon the side of his calf opposite that of Mel's dream tat. The artist's self-rendered work was incredible for somebody who had done it themselves, his snarling bear's dissolution into *Ursa Major* marked by a bloodlike splatter of red and wild linework like what Mel had only seen maybe once, on the Internet, when somebody she knew posted a cool collection of real artsy tattoos.

Junkie for sure. This dude had to at least have a bottle of pain pills somewhere. Took some kind of concentration to tattoo yourself—especially to such detail. Look at that bear! Crouching to examine his leg, she marveled, "Damn, dude! This is dope as hell—I guess you'd call this 'abstract' or something, huh? Man, I ain't never seen nothin' like this before. Not in real life."

"Thanks. Do you know Dr. Woo?" When she shook her head, he rested his cigarette in the corner of his mouth, cracked his neck in a way that stretched the black rose emblazoned upon his throat like it was doing the breathing for him, then got his phone out to show her this L.A. tattoo artist's work. Shit if it wasn't great, though not as great as this guy's. While she was flipping through a gallery he'd pulled up for her, she sighed. "I wish you wasn't booked up—I didn't realize it'd be so crazy here! Don't know why I thought I could just walk in and get my tattoo done."

"What were you thinking about doing?"

When she looked up from his phone to find his dark eyes brightened with curiosity, her stomach produced a flutter of cautious joy. "It's kinda hard to explain...I saw it in a dream one time. I guess it's an abstract tattoo, too." When he was still listening to her babble, she handed him the phone and went on, emboldened. "It's like...like you know one of them models of the universe? With the lines for the planets' orbits, and all?"

"Yeah, sure."

"Kind of like that, but at its center, there's a black hole, and it's also—it's like a diagram of an atom, and also the Kabbalah Tree of Life? So, like, the planets circlin' round this black sun are also, like, electrons, but kinda also Sefirot? Except it only shows five, and two of them are just black dots."

"What's in the other ones?"

"Numbers. The one closest to the sun, I guess that's Mercury, it's 6, and then Venus is 7 and…well, normally Earth would be there, but I don't think it is. Just the black ones and then Saturn—that's 9."

"So it's sodium."

"What?"

"The atom…if the numbers are protons and neutrons, then it's got 22, and that would make it a sodium atom. 'Course, if the numbers are just protons, and the black ones are neutrons, then that'd give it a mass of 24, and make it magnesium. If they're electrons, though, then it's just sodium…since there's nothing in 'em, they're probably electrons."

Laughing a little, she marveled, "You must be smart as hell! Shit, dude, my cousin Junie and I were fallin' asleep during chemistry class."

"I was always really into it. Science and art…but art was easier, I guess. Your tattoo idea sounds really cool."

Junie picked that peachy moment to whizz down the convention center parking lot in their beat-up-ass Oldsmobile, which was in fact old, and Mel resolutely refused to acknowledge her fucking existence. Why couldn't she respond to a text that quickly on a day when Melba actually needed her? Some people.

"Thanks. I'm just sorry you're all booked up! Your style looks just like what I want. I can't draw it myself, and I don't know who can."

"Southern Oregon has a lot of good artists, but I understand."

"Where are you from?"

"San Francisco," he said with a slight, apologetic smile at Mel's sigh of exasperation—for the artist as much as for the friend who pulled up to wait for her. "Yeah, it's probably not fair of me to say all the artists around here are great when I'm from out of town, but…"

"No shit. And I bet you've been all booked up since *last* convention, huh?" At his humble laugh, she shook her head and said, "Well, good talking to you," which was a strategy her Daddy taught her for when business negotiations were almost as good as agreed to and the other person needed a little nudge. Sure enough, as she turned away, the artist said, "Wait a second."

Turning back, Mel watched him snub his cigarette and check his fat smartwatch. "I don't think there's any way in hell I'm going to take a lunch break—at least, not to leave for one. If you can grab me a sandwich or something, and you don't mind kind of a rushed design, I can at least draw it for you while I eat. Maybe if I finish early today I can even get it done, though it'll be a long night for both of us."

"I'll pay you whatever you want," she enthused, refusing to look in the direction of waving, smiling Junie until a short honk elicited a glance sharp enough to wilt her ditzy cousin's happy expression. "Your work is perfect! Ain't nobody I can imagine doing a better job."

This pleased him as much as it did her, because it was the truth. She hadn't been able to imagine anybody on Earth could recreate the tattoo, but it turned out this guy was her man. After Mel and June brought him a big-ass sandwich along with a Coke and a whole big pile of fries, he turned right around and cranked out that drawing in the course of his thirty-minute lunch break.

Damned if it didn't look almost better than she remembered! A little different, of course—that was always the way with things like that—but when she looked at it, it made her heart skip a beat. It made her feel like Rexie was there with her already. To celebrate, the cousins waited out the rest of the expo by going to the theater and watching Rexie's current movie. Junie didn't even protest too much, though she did look around for cops.

Junie was too paranoid. It wasn't no big deal. The Rudolph Valentino biopic was still in post-production, so the best Mel could do was getting her cousin to buy them dollar tickets to what by then surely was the last week of *Happy Birthday*. It was a comedy movie where he only had a tiny background part, and he was its only saving grace. By the time Rexie had delivered his punchline and made his last appearance, the expo was wrapping. Mel jostled Junie awake and the two of them returned to the eerie, emptying convention center.

While other exhibitionists cleaned up, the artist worked hard into the night and the convention hall was moderately understanding. By the time it was finished around eleven at night, everything about it was perfect. At home, as she smoothed a thin layer of ointment across its surface, she whispered, "Isn't it beautiful, Rexie?" It was much more beautiful once it healed. It also needed a little bit of touching up, and that was how Mel got the idea for the alibi she'd need if she and Rexie decided to have their honeymoon in the consensus reality. Paid for three nights at the hotel, stayed one. Nobody could kidnap somebody visiting Oregon while they were in the Bay Area.

Besides: that tattoo really did need to look its best.

After having her artist fix the darkness of the lines around the three numbered planets, she took a picture and sent it to everybody she knew. Most women were like that with engagement rings, she thought with a giddy thrill. While settling into her car, her phone buzzed with hearts and smiley faces and other little emoticons sent to her by approving former colleagues and those old pre-medication buddies who regarded her as safe to interact with since they were still in

Tennessee and she and Junie were living all the way up in Oregon. She felt similarly toward them.

She got homesick sometimes, but it was for the best. Rexie had been very firm with her on the subject: no more drugs. If she did any more, they wouldn't be able to go away together. She could never stand to let that happen. She was being good, and not due to the demands of that cracker-plain Alabama transplant, Patricia Sunday, who called Melba's phone while she was trapped in the northbound commute of San Francisco workers for whom getting home early meant they only had to drive an hour instead of two. Disappointed to turn down Guns N' Roses and answer it, she put on the cute voice while tapping her speakerphone button on the face of the phone.

"Heya, Patty. Sorry on account of the speakerphone, I'm drivin' right now."

She had hoped that would be enough to encourage her parole officer to hang up, since Melba was endangering public safety by distracted driving and all, but nothing was enough to deter Miss Sunday when she felt she had reason for some good-old-fashioned bird-dogging.

"Hello, Melba"—she was using her friendly voice—"pretty tattoo!"

"Thank you!" Behind the big sunglasses she bought because they made her look like the sheriff of beauty queens, Mel wiggled her eyebrows and rolled down the window to light a cigarette. "I sure do appreciate you making it so easy for me to stay out of town. This tattoo means so much to me."

"I won't pretend to understand, but it's about the nicest tattoo I think I've seen. You picked up your medication before you left town, right?"

Mel rolled her eyes, cheek propped against her fist as the car jerked forward. "Yes ma'am."

"Good girl," said the woman, her husky voice laden with maternal approval. "And you're gonna be back in town in time for our meetin' on Wednesday?"

"Oh, yes, ma'am, yes. I'm coming right back after I stay the weekend in San Jose."

"San Jose! What's in San Jose?"

"Cheaper hotels than San Francisco and the best donuts you've ever had in your life, ma'am."

"You gonna bring some back for me?"

With a wry grin, Mel said, "I would, ma'am, but it's a long drive from San Jose to Medford, and a girl gets hungry."

"I can't blame you." Patricia's next word was obscured by a beep, and her whole next sentence was obscured by the rush of adrenaline because the word 'Junebug' flashed on her screen. All Melba could think thereafter was the phrase "Get off the phone," and at such a furious rate that she didn't even realize she'd been asked a question until Patty was saying, "...all right?"

"All right"—get off the phone—"but, um—"

"No 'buts.' Nothing about waking me up or none of that. My phone is always open."

Divining through this that Patty had told her to call her if she needed to talk or otherwise met some temptation while in the Bay Area, Melba suppressed an eye roll. "Yes, ma'am, I only mean—" She missed Junie's call and clenched her teeth. "There's an accident up ahead here, ma'am, and I have to pay attention."

"Okay, sugar, you drive safe. Don't do anything I wouldn't do."

"Yes ma'am, thank you, have a good day..."

The singing notes of her words dropped flat once the phone beeped to signal the call had ended.

"Fuckin' piece-a shit old cop."

Melba shifted her cigarette between her fingers to take up the phone and call Junie back, meaning she had some little bitch try to sneak into her lane while she wasn't paying attention. Almost dented a damn bumper in her effort to retain her precious space in the dense California traffic.

"Fuck this city," she added to herself the very second Junie picked up.

"Everything all right," Melba asked before her cousin could say anything. "Did you get our cabin?"

"Oh, yeah, it's real nice—"

Mel's heart throbbed. She leaped in her seat and gave a joyous whoop: a noise containing every dream she had ever had, every imagining, every private visit and phone call and everything that Rexie had done to court her like the gentleman he was. She was so overwhelmed with that outburst of joy that not even Junie's next concern could touch her.

"I just, uh, I just happened to notice when I's packing up my toiletries that you left your pill bottles here."

"Uh-huh."

"During your trip to get the tattoo, I mean."

Melba didn't reply.

Junie's palpable anxiety forced her to change the subject for at least a moment. "How's it *look*, by the way?"

"Better'n I dreamed it."

"That's good! That's real good. I can't wait to see it."

A few seconds of hesitation.

Come on, bitch! Say it.

"It's just—it's just, there's an awful lot of pills here, Mel."

"So?"

"So…so, I don't know. I guess I'm—I guess I'm just worried."

Her hands tightened around the steering wheel, the narrow spires of her knuckles whitened by the possibility that Becky June was about to get on her case when she was feeling so damn good.

"You know that shit turns me into a fucking zombie, Junie."

"I know—but—"

"You want me to be a fuckin' zombie on our lake vacation?"

"Well, of course not—only, it's just—"

"God damn it, Junie, it's always *just* something with you. Take a fuckin' position and defend it!"

"I only mean that it's dangerous. You have to take your pills, Mel! The doctor said, and the judge. Suppose Patty comes by and counts them?"

This was the kind of shit Rexie warned her about. When he said nobody would understand, he meant it. Nobody: not even his other self understood it, or remembered it consciously, at least. Although Melba did not always comprehend the logic of his commands, she believed one hundred and twenty percent every word that came out of Rex Virgil's perfect mouth and settled telepathically into her head. All this fussing about pills was some kind of test—a test of her faith, or of her strength of will. A test of her obedience.

Whatever it was, it was for Rexie to know for sure, and for Mel to heed. It was *certainly* not for Junie to question one way or another.

"If you're worried about Patty comin' by, check the date on the bottle and flush a few accordingly. I ain't takin' no god-damn pills before our lake time, June."

"Okay," said her wary cousin, rolling over as always. "I guess I'm just nervous, is all."

"Don't be. We're fixinta have a great weekend, Junie, I promise. No work, all play. Pick up a couplea cute redneck fellas hangin' around the barbeque and boost our morale."

Junie laughed despite herself. "I love you, Melba."

"I love you, Becky June. Hey, speaking of Pat…"

And that was that. With a little more wiggling off the hook, Melba soon dropped the line. Freedom! Fuck that damn phone. She settled back into her seat to turn on the radio again. As the constipated traffic crawled along (what did you know but there really was a big old wreck on the shoulder of the highway) toward expansion into a more acceptable number of lanes, the music turned out to be over. Melba sucked her tooth at the voice of Ted Dormant, Junie's favorite crazy tele- (and radio-)vangelist.

"Jesus Christ made it very clear in the Bible. There's no mystery here, folks! Here, in black-and-white, "Jesus answered: 'I am the way and the truth and the *life!*'""

A cheer arose in the background. Melba, annoyed at Miss Sunday for making her bump Junie's station while scrambling for the volume knob, passed the meandering old fart in front of her and tried to turn the radio back to her music. "*No* one comes to the Father except through—'"

Except through the most bitchin' guitar solo of the world's favorite Lynyrd Skynyrd song, which replaced Dormant's screeching pitch and elicited a giddy noise of delight from the back of Mel's throat.

Rexie had told her once that it was a song about her— that *many* songs were about her, love songs he had inspired long before she was born to celebrate the eternal love that was the secret between the two of them. But she didn't always *feel* that they were about her. Not like this. Not like in this moment, drumming her hands on the wheel, her heart racing with delight.

Shit! She wasn't even to Winters yet, and she was this amped! The knowledge that Rexie's real, flesh-and-blood hand waited for her a mere six hours away was better than any dopamine receptor-flooding drug.

Yeah, baby, it was going to be a good weekend. She wasn't sure how she'd play off the coincidence to Junie, but once they were both up there and settled into the cabin, there wouldn't be a problem. Junie wouldn't turn around once everything was set for the weekend. She wouldn't interfere at all.

Mel was so excited, and her own heartbeat was so loud in her ears, that she almost missed the cell phone's third ring. It was softer and different from the rest, and her phone's screen did not illuminate. This was sometimes a problem with Rexie's calls, but also with her Daddy's calls—and always on those rare, ugly days the phone would just ring and ring and ring and ring and ring and ring and ring and ring and nobody would ever be there.

But today! Today: Rexie was calling her. She knew it with a flutter before she even picked up the phone. Her hands were more responsive now, her whole body eager to hear his voice.

"Hello?"

She breathed the word in the quiet of the car, listening, waiting. As often happened when she answered his calls from the car, his voice emitted from the radio.

"You're ain't really gonna take them pills, are you?" His voice was tinny: hard to make out against the gentle background of static and garbled conversation. It were as if he called her from a room full of a great many people and all of them spoke at once: some at various volumes among themselves, some to Rexie, some at her, although she could not always discern their words. Just a problem with the radio; some crossed station.

"No! Hell no, Rexie, of course not. I never will again. You know I promised."

"I know you did, because you're my good girl."

Her face warm, she glanced out the window to see if any other driver nearby was paying attention. In a moment like this she always worried other radios were picking up their private conversation. Nothing was really private in this crazy world. "I can't wait to see you, Rexie."

"You're gonna have to be patient. You know how hard it will be to get through to me."

"I do. I promise, Rexie, I won't give up. I've waited too long for this. For you."

"The whole world wants you to be scared that the things you know to be true might be false. The Gray Man wants you to live in terror. But I'm here to tell you, baby: if you believe in me, and do what you're supposed to—you and me? We'll be together forever."

Her heart throbbed in her chest so hard that it almost hurt her. She thought briefly about pulling off to the side of the road to catch her breath, but he told her, "No, don't pull off. Keep going, baby. Come see me."

"I just don't want some accident on the way," she said, half-laughing but really very afraid that might be the case.

His voice gentled up a little.

"Now, baby, you know I ain't ever gonna let a thing like that happen to you. And anyway, you can't pull off before you seen your surprise."

"Oh, surprise! What kind of surprise?"

"You gotta wait and see, baby. Now, mind you don't act too excited when you get home, or else Junie's going to get suspicious. You know when you get too excited everybody can hear your thoughts—just relax."

"How am I going to avoid being excited once we're there, though? Oh, Rexie, I can't hardly wait."

"Just think about something else. Repeat my lines to yourself. That's safe."

Nodding, Mel exhaled, looked at the radio as it uttered the word "Stupid," and told him, "You gotta get nicer friends, Rexie."

"Keep repeating my lines if you don't want everyone to know your thoughts," was all he said.

The line went dead. With an audible whine, Mel reached forward, twisted the knob of the radio, and only ended up blasting "Ace of Spades" by Motorhead.

Damn! She hated, hated how quickly he came and went sometimes. Oh…well, she shouldn't have ever thought the word 'hate' along with anything about her Rexie, but damned if she didn't get frustrated every time he flew off. What she wanted was a nice, extended length of time with him all to herself, but no amount of time would ever be enough. Yes— they could have eternity together and she would still want more. She would still be caused physical pain by the memory of all the time they were forced to spend apart. All the time the world spent calling her crazy.

But she wasn't crazy. Nobody understood her, was all. Maybe if she took more time to read some high falutin Old English treatise written by ye olde alchymists or whatever, she could have discovered some way of contextualizing her thoughts. What kind of nerd had time for something like that, though? Mel barely had time to stay caught up with Netflix.

The truth was obvious to her, anyway, and that was all that mattered. There was no convincing anybody else of any kind of truth. Hell! Mel wasn't much of a Christian anymore, but look at what they did to Jesus. What'd that poor old son-of-a-bitch say stuck up on that cross? "Forgive them, Father, they know not what they do."

No. Nobody knew what they were doing when they did the things they did to Mel. Nobody understood that, because of the way Rexie's soul had been corrupted by coming into Earth, his linear self just couldn't *remember* the love he had for Mel. That was all. That was all.

The cops, the judge, the doctors, everybody really meant well. They thought they were doing her a favor because they were all also trapped in the planetary flesh machine that the Devil had constructed to keep them away from unity with God. Oh, they were far from innocent, these passive helpers, these empty vessels waiting to be filled by infernal designs: but they weren't intentionally malicious. Not in a way that could have been helped. They were just people who were lacking a certain something. A spark; that Rexie spark. That ability to see the connectivity behind all things.

Who could see the things she saw and help themselves but believe in Rexie, after all? For instance, he'd promised her a gift: and by God, it was a gift she received. She gasped in absolute delight, recognizing the faded yellow of its background from a mile away.

Melba slowed in order to linger just a minute. Appreciate it from the shoulder of 5.

There he was.

Third from the left in the second row, head just overlapping with the 'B' of *Happy Birthday!* The billboard was long overdue for being pulled. In fact, Mel hadn't seen one of this design for at least a couple months. She bit her lip, grinning up at this color-bled icon, his black hair and roguishly cocked brow faded by the sun but so much more alive than the other actors on the billboard. What a stupid pose! Didn't you hate having to work on such a stupid movie, Rexie? Didn't you feel alone with all these empty faces around you?

It was okay. Melba would make it all okay.

Warm with joy, she hit the gas and drove on toward her weekend plans.

TWO

ONE OF THE things Mel loved about Junie was that, if Mel waited long enough to perform a certain task—for example, packing for their trip—Junie would get so nervous she'd finally just do it all herself. Having Becky June for what the courts called a "caregiver" was sort of like having a live-in servant, which was nice on the one hand but annoying on the other. For instance, when she walked into their squalid studio apartment, eager to show Junie her tattoo, Melba was greeted not by her cousin but by the angry orange pill bottle waiting on the prepacked luggage.

"Junie, what the fuck!"

"Oh, Mel—Mel"—the mousy, high-strung woman came rushing from the short hallway/storage area adjoining their living room/bedroom/kitchen and the bathroom that was by that point past all saving—"don't be mad at me, Mel—"

"I'll be mad if I feel like it. What are these doing here?"

"I just thought—well, you know, these sorts of drugs take a few days to kick in, so…so if you start taking them now, you'll still have a good weekend! By the time the week has started, your pills will be working again."

"And I'll be a zombie just in time for Monday." Disgusted, Melba threw down her overnight bag with one hand while snatching up the pill bottle with the other. They rattled while she shoved past Junie, who cried out and hurried after with a steel grip of Mel's hand.

"Don't, Mel! Don't throw them out—"

"You fucking drama queen! I'm putting them away."

Although Junie relaxed, she still insisted on following Mel to the bathroom as if to supervise. How many parole officers did Melba have?

"I'm sorry your pills make you feel fuzzy, Mel. Maybe next time you see the doctor you could tell him! He could try something else."

"Like hell…*all* these pills make me feel 'fuzzy.' And I hate it when you call it that…it makes me think of dogs. Cats. Nice shit, in other words—and this ain't nice shit." Mel slammed the pills back on their shelf and banged the medicine cabinet shut so hard that its mirrored door bounced off its magnetic latch and swung wide again. Her eyes fell on the bottle and

DON'T TAKE THE PILLS

DON'T

DON'T

DON'T DO IT

YOU KNOW THAT THEY'RE

JUST

POISON.

"I'm not taking the fucking pills," Mel assured the voice as much as June. "And that's that."

"Well…I suppose as long as you're feeling all right, that's all that matters."

It was obvious the discussion didn't go as planned. For a few seconds, Becky June looked crestfallen: then, as usual, she abandoned the thoughts of disappointment. Couldn't stand to feel a negative emotion for more than five seconds. With a sudden look of bright, almost canine joy, Junie clasped her hands together and asked, "Oh, but Mel, aren't you excited for the lake? I'm so happy we got a cabin! It's awful busy this time of year."

Remember: remember not to get too excited. Try not to get excited at all, in fact. It was safer that way. Shrugging meekly, Mel slipped past June, belatedly removed her shoes, said, "Yeah, should be nice. I could use the time off…nothing to do…space to breathe…"

While she spoke, Mel squeezed past June and returned to the cramped living area. There, she stood with her hands on her hips and a grim assessment of the room around. "Junie, I thought you said you'd clean up the house while I was out. It looks like shit in here."

"I'm sorry, Melba, I really tried…but the vacuum cleaner's busted, and I had to work all day yesterday, and—"

"Jesus! Fine, take care of it when we get back…hate leaving the place behind looking like this, but it is what it is."

With a sniff, Mel unzipped her luggage and flipped it open to inspect Junie's packing job. Not half-bad. She even remembered a bathing suit, and the portable Bluetooth speaker that Mel took out of its cozy nook among her clothes.

"I still need this for tonight," she said, "but other than that, good job." As June beamed amid what amounted to praise, Melba pulled out her phone to put on a little background music and ease her mind—and to give her something to do to look casual while she told Junie, "I skipped lunch today on the way back home. You wanna grab us an early dinner?"

"Oh, that sounds good, but—"

"It's my treat," Mel assured her before she could express her concerns about having already spent her money for the month on going halfsies for the cabin. While June's eyes lit up, Mel shrugged and said, "Like I told you, I missed lunch today. Can't stand to have that cash burning a hole in my pocket.

After setting down her phone and rustling through her purse, Mel produced $40 and passed the two crisp twenties to June. "How about you get me a burger and fries…oh, and a chocolate shake…and why don't you stop off on the way to get us some beers for the trip?"

She paused, added her second-to-last (ever?) twenty to June's hand, and put her wallet away again. While her purse dropped onto the floor, Mel flopped back upon the unmade bed with a hefty sigh. "Don't take too long, Junie. I'm already exhausted from the drive today. If I'm going to pull off another one tomorrow, I'm due an early bedtime."

"I'll be back A-S-A-P," assured Junie with a cheerful little salute. After getting on her shoes, however, she hesitated to exit the squalid apartment and instead hurried back to Mel's side.

"I missed you," June said, embracing her cousin and kissing her cheek.

Patting Junie with the same fondness a tired parent had for their least despised child, Mel told her, "I'll admit it, Junie—I like my life a whole lot better when you're around."

June smiled and bounded out the door. Her merry steps clopped along the breezeway until muted by the grass.

Melba sprang up and dashed to work, adrenaline pumping through her to dispel any hint of genuine exhaustion.

First thing she did was take care of those fucking pills. The other stuff was important, but the pills were a detail Melba couldn't forget. Checking the date on the bottle against the date on the calendar, she shook the difference into her hand and tossed the mean little bastards into the toilet. She had three such bottles to be properly reduced and, when they were gone, she flushed the toilet, washed her hands and went on to the next issue.

The 8½ by 11 script fit neatly upon her clothes in the suitcase, thin enough to avoid deforming the exterior. The ropes, which would hopefully be unnecessary but were better had and not needed than needed and not had, were notable enough from outside the sealed bag that she had to remove an extra shirt Junie had packed.

And the drugs, hidden in the bottom of her purse and picked up while in San Jose, were easy enough to slip in her pocket or keep in a compartment of her bag until required.

The final accoutrement—the camcorder—was not as easy to conceal, but easier to excuse. Why shouldn't they want to immortalize their first vacation since Mel's release from prison? Seemed the perfect thing. Instead of worrying about hiding it, Mel put the camcorder battery on the charger and set the device's bag atop her resealed suitcase.

When June and Mel sat on the futon beside the bed (many could not see the point in having one of each, especially in such a small apartment, but Mel couldn't sleep on the uncomfortable non-mattress so it was therefore relegated to a cheap couch) and ate dinner twenty minutes later, June smiled to see the black battery on the end table.

"Are we bringing the camera? I ain't seen you even look at that darn thing for months, Melba."

Shrugging, Melba licked her fingers, plucked up a few more fries and said, "Just figured it was a good time."

After wiping her hand on a napkin, June patted her cousin's knee and said earnestly, "I'm really proud of you, Melba. You've been doing so good since you got out, I—I'm just happy."

Melba rolled her eyes slightly at the praise…especially since she knew better. If Junie had the least inkling of what Mel was up to, she never would have agreed to rent the damn cabin. As a general rule, Mel didn't worry about things like lying—but she had to admit she felt a little bad for deceiving Junie, who was just so innocent and trusting.

It wasn't the lie that made Melba feel bad, though. It was having to pretend like Rexie wasn't the whole damn world to her. She wasn't allowed to speak the truth of her soul: to express the reality functioning behind the scenes of this one.

Sometimes Mel thought about Christian martyrs and really got worried about having to pretend like Rexie didn't mean nothing to her no more. So many of people went to their graves because they wouldn't deny Christ, and they were rewarded for it their steadfast spirit. Would Rexie punish her for denying him to all these people?

"You know I'd never do that to you, sugar."

The television glowing before them had changed from Junie's favorite sitcom to a commercial staring Rex. It must have been consensually real on some level, because Junie tensed up so sharp that she elbowed Mel in the ribs. While sitting at a table sipping coffee with a sigh of appreciation, Rex continued in a way that only Mel could hear—a way that did not match the pattern of his lips, incredibly.

"Just because the Good Lord rewards somebody, that don't immediately mean He'll punish somebody else. Don't forget: whatever I tell you to do is right. If I tell you to pretend to be normal, you just keep pretending."

She almost—almost—answered him out loud, because she had fallen back into the habit while alone in San Jose. Instead, glancing over at Junie's nervous stare into and beyond the screen, Mel forced herself to pick up the remote and change the station.

June's body relaxed. She smiled, took a bite of her burger, and, thank God, she said nothing about any of it. Instead it seemed her mind turned to other matters that, while distressing to them both in various ways, were nonetheless safer to think about than Melba's relapse into what was diagnosed as schizophrenia. Her smile grew sad.

"Guess it's a relief that we don't have to find somebody to watch the cat while we're gone."

Poor June. A genuine pang of guilt struck Mel in the chest. She continued watching the screen while settling on the food channel. "I guess."

"I miss him so much, Melba—oh, but—" With a fearful, sad little gasp, Junie looked up at her cousin. "What if he comes home while we're not here?"

Melba shut her eyes.

"That'd be a damn shame," she said at last, polishing off the last bites of her burger and dusting off her hands. "Maybe you should leave out a little food while we're gone."

Nodding, Junie said, "That's a good idea," and whisked away her cousin's trash along with her own. Melba sat there on the futon, idly wiping a red ketchup smear from the heel of her palm. When Junie returned, still with that beautiful smile, Melba smiled back but barely.

"What's wrong, Mel?"

"Nothing," said Melba. "Just feel bad about your cat, is all."

"He's *our* cat, silly. and he'll be back someday. Just wait… I'll bet you anything he's just on an adventure somewheres."

Junie! Oh, Becky June. Mel's heart broke when she thought about it all too long. How optimistic Junie was, and how wrong she was sometimes. How wrong she was about the cat—how wrong she was about Mel.

But some things were just too complicated to explain to somebody so soft-hearted. Junie couldn't take certain truths. When it came to Mel's condition, Junie wouldn't be able to understand or respect everything it implied. She would see the point of the weekend—and the implements that were designed to facilitate it in case truth proved insufficient—and would panic. She would call the doctor, and the doctor would call the parole officer, and Patty would call the cops, and then it would be goodbye, blue sky.

Sometimes, it was just easier to lie.

An hour or so later, while the cousins inhabited their distant edges of the full-size mattress, Melba turned the music down and put in her wireless earbud. As the music synched with the small device, she patted June's shoulder and told her, "Good night, Mrs. Cleaver."

Giggling, Junie shook her head and turned over to face the back of the futon. "Nighty-night, Melba…I'm glad you're home."

"Me, too," Melba said softly, although this was yet another lie, sort of. After turning out the bedside lamp precariously perched upon the edge of a low-set bookshelf overflowing with magazines and tarot guides, Melba settled down upon her side in the direction opposite Junie. She couldn't sleep if she didn't face the door: not even with medication. Without meds? Forget it.

Arms folded across her chest, Pink Floyd softly reciting the comforting disintegration of the greatest rock opera yet to be produced by Melba's lifetime, the elder cousin tried to tell herself that the door was locked. Most assuredly locked, and yet

IT'S OPEN

THE DOOR IS OPEN

WIDE OPEN

AND PATTY KNOWS

ALL ABOUT THE DRUGS YOU FLUSHED

SHE KNOWS

No, she doesn't.

SHE KNOWS

AND SHE HAS SENT POLICE

TO COLLECT BLOOD SAMPLES

FROM THE TATTOO PARLOR'S NEEDLES

DOWN IN SAN JOSE

YOU'RE FUCKED

AND ANY MINUTE

OFFICERS WILL COME IN

WITH KNIVES

AND SLIT YOUR

Melba hopped out of bed and hurriedly checked the lock on the burnished chrome doorknob affixed to their door. She unlocked it, proving it was locked, and reached out to lightly rattle the knob of the external security door. That was locked, too.

Quickly, before anyone could find her there, she shut the wooden front door, locked it, unlocked it and re-locked it again just to be sure, then made her slightly steadier way back to bed. Hesitating, she instead crossed around it and repeated this routine with the slider to the back patio. There were no windows in the bathroom, but she did try the one in the kitchen. Just to make sure she could get some sleep.

To no avail.

There was no sleep for Mel tonight. Too much anticipation flooded the molecules of her body. She trembled enough to move the bed across the floor. Miraculous that Junie was able to sleep at all; but, used to Melba's ways, she was contentedly dozing by the time Mel had returned from what Junie often referred to as "the nightly patrol."

"I sure do feel safe with you," Junie remarked happily once, meaning it with genuine kindness.

Mel wasn't so sure that she should.

He came in around eleven. Usually, he waited until midnight to see if she was awake…but he was cheating tonight. She felt him slither into the room like a cold, humid terror: some kind of oozing fish whose noxious presence was felt before seen.

Mel refused to look. She squeezed her eyes shut and took a small breath. She held it.

He made his slow, agonizing way to her side. The penetration of his stare was so vulgar, so intense, that if he had any orifices or organs at all she would have thought of him as some sort of sexual creep.

But he didn't want that gratification.

Even after all these years, Mel just didn't understand what he—it—wanted.

The towering figure bent over her. She felt the stoop as one felt the nearness of a parent bowing to kiss a young, sleepy self. Melba lay as still as was humanly possible, willing her trembling to cease. It had never attacked her, but still the entity seemed somehow to Melba like a wild animal. It certainly had an ability to persuade that frightened her.

The nearness inspired another wave of cold trembling: this, out of pure fear.

Her pursuer drew closer, closer still. The horrific thing seemed, as always, poised to touch her if she did not look.

So, tears streaking down her cheeks, she opened her eyes.

Nothing was there.

THREE

MELBA PARKED IN the gravel lot at Lake of the Woods and rested her head against the seat with a sigh. Her eyes shut behind Junie's borrowed sunglasses, where Rex was singing a song about swan-divers that she would never remember and never hear again.

"We oughta go swimming this time, Mel!"

She barely heard that, either. The drive wasn't an exceptionally hard one—in fact, it was soothing. But, from the moment they got in the car, something had felt—off. Melba realized after ten minutes that she had forgotten her sunglasses, which was a real pain in the ass. The rest stop had been closed, too. Junie'd had to take a piss on the side of the highway while Mel squinted down the black road. When her cousin got back in the car and rinsed her hands with the remains of a water bottle, Mel forced her to yield her tea shades as a form of payment for the embarrassing inconvenience and the dangers presented by sitting on the side of the highway. Just asking for a cop to show up.

Or something worse.

As the drive went on and, in her groove, Mel put on a little music, it occurred to her that it was not the trip itself that felt wrong. On the contrary, Mel felt freer than ever when careening down the highway with "Pinball Wizard" blasting and Junie singing along just a little off-key.

Yet a dark cloud still seemed to stretch across the horizon. The sky was clear: but, in Mel's head, a cold bell rang the alarm that signaled an oncoming hurricane.

"You know *he's* gonna be here, too. Right, sugar?"

While June climbed out of the car, Mel glanced into the rearview mirror. Shards of Rexie were there. He lifted his eyebrows at her. Expected a response.

"Hell. Yeah…I know."

"Now, don't be so distraught…Gray Man's just a fact of life, Melba. Like storms and shits."

Mel rolled her eyes and turned in her seat to address him properly. He was gone, of course. Typical…but it was always comforting to know he was jangling about somewhere in this higher, disparate form.

"You sure you're feelin' okay, Mel?" Junie paused by the driver's side door, already pulling her suitcase along as Mel extricated herself from both the car and a fugue of unpleasant thoughts.

"I just didn't sleep too much last night. You know how I get before a trip."

Melba knew a whole hell of a lot about this place accounting to her research, so when the lady in the central cabin signed out the keys and proceeded to try and elaborate on things like the barbeque that happened every Friday, Melba cut her off by claiming she'd been to the resort as a kid. Then, more graciously accepting the directions to their cabin, Mel bid the lady good-day and led her cousin back out to the blue sky.

Really was a cute, cozy little place. Not the glamorous spot you'd expect a celebrity to summer, which was probably what attracted Rexie to it.

"Sheesh, Mel, this place is gorgeous! Where'd you find it!"

"Just some magazine," commented Melba, scanning the landscape in search of that stimulating spark that would wake her soul up from the first glimpse. That was what she wanted: to wake up inside herself. To stop this restlessness and shrug off the Gray Man's hideous cloud like an optional cloak. Who needed a cloak on a beautiful day like today?

GET INSIDE

GET INSIDE

GET INSIDE

GET

Mel ground her teeth at the chorus of demands. By peering across the sparkling waters of the eponymous lake, she tried to focus on tangible reality like what all her therapists told her to do. It must have been real easy for *them* to focus on tangible, consensual sensory information. They would say things like, "Pay attention to everything happening inside your body. Touch the grass and feel as many things as you can about it. Is it sharp? Dull? Flat, round? Wet? Rough? Smooth? How does it smell? How many blades can you count?"

But when Mel tried to think about things like that—when she tried to focus on anything, really—Rexie would take advantage of the stillness to talk to her a little bit. To fill her mind and her heart with his voice and make her feel less alone. Less scared all the damn time.

He was too good for her…it was nice to have his company. She wasn't stupid, of course. She knew that his presence meant she was ill by any legal or medical definition, but that was only what some old white dudes said while writing a textbook half a century ago. They weren't inside of Mel. They didn't understand the way everything came together for her when she listened to what Rexie said—and the things that happened when she didn't.

Lake of the Woods was—appropriately, given its generic name—in the middle of nowhere, a cluster of Lincoln Log cabins interspersed throughout an exquisite forest of redwoods, Douglas firs and an assortment of beautiful forest ferns. There was something almost primordial about the environment. Mel expected some kind of dinosaur to appear from the underbrush.

No, no lizards. Only people, and one tawny dog that bounded up with a happy bark. Not so much as a collar, let alone a damn leash.

"Buster! Heel!"

Somebody whistled in the distance. Before it could spring up and lay its muddy paws on Junie, the brute (well-trained, if nothing else) wheeled about and loped back to its master.

Melba looked the guy—scrawny, covered in disjointed and faded tattoos, hair too thin and facial hair too wispy—up and down. Like the hillbilly Sherlock Holmes, she read him in a second: Has at least tried meth and/or heroin and probably still knows where to score; Has at least one form of hepatitis; Has at least thought about punching a girlfriend or female relative, and is highly likely to have actually done so.

"Sorry 'bout that," said the guy. "He just gets a little excited, 'sall. Buster's a ladies' man, aintcha boy?"

"That's all right." Laughing, her eyes glowing bright with the pure, innocent animal-love that made her seem at least a decade younger than she was, Junie admired the pooch. "He's so *handsome*! Is he a pit bull?"

"Mix," said the guy, slapping his dog on the haunch a few affectionate times before picking up a nearby stick and tossing it away a few yards. As Buster bounded after it, his owner continued, "His mom's a—golden retriever."

Sweeping his blue-tinted sunglasses to the top of his prematurely thinning head, the guy offered his hand. "I'm Taylor."

"Nice to meet you! I'm Becky June, and this over here's

my cousin, Melba"—who was feeling very impatient and not shy about showing it. "You here by yourself?"

"Me? Nah, nah, I'm here with my sister and her friend. I was thinkin' 'bout gettin' sweet with her—the friend, of course—but"—he grinned in a way that made Mel roll her eyes while Junie blushed like a complete idiot—"well, you never do know when a better thing's gonna come along and interrupt your plans."

"That's great," said Melba, dragging her suitcase off the path and down the grass to discourage the guy from walking with them. "Hope y'all have a good time over here. We'll be in cabin 13, which is…"

"Oh! Right next door." Smiling in a mockery of pleasantness, clearly able to tell the difference between a woman who liked him and a woman who instantly hated his guts, Taylor took the stick from his mongrel's jaws and threw it off into the distance. "Guess we'll be seeing a lot of each other, huh?"

Mel said nothing, already several yards away. Junie responded in the happy affirmative and sprang off after her cousin, her face still aglow with the thrill of attention.

Why was Junie like this? It boggled the mind. It wasn't like attention from either sex was rare. June was a cute, slim woman with long, usually ponytailed hair that, Mel knew from a lifetime of dealing with her own, men and women both wanted to grab and pull and bury their faces in. Consequently, Junie got hit on all the time: at least as much as Melba, if not more. But, unlike Melba, Junie always seemed to want to do more than just play along. It was like she *bought* it—every sweet nothing and cheesy one-liner!—and that quite frankly scared the shit out of Melba. Was it any wonder they lived together? Caregiving went both ways. Had to keep an eye on her baby cousin…without Mel around, June was bound to get into trouble.

Plus, well…Junie had plenty of benefits to Mel, too.

Cabin 13 was a small box from the outside, and from the inside. When Mel referred to these buildings as being like Lincoln Logs, she meant they were *literally* like Lincoln Logs. As in, built in the style that the popular children's' toy emulated. Round logs, green roofs, tiny little window with cartoonish crossbars dividing the panes, bright red doors into every little hut.

"I *love* this place," Junie yammered in delight, beaming to admire the structure while her cousin rattled the key into the lock. The door stuck a bit but gave with a push. It swung wide enough to reveal a dim, small, cluttered cabin that was so busy Mel almost didn't see the Gray Man facing the corner.

While she jolted back from the threshold as though the door had electrocuted her, oblivious Junie marched right in with her bag rolling behind her. "Wowee! There's a tub right here in the open room? Gosh…guess this is kinda meant for lovers, huh, Mel?"

"Something like that." Her mumble had to be maintained at a low volume: both to avoid aggravating the faceless, seven-foot entity and to keep from giving into the impulse to scream.

She hadn't been expecting him so soon somehow.

TOLD YOU

TOLLED YOU

THE FERRYMAN IS HERE

LAKE OF THE WOODS

THIS IS NOT A LAKE

ALL LAKES ARE THE SAME

ONE RIVER

Averting her eyes from the still demon around whom Junie effortlessly worked, opening blinds and turning on lights and pulling back the quilted bedspread, Mel edged into the cabin and tried to admire the deer head displayed on the wall. Reminded her of being a kid…except—

"Hell," said Mel, so surprised she momentarily forgot about her pursuer. "That damn thing's made of plastic!"

"Oh, gosh, it *is!*" Laughing, Junie paused to lean back against the rustic wooden frame of the bed. "Isn't that the funniest darn thing! Like the real ones aren't spooky enough…"

Shaking her head, Junie trotted into the bathroom and shut the door behind her.

The Gray Man shuddered, its head rocking back and forth upon the column of its too-long neck.

"Get the fuck out of here," whispered Melba harshly, forcing herself to stare the heinous thing down. Just doing so left her out of breath. Her heart pounding, Melba clenched her hands in fists at her side and stepped a little farther into the cabin. "You know damn well you ain't welcome in any house of mine—especially not now. Hell! This ain't even *my* house. Don't seem right for you to be breaking and entering private property like this."

The creature, lacking in orifices of any kind, nonetheless heaved with breath. In the tiny bathroom on the other side of a corner that barely qualified as a kitchenette, the toilet thundered. The sink ran soon after.

"I can't have you here," Mel pleaded, looking quickly at the bathroom door before clasping her hands toward the thing that was disappointingly still there. "I can't look at you this weekend. Please—please, let me just have this. Let me have Rexie."

Still in the corner, the Gray Man began to turn.

The bathroom door opened. Junie, smiling in blissful ignorance, pranced out while asking, "You say something to me, Mel?"

"Nothing, sorry…I's just thinking out loud. Place is smaller than I thought."

Casting a sharp glance toward the entity and telling it in her head to get gone by the time she was back out of the bathroom, Melba made her way past her cousin. "Don't worry about unpacking my stuff. We'll only be here for a couple of days…just be sure to get the bag off the floor so it doesn't get bugs in it."

In the bathroom, all was quiet. Mel took a desperate breath and ran the water of the small sink. There was, thank God, a shower in the bathroom, which was good because the idea of sitting in a tub with a bunch of other people's skin cells made Melba want to set herself on fire. Now…taking a bath with Rexie, that might be nice.

Yes, there. Focus on that thought. Exhaling, Mel bent to splash a few handfuls of warm water across her face. She pressed her hands there and, closing her eyes beneath the warm darkness of her hands, she imagined reclining in Rexie's arms in a pool of rose petals.

"You won't have to imagine soon," he said from behind her, his tone of gentle love a cool breath of relief after the hideous intrusion of the Gray Man. Tears filled Melba's shut eyes. "Soon, angelbaby, you and me'll be together forever."

"I know, Rexie," she said softly. "I know, I know. I'll stay strong."

After a quick piss (the toilet was, of course, one of those with the type of wooden seat that made her want to kill herself worse than the idea of a hotel tub) Mel rinsed her hands, wiped them off on her shorts and stepped into the main cabin.

The Gray Man was gone, which was great. Unfortunately, it was difficult to tell this for a few seconds because the cabin was flooded with the sunlight of an open doorway. Junie's giggling silhouette shifted from foot to foot, braced against the doorjamb, reached a hand up to play with her ponytail. Outside the cabin, Taylor flashed his stupid grin and flirted with a frankly gross amount of confidence.

Aha! A missing tooth, a molar in the back. His lips folded

over it quickly, but Mel knew what she saw and treasured the flaw. A good starting point to begin dismantling Junie's ill-advised interest.

"…uh-huh, and—oh say, Melba!"

When he smiled at her, her skin crawled. It wasn't so much that she didn't trust him—though she didn't—but that she felt he was beneath them. Beneath June, especially. It was one thing for somebody to be worse-off than they were. Lots of folks were worse-off, which was sad because Mel and June weren't exactly set for cash.

But there was the kind of worse-off where somebody wanted to rise, and there was the kind of worse-off where somebody wanted to drag down everybody else.

"He's an evil, ugly man," Rexie murmured in her ear.

Mel evaded further eye contact and turned to attend to her luggage. Junie had not yet moved it off the floor and Mel, with an annoyed glance at the flirting duo, got so lost in thought that she forgot he was trying to talk to her.

He was saying *something*, though, at least until he wasn't. When Mel didn't respond, Junie exchanged a glance with Taylor and turned back to her cousin.

"Doesn't that sound nice? Mel?"

"I'm sorry," she said bluntly, straightening up with a pack of smokes in one hand and her script in the other, "I wasn't paying a single goddamned bit of attention. What were you saying?"

"Hell, never mind." His jocular expression faltered in the aggrieved response of a pick-up artist used to getting a reaction, whether positive or negative—but not being ignored. Taylor swiftly regained composure and said with a nod at her script, "You keep a journal?"

"A printed journal?" She flashed him the top page of the stack before tossing the bound document upon the bed and pulling the portable speaker out of her luggage. Shutting it before the interloper—or, Rex forbid, Becky June—saw the ropes slightly visible beneath her clothes, Melba zipped the works back up, sat the speaker on the edge of the night stand, and perched beside her script to look up some music on her phone.

All the while, Becky June and her redneck Prince Charming continued conversing.

"That's Melba's script, Taylor. She's on the fourth draft. Do you like movies?"

"You girls ain't from Hollywood, is ya?"

Blushing, giggling. "Of course not, but Melba's trying to be. I'm so proud of her! She's been working on this darn thing for a whole year, gettin' it all nice and perfect."

"Ain't that nice…anyway, Melba, I was just telling your cousin here that you two should come meet my sister and her friend. We're gonna be havin' our own barbeque, then spend some time hanging on the lake. Shit, you seen summa the boats out here? Wonder how much they are to rent."

"Some of 'em are privately docked," said Melba without looking up from her search for a playlist. "I think the office'll rent out kayaks and paddleboats and all, but if you want somethin' real nice you gotta bring it yourself."

"Sweet Child O' Mine" began playing and, soothed at once, Mel relaxed enough to lean against the headboard, put her phone down, and actually look Taylor in the shadow-obscured face. "Whatchy'all cooking?"

"Gotta few steaks and some burgers for the next few days, but since they've got the big cook-out here with the band and all I reckon we could feed you two tonight and see what's good 'round here tomorrow."

"Doesn't it sound fun, Mel?" Junie turned her hopeful eyes toward her cousin, who smiled genuinely and nodded. Free food was free food…and anyway, it was a fair enough distraction.

Just like that, her attitude changed. Melba's focus was infinitely better with music on. With something playing, Rexie didn't have to fumigate her mind with chatter and singing and her own harried thoughts to avoid letting other things fill the empty pit. Sometimes it didn't work, these musical attempts to distract herself from her own worst visions, but that was just the way it was. The Gray Man was too powerful, and the ghosts he brought with him were too loud to be compensated for all the time.

Today seemed like it was a good day, though. Now, breathing easily through the music and able to converse and think, Mel considered that Junie would have to leave the cabin at some point, for some extended period of time, if Mel was going to accomplish her goals. Although she didn't like this Taylor guy and certainly didn't trust him at first glance, she supposed if she were going to throw Junie to a wolf it had might as well be one missing a tooth.

"It does sound like a good time," said Mel accordingly, the glow of Junie's smile far from her only reward. "How 'bout you give us an hour or two to settle in and we'll come by? We got a cooler of beer we can share."

"All right," he said with great pleasure, rubbing his hands together and looking briskly between the ladies. "Sounds like a party. Hey—sweet tattoo, by the way."

"Well thanks," said Mel somewhat drily, extending her leg and glancing at the freshly touched-up intermingling of atom and galaxy and godhead. While Taylor came over to check it out, conspicuously brushing against Junie as he did, Mel tensed. She was ready for him to try to touch her, as most assholes would, but thankfully he read the room and kept his hands to himself.

"Damn," he said again, more genuinely. "This is really something. Where'd you get it done?"

"Down in San Jose."

"California? Shit, see! I knew you two were Cali girls, at least." The girls exchanged a glance—and June threw in a grin—while neglecting to correct him. "I hear all the Hollywood types are coming here these days."

"Oh yeah?" Junie's question prompted Taylor's happy opportunity to talk to her again.

Mel's stomach dropped down into her ass. No! No, idiot, don't tell her!

"Hell yeah. Lake of the Woods is the new secret. See that side of the lake? Most of that is private real estate…"

He touched June's shoulder with one hand and pointed out the door with the other, glancing over, waiting for Mel to join them, going on when he realized she had no intention to.

"Bad Moon Rising" played; a cursed song. She liked it, but hated to hear it. Always meant something bad was going to happen. She skipped it in favor of The Rolling Stones.

Taylor went on. "I guess there's a couplea different folks what come around to avail themselves of the private atmosphere, some music producer or something…but you ladies'll never believe the *big* one who comes here sometimes."

June, her lips curling into an 'o' of interest, asked gaily, "Oh, who, who?"

"The one and only Rex Virgil!"

While he laughed and slapped her playfully on the shoulder, Junie's expression of intrigue disappeared. In fact, it flipped upside-down. The happy smile of anticipation twisted into a dismayed pair of parted lips that hinted at teeth in anticipation of a gasp, or maybe even a scream. Junie's luminous eyes widened and whipped toward Melba.

"Is that so," she said, not a question so much as a confirmation.

"Swear on my daughter's life," said the deadbeat solemnly.

Rather than sustain Junie's judgmental stare, Melba slid back upon the bed until, supine, she draped her hand over her eyes and heaved a pained sigh. Misunderstanding, Taylor laughed.

"No patience for celebrity crushes, huh? Me, neither… but damn, my sister almost cried when I told her. She's been in love with that man since the *Flash Gordon* remake."

Ugh. Melba hated the *Flash Gordon* remake because of the way the bleach had damaged his hair. Why didn't they just get a better wig maker? It pissed her off to think about, and she was even more pissed off to think of some teenaged bitch swooning over *her* Rexie. There was no point in being jealous, of course, since it wasn't like Rexie could help the condition of his temporal mind…but every time she thought too hard of random girls lusting after her one true love, Melba started getting all upset. Part of her hoped Rexie would retire when they were married, but then, well. He loved his work so much. She couldn't take it away from him, could she? Reckoned it all depended on whether they stayed on temporal Earth.

Taylor continued chatting the women up, or trying to, but the mood had soured for reasons he could not possibly grasp. Soon he excused himself with another smile between the women.

"Guess I'll catch you two at dinner tonight, or a little bit before. How you ladies like your steaks?"

Junie answered for both, shut the door behind him, and stood with her hand on the knob for a few seconds.

"Melba," she began, tone delicate.

Mel wouldn't let her form the thought.

"I don't wanna hear it, Junie."

"But—"

""But," nothin'. It's an honest coincidence and ain't nobody can prove nothin' otherwise."

"I wish you wouldn't lie to me, Melba. I know—I know sometimes you can't help what you say, but I just wish you wouldn't *lie* to me."

"Junie! Baby, I'm telling you the truth. The real, honest truth is that I didn't know about Rexie—about Mr. Virgil visiting here when I first heard about this place."

And that really *was* the truth. It had been presented to her several times prior in her life. First in the mere abstract form of a roadside sign at which she had meanly scoffed while on a different trip with Junie. The name, "Lake of the Woods," had struck her as so generic that it was almost silly.

But then it had appeared again, manifesting now in the open vowels and careful consonants of a client's tongue while discussing a recent vacation. And the third time, at last, it appeared in the flesh, the ghost presenting its form in the glossy photographs of a magazine article titled "Back to Nature: Seven Celebs' Secret Hideaways."

She had not expected Rex Virgil to be highlighted in an issue of *Architectural Digest*, which had been deemed a "safe" magazine with the guidance of her counselor. Clearly, the woman had not realized that *AD* often featured celebrity homes and related projects. It—like the tabloids, pop culture, and movie magazines Mel once hoarded and mutilated to collect new Rexie pictures—was just another trigger for her lovelorn thoughts.

That was all it was. Love. That was what nobody understood: not even Junie. This was Romeo and Juliet. This was Pyramus and Thisbe. This was two people—two interdimensional lovers—separated for an eternity. This was a fairy tale. *The Snow Queen*. Melba had always loved that story as a little kid. She wanted more than anything to pluck the mirror shards from Rexie's perfect eyes.

"I don't want you to get into trouble, Mel," June said, sidling over to sit upon the foot of the bed. "I love you, you know."

"Then please. Just let me have a nice weekend in the middle of nowhere."

"But if something happens—"

"*What's* gointa happen?"

Taken aback by Mel's sharp tone, fixed by her eyes when Mel whipped her hand away to look her cousin in the face, Junie recoiled. Instead, she toyed with the strap of her tank top. Nervously tugging it up near her neck, she admitted, "I don't know what's gointa happen."

"Then don't worry about it," said Mel firmly, pushing herself up from the bed and reaching for her cigarettes. "I'm gonna go take a walk."

"By yourself?"

"I ain't fixinta do anythin'," Melba snapped, making her way past June without contact. "I just need some fresh air… smells like an empty can of Axe body spray in here since your friend left."

"Okay, well—"

Mel didn't wait for June to finish her plea before shutting the door. The words hung in the air and Mel fought off the same guilt she always felt when dealing harshly with Junie, but if she didn't sometimes deal harshly with Junie, the message would never get across.

Becky June had trouble with boundaries sometimes. She thought that, just because she was helping Mel take care of herself, that *she* was taking care of Mel. That was certainly not the case. Anybody could take one look at them and see it was Melba taking care of Becky June.

Outside, inhaling a deep breath of humid high-altitude air and glancing toward the forested mountain that peered over the lake, Mel pushed her tumbling hair back from her face, admired her tattoo in the light, and lit a Kool that at once unbunched her nerves. The familiar tension that came upon the body when lacking nicotine evaporated in an instant and, loose and merry, Mel slid her cigarettes into her sweatshirt's shoulder like Daddy used to.

She smiled at the thought. Old bastard wasn't always so bad. Summertime with his white t-shirt squared at one shoulder while he fixed Ma's birdhouse in the back yard. No, not always so bad when another adult was around to watch him. Woulda liked this place. Was his speed, for sure.

But what about June? Damn that Taylor idiot. Mel spied him at the end of a dock, talking to a pair of girls she assumed were the ones to whom he had referred repeatedly—as though the repetition would make Melba comfortable. Avoiding this clod and his clodettes, Melba made her way up the hill to the central parking area.

Despite the ample trees around the large clearing of the resort's main area, the rocks of the parking area were still so hot that Melba felt it through her thin foam flip-flops. She frowned down, flicking a bit of ash off her cigarette, and wondered if Junie had packed her any other shoes. She'd have to check later…failing that, they might sell things like that at the little store here. Mel wasn't made of money, but she was betting on the come.

If this weekend went as planned, she would never need to worry about money again—a secondary reward for her love and devotion to Rexie. One that paled in comparison to the mere privilege of waking up to find him beside her every day. Face still slack with dreams. Lips ready for a kiss.

Mel smiled shyly down at her own feet, puffed on the cigarette, and looked for an ashtray to hover near.

LOOK

Like a poker had been thrust up her ass, Mel whipped back around to obey the command.

The tail of a red convertible vanished in the trees.

FOUR

MEL'S HEART CLENCHED with dangerous ecstasy.

Yes! Oh, yes, he was here! He was really here!

Her research had been so intense that it was not a surprise to see it paying off, but there was still something about it that seemed so impossible. His physical nearness made her body shake as, her foam sandals slapping upon the ground, Mel hurried along the path to the access road that split its attention between the private drive and the path to the shared resort.

There he was, off in the distance, rounding a bend fully out of sight just as she managed to take a good look at him. At his fender, anyway. It was hard to tell because the windows were slightly tinted and the roof was up, but she knew that car extremely well. For legal reasons, she was no longer able to own a website in or participate in the online fan community devoted to Rexie's artistry; but by lurking in existing groups with a private browser on Junie's devices, Mel was able to learn about his latest cars, his latest shirts, his latest favorite forms of food. She'd seen more than one shot of the brilliant red Firebird, and to be met with it in real life, oh! She twirled in place like a schoolgirl, laughing, then glancing toward cabin 13 and its many fellows.

Just a look wouldn't hurt nothing.

Grinning around her cigarette, Mel followed the car. She had looked at so many photographs, maps and reviews of the area that she was certain she could have found the house with no other clues than what she had garnered through research—but, kindly, Rexie had parked outside rather than pulling it into the garage.

The house was a truly extraordinary design, which was of course why it had been featured in *AD*. Much like Rexie, though, there was a difference between seeing it in real life and seeing it in the pages of a magazine. Tucked amid the trees and against a slight slope into which it was recessed, the home was split-level. Its wonderful deck, like the floor-to-ceiling windows of glass on the upper story behind it, boasted an extraordinary view of the lake and all its many glittering sunsets. Melba bit her lip in admiration for the home, modern in its design but rustic in its use of wood. The gate that enclosed it was really a symbolic affair—short enough to be climbed, but high enough to demonstrate the property line in a way everybody could understand. Rexie was famously friendly with fans, or had been. He did not feel an oppressive need to lock himself up like the precious treasure he was.

Admiring the car from the middle of the street as she was, hypnotized by the glamor of the place and the masonry that made up the first floor of the facade, Mel was very nearly caught right there.

One of the panes of glass leading to the deck slid open. Grinding out her cigarette, Mel dashed to the roadside and hurried into the trees across the street.

Oblivious, mid-conversation with his phone, Rexie stepped onto the deck.

"Uh-huh…yeah…well, that sounds interesting and all, but you're really missing out. You sure you don't have some time to come down? Oh, come on…it'll be great."

She almost couldn't look at him. Imagine! All this time, all these conversations in her head, and she still couldn't stand to look at him directly. She'd have to get over that soon—but for now, the crisp sound of his voice, directed not from simultaneously within and without her but actually, truly emanating from a visible, verifiable body, was enough to bring her to a state of trembling bliss. It was a different voice, unaccented, but it was most assuredly his.

"You mean to say I came out here, I've got three guest rooms, and you're not going to be in one of them? Ah, forget it…I won't beg you to be fun if you're not in the mood to be."

While Rexie laughed and the subsequent comeback, Mel closed her eyes and let herself get lost in the wonderful, thick sound of his mirth. She loved his laugh most of all. It sounded like sophistication and cocktail parties. Like security. Satisfaction. Her entire body ached with the fever of her heart and, dizzy, she knelt amid the ferns while he went on flirting with the woman on the phone.

"Oh, there's plenty of that…and lots of wine, too. The cellar is practically an art gallery. Come on…don't you want to get away?"

He waited, a tawny chuckle emanating from him while the woman vacillated. Didn't want to make the obvious choice too soon and seem too desperate, probably…but Melba couldn't help hoping that this chick really was stupid enough to refuse.

"Tomorrow? All right. What time?"

Mel shut her eyes and exhaled in relief to know she still had a little bit of time. Especially when he said with an audible pout, "After*noon*? Ah, come on…that's half a day gone. The most beautiful hours, too. Don't"—pause—"ah, well, okay. I should just be glad you'll be here at all."

While he wandered back and forth over the deck, still talking on and on with the assumption of privacy, Mel studied the property around the edge of her guardian tree. It had been hard to tell through the tint of the windows, but it hadn't looked like he had come with anybody.

That included security guards.

Good. It would be a huge hassle to sneak around some meathead to get to him…especially in a timeframe like this one. But this new timeframe was worrying.

She should have figured he'd be here with somebody else. Somehow, when she thought about this weekend, it was always them alone—but, realistically, that never could have been the case. Men like Rexie were surrounded by security, assistants, gorgeous women…even twenty-four hours of him alone were more than she ever should have hoped for.

Still—pressure was really on now. While Rexie, still jawing, made his way back into the house, Mel looked one more time at the layout of the property.

That squat fence was inviting, but Mel quickly identified two separate cameras. One pointed at the car, and one pointed at the dock and the boat already waiting at its side. In addition to that, he'd probably had one of those ritzy digital doorbells installed—ready to snap a shot of anybody who came too near the porch.

That was just the visible equipment. There was no knowing what he had aside from that—*in* the house, especially.

Feeling discouraged but not entirely hopeless, Mel made her way back down the way she'd come. Lips firm-set, her hand occasionally rubbing over her jaw as though in search of a beard to stroke, Mel considered her options.

"Don't worry, angelbaby…you've got all the tools you need."

She sighed, nodding at his reassuring whisper. That was always the way it worked out. Whenever Rexie set her on a task, no matter how impossible it seemed, she would accomplish it simpler than anything. Usually in ways that seemed somehow silly. The only time things didn't work out like he promised was the time she went to prison, but that had also been for a purpose. A purpose not yet revealed to her, maybe…but a purpose.

All things had meaning. The trees around her seemed chaotic and yet so orderly, as if their trunks could have been divided along a grid of hyperspace. They were, of course. Every swirling fractal of fern reminded her of a few important facts that she always needed to remember. One, that the universe would not exist without her eventual success in at least one iteration; and Two, that success meant that she and Rexie would inevitably be together as long as she was her best self.

And she had to be her best self, because this was the life she was consciously observing.

Her plan could not fail. The question was one of its enactment. Before she got the dirty deets, Mel had imagined something very straightforward. When alone, she would be able to tell him the truth in a way—a leisurely, unhurried way—that he would understand. He would understand her at last, and they would finally have the sweet relief of true soul-companionship.

It occurred to Mel that she was walking with her own thoughts without music on, and that filled her with unusual optimism. She was aware of only a slight haze on the fringes of her vision, and was subject to only the occasional nervous push from the chorus that haunted her with declarations like

HE SAW YOU

THE POLICE ALREADY KNOW

and

HE'LL NEVER LOVE YOU

KILL YOURSELF

or, the classic,

AND HIM

KILL HIM

TOO

so maybe Mel would put in her earbuds, after all.

By the end of the road, with Jethro Tull ordering her thoughts the way the electric grid sometimes shimmering around her ordered space and time, Mel merged back into the resort area and peered around with her hands jutting into the red pockets of her hooded sweatshirt. Her gaze tracked around the common area and its cabins while she regained her bearings.

Her assessment paused, her jaw tightening along with all the muscles of her neck.

One hand withdrew from her sweatshirt to shield her eyes and confirm what she thought she saw—namely, that Junie was down there lakeside, chatting away with What's-His-Face. Taylor. She'd already forgotten.

Sniffing lightly, Melba lit another cigarette, blew a menthol smoke ring into the air, and made her slow way across the warm tar of the parking lot. Her eyes flickered down to the chipped nail polish of her toes. Gonna have to fix that before she tried to talk to Rexie.

Had to fix a lot of things. Like her nerves.

"Hey y'all," she called ahead of herself, keeping her tone breezy and oblivious. "What's going on?"

"There you are, Mel!" Sheer relief expanding the features of her face, Junie glanced one quick time at Taylor before hurrying up to meet her cousin. "I was worried you got lost in the woods or something…Taylor said there's bears around here."

"They're pretty shy unless you've got an open can of food, though." Taylor nodded at Mel in a way that was friendly, respectful enough, and…something else.

Interest? Fucking hoped not. Mel had about as much interest in him as she would in a tick.

"Well, I managed to avoid any bear attacks. Just took a walk up the road a little bit to see some of the sights. It's gorgeous around here. What?"

Junie had been staring at her in skeptical intensity. One eyebrow very nearly arched, but not quite. By some inner strength she resisted, yet her posture—arms crossed over her diaphragm, shoulders slightly hunched as though braced against bad news—still betrayed a mistrust and renewed annoyance with Melba's so-called illness. With a slightly shit-eating grin she couldn't help, Melba waited for her cuz to come up with the improvised answer, "I just got nervous when I came out of the cabin and you were nowhere to be seen, that's all."

"She was talking about you."

Rexie's murmur made Mel's hands ball in her pockets. She peered across the lake, setting aside her partner's private comment while willing herself to go on as though Taylor did not exist.

"You worry too much, Junie…you'll worry yourself sick."

"No kidding," said Taylor in helpful, chipper tone, meriting another bleak little flick of Mel's eyes. "No reason to stress yourself in a place like this. Besides—oh—"

Someone had called to him; he twisted at the waist toward the sound. The motion revealed an ugly trio of tribalist wolves on the back of his shoulder blade. Mel wrinkled her nose at the sight of the tacky tattoo and glanced at Junie, who was too busy scrutinizing her cousin to take in her suitor's flaws. With a shake of her head, Melba followed Taylor's adjusted direction toward the pair of girls who approached with towels wrapped around their waists.

"Mel, June—this is Candy and my sister, Daisy."

"Nice to meetcha," said Daisy briskly, pushing a few strands of tangled hair highlighted blonde back from her cheek. She offered her hand to Mel first and, taking it, Mel smiled as much as she could for a young chick with so much sun damage she looked like a walking lesion. "You're Mel?"

"Thank the Lord…you wear a lotta sunblock, Daisy?"

While Daisy's face screwed up in a look of vague affront, Junie hurried up to offer her hand and smoothly save the day. "Mel's an esthetician!"

At the girls' impressed look, Mel corrected, "Tarot reader. I retired from beauty parlors."

"How old are you?"

Candy asked this, boldly, and Mel gave her a sidelong look. "Thirty-four."

While the girls made noises as though in amazement, Melba's blood boiled beyond her control. "Well? Hell, what do you expect? You don't turn thirty and wither up like a bad apple…and I'll have you know your tits'll start saggin' *long* before."

Daisy produced a little gasp of semi-terror and glanced down at her bikini top while Taylor slapped his knee. "Hoo! She was their enemy because she spoke the truth. Damn, Daze, listen to the woman…I got sunblock in the truck up there, go on, help yourselves…"

While the girls marched off, Taylor turned his pleased eyes toward Melba. "You a drinkin' woman? Harder drinks than beer, I mean."

"I can do one or two," she said with a shrug.

Rubbing his hands together, waving the women with him, Taylor hustled to the grill pit already claimed by his cooler, lawn chairs, and various props that made evident the intention of a picnic. "I have got the most *b-e-a-utiful* pineapple daquiri mix," he said, producing the bottle along with another of rum. "You like 'em strong?"

It wasn't long before everybody had a red cup of some kind of cocktail in their hand. Suspicious as the day was long, Mel kept a careful eye on their so-called bartender; but, unless

Taylor was some kind of magician, he wasn't slipping anything into the drinks except Bacardi.

The day wore on. Melba relaxed. Everybody drained at least one cup and soon the air filled with the sizzle of meat. Candy and Daisy sat on the ground while Mel and June reclined in chairs, their cooler of beer beside them being drained mostly by the younger women.

"How come you retired," asked Daisy, peering curiously up at Melba with a pair of bright blue eyes. Her hair was drying to a bright shine and Melba, her auburn hair always having been a little frizzy before she learned the many steps of taming her curls, supposed she envied it. It would have been nice to look in the mirror and feel that everything Rexie said about her was true—but it had to be true, or he wouldn't have been saying it. She knew she was pretty, but was she extraordinary? It was confusing that Rexie loved her so much.

"Hogwash. You *are* extraordinary, Melba. Before the night is through I'll tell you that myself, with my own two lips."

"Will you?"

"What was that?"

Daisy was looking curiously at Mel, who realized she had almost completely forgotten a question was asked of her.

"I went to prison," answered Melba honestly, meriting some noises of astonishment from their new friends.

"She-it," swore Daisy in a tone of new respect.

Candy, batting slightly more blankly bovine brown eyes over at her friend, asked of Mel, "What'd you do?"

"Don't ask *that*," hissed Daisy in response, though Mel laughed.

"What the fuck else is she supposed to ask? I was convicted of trespassin' and breakin' and enterin'."

She could feel Taylor's ear focused on her as Daisy, forgetting her previous mores about asking after crimes, leaned forward. "Were you, like, a burglar?"

"Nah, I didn't steal nothin'."

"It doesn't matter," said Junie, leaping in with such nervous, desperate energy that she quite literally leaned forward in her seat. "Mel just made a mistake. She spent more than a year in prison. It's high time she gets a chance to forget about it and just have a good time."

"Hear, hear," agreed Taylor, lifting his beverage before plucking a steak from the grill. "In light of that, I say we give the first steak to Miss Melba."

Classic tactic. Trying to pick up a girl whose relatives aren't exactly sweet on you? Butter them up as soon as you can.

Sniffing, Mel forced herself to be polite and said, "Thanks," accepting the steak and premade chimichurri deposited from a nearby deli cup. With plastic fork and knife that did a surprisingly acceptable job of cutting the tender meat, Mel chowed down.

At the first bite, she sighed.

"All right, you sonofabitch," she openly groused, waving the plastic tines his way. "This is one damn good steak."

"Why thank you kindly." Taylor grinned to himself while plucking up the next steak and cutting it into slices for more even distribution. When all the food was passed around, Taylor took a seat between Mel and Daisy and committed himself to whatever conversation the women would have.

Mel still didn't trust him, but the food was good and the drink wasn't drugged and the girls seemed to be there of their own volition, so Mel relaxed a little bit. Soon she brought out her speaker and they were having a regular little party in back of the cabins. Another set of neighbors, attracted by the sound and the happy dog, came by with a six-pack that, though insufficient, still bought their entry. The red sun glittered on the lake, slowly cooling to the indigo of evening.

"This is a pretty good time," she said when she had a few seconds to murmur with June over the beer cooler. Playing DJ had given people an easy ice-breaker for talking to Mel, and the responsibility of maintaining the playlist meant she had perpetual dibs on one of the chairs. There was something regal about reclining there, watching the lake and holding court with whomever dared interrupt the magic of Captain Beefheart with their lowly requests.

"It really is pretty fun! Like a whole community." Junie smiled in an endearing way and raised her shoulders in time with a cute wrinkle of her nose. "Guess it's good we came after all. You're really doing okay?"

"I'm doing great," Mel said, which was for once not a confabulation. Junie smiled warmly and touched her hand— then Taylor's girls called from the other side of a mumbled conversation that grew as more and more people got wind of an impromptu party by the lake.

"You should circulate with me," urged June, her face glowing in the light of the modest bonfire established as the sun began to doze.

"And lose my seat? Nah, baby, I'm good."

Laughing, June shook her head and bounded off toward the girls who were trying to show her an owl they swore they had seen swooping overhead. Alone amid the commotion of the party, Mel let the music service switch out of a spate of requested party songs and back to her preferred classic rock. Her eyes slid closed.

For just a second—for one half of a second, really, but the thought was there—Mel thought about how much easier and safer it would be to just take the medication everybody wanted her to take.

It wasn't too late. Junie had probably insisted on discreetly bringing it with them against Mel's wishes. Melba could get up right now, go rifle through her cousin's belongings, find the pills, be normal. Join the party and feel part of the party, and go on to enjoy more parties. To enjoy people. To meet a normal, accessible man who settled down and settled her down with him, and who would keep an eye on her medication with a little more force than Junie did.

And who'd have to slog away in misery, break his back to maintain a trailer, die at sixty and leave her all alone to be devoured by the Gray Man.

Maybe there was nothing safe about being normal. She decided just as that idiot Taylor saw her lost in thought and decided to interrupt by filling the seat beside her.

"What's goin' on? You got any Creedence on that thing?"

"I got the whole damn Internet," she said, opening her eyes and thumbing through the phone to search for the band. "Kind of fucked up that I get such good service out here."

"Ain't no escape from the world anymore." Offering her a beer still sealed in his hand only to be rebuffed, he set it aside and leaned back in his seat. "You don't drink much, huh?"

"Try not to," she said, focusing on getting up *Cosmo's Factory*. "Makes me feel like shit the next day."

Melba felt his eyes flicker over her with the caution of a near-stranger gauging how cool the other was. "You do shrooms?"

"Used to," was her response with a quick glance over, a flutter of temptation, and then, from Rexie, a quick impulse that signified "No."

"I can't anymore." The album started and she rested the phone upon her thigh again, her hands folding over her stomach rather than hiding in her hooded sweatshirt. "Shrooms and acid—even Molly fucks me up too much."

"That's a damn shame."

"Sure enough is."

After his continued contemplation drew her attention and a deliberately unpleasant, "What," Taylor leaned in.

"You dykin'?"

Mel's brow furrowed and her mouth opened in annoyance and disgust. "What the fuck kinda question is that?"

"Well—are ya?"

"So what if I was? So what if I'm not, for that matter! What the fuck are you, the type of asshole that thinks when a girl's not into him—"

"All right, damn, all right, my sincere apologies. Didn't mean to offend."

"I'll bet you didn't…horse's ass! And people think *I'm* rude."

"Breakin' and enterin' is considered a bit of a faux pas," agreed Taylor, stroking the shifty little patch of facial hair that strove to be a goatee. While Mel glowered over at him, Taylor grinned wide enough to reveal that little black hole amid all his other, nicotine-yellowed teeth. "But I wouldn't hold it against you if I found you in my cabin sometime…less you asked, anyway."

"Get lost, troglodyte."

"Troglodyte! Damn, girl, that's a big word."

"I'm sure it's a huge word to somebody who didn't finish grade school. Hit the fuckin' road and go pester somebody else…my cousin seems to like you."

"Yeah, well, she might like me, but *I* like a challenge." With a slap of the wooden arm of the chair, the creep flashed another ugly grin that contorted his cheeks in an unpleasant way, stood up, and said, "Catch you later, Melba."

Mel gave him the finger with one hand while digging for her pack of cigarettes with the other. The hollow feeling of the box in her hand inspired a surge of panic.

Shit! Damn. This happened every time Mel did a little bit of drinking. Her mind would settle and there would be no Gray Man—at any rate, he would appear less frequently and only under great duress—but she went through smokes like they were goddamn tortilla chips.

Sighing, shaking her head, Melba forced herself to vacate her comfortable lounge seat and stretch her legs. Catching June's eye across the party and waving her empty box of Kools, Mel mimed a person walking with two fingers of her free hand and mouthed the word, "Store." Her cousin nodded, flashed her a thumbs-up, smiled, and resumed her conversation with the younger women.

Smiling a little herself, glad to see her cousin having a good time, Mel slipped beyond the murmuring ring of light in favor of the darkness.

The night air by the lake was crisp and cool, and the further she got from the fire the more she remembered they were truly in the mountains. Goosebumps crawled up legs bared by her shorts and, grinning at the brisk air, Mel made her way across the parking lot with a pleasant noise of relief to find its greedy surface still warm from the day.

As she had on her return, she looked around the premises to take stock of the buildings. Everything was so samey-samey that it was a little confusing, but she figured the marina store would sell cigarettes of one kind or another. At least, they'd tell her where to drive to pick some up. Following the slope to the quiet marina where a few boats trickled in late, Mel patted around for her wallet, pondered the slim bill within, and wondered if she might be better off trying to shake down Junie for some pocket change.

She was so lost in thought, so busy rifling through useless receipts in search of a few more bucks, that she didn't see him.

Only, as usual, heard him.

"Don't bother—they're closed."

"Damn, really?" Mel lowered her wallet and tried the door, frowning to shake the handle. Rexie was, as always, right. "Hell! But I thought I saw a bunch of people returning boats in the marina."

"Yeah, that's the other side. They said they won't sell after-hours…I went in the marina door just now and tried. If they won't sell liquor to *me*, I don't think they'll sell to anybody."

Melba froze in place.

Pale, heart flying, body starved for breath, Melba peered through the dark.

A man stood smoking against the marina's facade.

"Rex Virgil?"

With a laugh of near-surprise, Rexie said with his own two lips, "What a pair of eagle eyes you've got…guilty as charged."

FIVE

MELBA FELT LIKE she was going to puke.

A lot of people probably felt that way when meeting Rex Virgil, but Melba *really* felt that way. Her insides lurched as though suddenly tilting on an axis separate from her skeleton—her muscles, her flesh, her sweating face. She stepped back, fear raging through her.

It was happening. It was happening, it was happening.

YOU KNOW WHAT THIS MEANS

She knew, she knew.

IT MEANS

YOU ARE GOING

TO

"I know," she said aloud, too sharply, cutting off the awful voices. Her eyes strained through the dark; she could look at him with abandon when they were mostly unilluminated. "I mean—I know it's you. I saw your car."

The fast save came to her and she added carefully, trying to affect a slightly more Valley Girl twang than her usual southern one, "You, uh—you were on some car show talkin' about it. I just saw the rerun the other day. I—I can't believe it—"

She could believe it, and she did. It was the only thing she believed in. While Rexie laughed gently, he put out his cigarette and approached her with that same hand extended. "Nice to meet you, too, Miss—"

He wanted to touch her! She was going to explode into flame. If she was going to die any way, it was surely going to be of a heart attack. Wiping her hand off against her shorts, Mel offered her hand and uttered the first name that came to mind: "Gwen," she said, thinking of Ma. "I'm, uh, I'm Gwen, Mr—"

"Please, call me Rex."

"Don't let me know who you are," he also said, now in his country accent, though Melba wasn't sure how he managed to say the words while smiling expectantly.

"Uh—of course, of course, Rex. Sorry, I'm just so—"

"It's all right. I guess you like my movies?"

"Yes!" Laughing, staring down at the hand he released from the grip of his own firm, big, warm but somehow soft and pampered one. "Yes," she repeated, looking up to find— with a bolt of fear and thrill—that he studied her closely through the dark. "I like your movies, Rex. I think you're the best actor in the world."

"That's a pretty high bar! Hope I never disappoint you." Glancing toward the party, Rex asked, "You from over there? Sounds like a good time."

"It is! You should come by." Wouldn't *that* freak Junie out! She didn't really mean it, though…just said it because it was the done thing. The normal thing. She needed him to think she was normal.

"I've been considering it," he said, glancing over his shoulder. "especially since there's no sale."

"I'd think a fella like you has a big ol' wine reserve or something," she said, her accent slipping in and out but evidently not enough to catch his attention. "Kind of strange to see you at a place like this at all. Seems kinda low-down."

"Oh, me? No, I'm not actually staying *here*. I own one of the houses on the other side…and you're right. I've got a lot of wine—just no liquor."

"I think there's a place in town that'll still sell to you."

"Probably…but, to be honest, I'm a little too high to drive, and I left my assistant at home." Rex laughed a bit and then, pondering through the dark, studied Mel in a way so thrilling she thought for sure she was going to pass out. "Do I know you?"

She focused on his prior urging that she lie to him, though she hated to do so.

"No, sir," she said.

"Are you sure? You haven't done any background work, have you? Haven't been an extra in anything? No? Wow… hard to tell in this light, but…"

He looked at her so closely that for a few seconds she was afraid he *would* remember her, but in the wrong way.

After a few seconds, Rex shook his head.

"Well, who knows. Maybe you've got a famous sister, huh?"

"I had a cousin disappear one time," she said absently, before adding, "Oh, but—what if I swing through the liquor store for you, Rex? What can I get you?"

With a noise of sheer delight, Rex asked, "You'd do that? You're not too wasted?"

"Nah, I don't really drink that much."

Clasping his hands together and looking up at the sky, he sighed. "God sent me an angel tonight. Ah, Gwen, honey! You're the best. Absolutely—here—"

Mel tried not to look too stunned when Rexie pulled out his thick wallet and, like it was nothing, greased her unready palm with three hundred dollar bills before thoughtfully adding two more. "If you promise to spend three hundred on the booze, you can keep two more…and if you run away to Mexico with all five hundred, then I guess I'd say, "Canada is closer.""

Mel laughed and looked hesitantly at the money. She had just been wishing for some but now she felt a little silly, especially since her meeting up with Rexie meant she wouldn't really need it. A normal person wouldn't refuse, though, would she?

Besides…there was still that little twinge of attachment. Still that temptation to stay with the world and all its trappings. Clothes and cars and sex and money. Somehow, money most of all.

"I promise I won't run off anywhere with it," she said, "but three hundred dollars' worth of booze! That's a lot."

"It is if you're not having an impromptu party." With a gallant smile and a glance toward the gathering over by the lake, he said, "You think everybody'll be into taking this thing indoors?"

Mel's heart hammered in her chest.

Opportunity after opportunity unfurled itself. While Rexie explained the directions to his house and roughly named a few brands and types of liquor that sounded good to him, Mel swore she felt the whole world falling apart. The molecules of reality rearranged around her to form a tunnel, all the trees and sky and ground bowing, twisting. Concealing her and Rexie in the passage that only *seemed* like it was of the world.

She was really going to miss June.

"And the gate code is 1974," he explained, jolting her with the sudden, full realization of how simple this knowledge made everything—everything.

"Gate code," she stammered.

"Uh-huh, keep it to yourself, of course…hey, Gwen, listen—"

Rex placed a comforting hand upon her shoulder. She flinched even as he looked gently into her face through the veil of darkness that, along with memory and time, obscured her identity.

"You don't have to be nervous, okay?"

"Okay."

"I know it seems like I'm some big deal, and I guess I am to a lot of people, but to me—I don't know. I'm just an artist, you know?"

Yes. She did know. That was one of the reasons she loved him so fiercely. Smiling, Mel nodded and said, "You're a *great* artist, though. That's what makes me nervous around you."

"You're a sweetheart—well, that may be so, but so far as I'm concerned I've always got room for improvement…always learning. And I, like most artists, love to hang out with real people. So just relax, okay?"

"Okay," she said, but it was impossible.

While he smiled in approval and released her with one last pat, Mel stepped back and said, "1974?"

"That's the one."

"All right. Be there in—in an hour at most, okay?"

"Sounds good. If you're late, I'll assume you fled the country."

Laughing, Mel forced herself to return to the parking area. Her laughter faded by the yard until, shellshocked, she moved through the darkness in absolute silence.

What just happened? What was happening now? Rexie was curiously silent on the matter, but that was because he was busy being himself. Things would be explained to her in time. For now, though, she could still fuck this up…and badly.

She had one chance to make it happen right.

Moving silently across the lot, Mel entered the thirteenth

cabin and glanced at the party just down the hill from the back yard. She held her breath to identify Junie amid the crowd. Her phone had synched to the speaker in the absence of Mel's. Bubblegum pop encouraged her, along with a few other exceptionally drunk partygoers, to dance.

Relieved that both the dancing and the lighting allowed her to do so unseen, Mel shut the curtains and quickly scanned the cabin.

There was no time to be picky. Junie would freak out, but maybe she would understand someday…however it ended up working out. Now was not the time for pining or regret.

With the quick jerk of a zipper, Mel shut the bag that Junie had left on the floor and stood it upright.

"Goin' somewheres?"

Mel yelped, stumbling back and producing a second, sharper gasp when she found Taylor's unexpected form dwarfed by the Gray Man. The creature's limbs undulated, quivering at its sides while Taylor looked her up and down.

"Think I better get your cuz," said the near-stranger, this intruder on the enactment of a multi-year long plan and two decade-long dream. "You plannin' on leavin' her all alone out here in the damn woods?"

"Of course not. Mind your own damn business…I'll be back."

"But when?"

"I got an errand to run, if you must know."

"With your suitcase?" The idiot arched a brow and Mel looked him up and down, trying to avoid the inexorable draw of her gaze toward the Gray Man's haunting face.

"With dickheads like you feeling entitled to come in and out of our cabin, fuck yeah I'm bringing my goddamn suitcase. You were probably followin' me in here with some nasty shit on your pea brain."

"You gotta learn to talk to people a little nicer. I'm tryinta be your friend, Mel. I could be *real* unfriendly if I wanted, after all—like by tellin' Junie I saw you down there talking to that movie star guy."

Hand tightening around the handle of her suitcase, Mel fell back on her heel. "She told you about me, I guess?"

"Told me enough. You may think I'm stupid, but I can do some basic math. Thought it was damn weird that the room took such a turn when I brought him up…didn't think about it again until seein' you two in the dark. He recognize you?"

"What the *fuck* did she tell you?"

"That you got some problems, Sister Susie," he answered flatly, tugging at a scraggly strand of his beard while leaning against the cabin door. "Said she was real worried you'd wandered off after our conversation, on account of some time you broke into a famous guy's hotel room and got in big trouble for it. One plus one, baby. That's two."

Mel's eyes flashed down toward the webbed feet of the Gray Man. They extended so hideously past Taylor's that, shuddering, Mel found it preferable to look the loser in the face.

"So? That's all in the past. I served my time."

"Out on parole, she said. Bet your parole officer wouldn't take kindly to your proximity to the guy you're stalkin'."

"I was *not* stalkin' him," Mel said sharply, her tone bleak as the expression that fixed itself to her features. The Gray Man looked on, trembling like a boneless structure of ballistic gel while Melba approached the absolute clown getting between her and a god.

"What I have with Rex Virgil is none of your damn business—none of anybody's damn business except mine and his."

"Sure does seem like you sincerely think that."

He remained leaning against the door, one elbow propping him up, while Melba got in his face. "The fuck are you playin' at, Taylor? You think I'm afraid of you?"

"I think it wouldn't take me any effort at all to go tell

Becky June what you're up to. Or...maybe I could just tell Virgil to look a little closer."

"Good fuckin' luck. You just gonna walk up to his house and let yourself in? Hop the fence? He'll call the cops."

"1974," was all the idiot said.

Behind him, the Gray Man buzzed so wildly that his—its—entire body quivered up and down.

Rage burned through Mel. She didn't need Rexie around for guidance on this one. Heart and eyes blazing, Melba drew her head back and slammed her forehead right into Taylor's tiny little shyster nose.

"Son of a bitch!"

The redneck reeled back, one hand flying to the curtain of scarlet blood pouring from his nose. Melba grabbed him by the thin cotton of his shirtfront and hissed, "I told you I ain't fuckin' *scared* of you, asshole."

"God damn, you little bitch, let me go—help! Hel—"

Melba slapped him in the broken nose and, when he howled in pain, she shoved him back toward the corner of the room. He probably thought he bounced off the bathtub on his way there, but it was really the Gray Man. The entity shuddered with excitement while Melba stomped after the disoriented loser.

As, pushing himself up from the rattling wall beneath the deer head, Taylor focused his surely blurring vision, he reached behind him and—to no one's surprise, let alone Melba's—drew a firearm from his waistband.

"Now you just back right the fuck off," said Taylor with a suffocating gasp through the river of blood released in gouts by ruined cartilage. "I ain't playin' around. You come one step closer to me and I'll put a bullet in your fuckin' head. Lock that door."

Melba complied, quiet and still.

Nodding in satisfaction, adopting an ugly little grin, the loser leaned heavily back against the wall.

"Take off your—"

The plastic deer head above him, hefty despite its falsity, dropped from the abused wall and slammed him right in the crown of the skull.

SIX

MELBA HAD NEVER seen somebody knocked out cold and waited a good five seconds to see if he would get back up. She assumed he would, anyway—but, slowly, the noises of the world entered her consciousness. Laughter and distant music from the party; the slow breathing of the noseless Gray Man hovering over her; the pounding of her heart in her ears.

And she was not aware, for all of that, of any sound Taylor made.

Moving across the floor upon the balls of her feet, nervous to turn her back on the Gray Man but not given a choice, Melba crouched over Taylor's prone body and pushed the fallen wall ornament out of the way. Blood continued flowing from his nose and, not wanting him to suffocate despite the temptation, she turned him over to face the floor and made sure he was still breathing.

Lucky for him, he was...although, again, a fatal accident might have been a nice "out."

Just as well. Mel looked around to make sure all the windows were closed while she slipped the gun into the back of her shorts.

This immediate violation of her parole was still less dangerous than letting Taylor wake up in a rage and come after her with the gun on his person…but the weapon's cold heft still made Mel super fucking anxious. She was going to drive like an angel to and from the liquor store.

After considering how it looked, Mel replaced the deer head on the wall and then used a rug by the door to move Taylor's limp body nearer the giant bathtub. Gritting her teeth, telling herself to lift with her legs, she grabbed Taylor by the armpits and dumped him into the tub. She covered him with the same rug she'd used to drag him along the floor. With the lights out and the rug over him, he might stay out for a while.

By the time she dusted her hands, the Gray Man was gone. Satisfied this meant she was on the right track, Mel made her way back to the bag and took it by the handle.

Before she made it to the door, something tickled across the back of her hand.

Melba glance down once—then again, this second look a more urgent and sustained glance.

A small black bug rushed across the valley of her knuckles.

"Fuck!"

White terror bolting through her heart, Mel released the handle and recoiled from it with a sharp shake of her hand. She didn't see the insect go flying and turned her hand rapidly around, inspecting it from all angles in an effort to locate the hateful little roach. She had just jerked up the sleeve of her hoodie when something moved across the handle of the bag—and something else caught her attention.

A noise. A rustling. A heinous whispering.

Nauseous, Melba looked around for Rexie. Really wished he wasn't busy being himself right now. Tears filled Melba's eyes as she gingerly lay the bag back upon the floor and tugged open the zipper.

The bugs writhing within flooded out in all directions long before Mel finished opening the case. She shrieked and leaped back upon the bed, cursing her sandals and the feet they left exposed to a scurrying sea of roaches, waterbugs, centipedes and bedbugs. How long had they been in there? Long enough to lay eggs, for sure. She was going to have to burn everything—it was no good if Junie tried bringing the bag back. The entire apartment would wind up contaminated.

Tears of frustration filled her eyes at the thought and, whimpering as they began to scuttle up the posts of the bed, Melba recoiled farther along the mattress.

"Damn it, Junie," she whispered, "damn it, damn it, what'd I fucking tell you? Can't leave the bag on the ground—"

IT'S NOT JUNE

"Yes it is!"

IT'S YOU

YOU BROUGHT THE INSECTS

THEY CAME FROM SAN JOSE

THEY CAME FROM BEFORE

YOU HAVE ALWAYS BEEN

FULL OF BUGS

YOUR EYES ARE FULL OF EGGS

AND THEIR CHILDREN

SQUIRM OUT OF YOU

ALL NIGHT LONG

TO BURROW INTO JUNIE'S BRAIN

KILL YOURSELF

SO JUNIE WON'T SUFFER

Mel had long-since covered her eyes, but now she covered her ears…for all the good it did her.

"This is a hallucination, right? Right? It's not real."

IF THIS ISN'T REAL

REX ISN'T REAL

Groaning, teeth clenched in a fury, Mel rocked upon the mattress and uttered only one short cry as a few tickly feet quivered over her toe. The contact was more than enough to spur her motion. Kicking out, Mel scrambled back from the encroaching wave before she at last forced herself to leap through the mass of insects.

She didn't need the bag. She didn't need the clothes. Fuck it—fuck it! They could live in her stuff forever for all she cared. She was going elsewhere, and she only needed what Rexie told her she needed. Moving fast, she swept her purse from the bedside table and then, wincing, flipped open her suitcase. The remainder of the insects, exposed to the light, escaped from her as fast as their tiny legs could carry them.

Overcoming her understandable reluctance to do so, Mel bared her teeth and reached a hand into the depths of her clothes. She thought nothing at all of disheveling them to remove the rope, and though a few articles burst out onto the bug-covered floor, she wrote them off. All she snatched otherwise was the script. Putting that under her arm and stuffing the purse with as much of the rope as she reasonably could, Mel fled the scene in favor of the car.

Thank God! No bugs. Thank Rexie.

Closing her eyes for one brief moment, Mel leaned back in the driver's seat and stared toward the abundant stars visible through the windshield.

This was it. She was going to do it. After all this dreaming—all this work—she was going to do it. By the end of the night, he would remember.

She just had to stay calm, not worry about the gun in her waistband, and not fuck this up.

What was Junie going to think? Mel hadn't thought about it in too much detail because it made her sad to, but now she had to confront the reality. Junie was going to be left behind when Rexie's resonance aligned with that of his true self.

That was terribly sad. If money was the material thing that seemed the hardest for Mel to leave behind, Junie was the person. She was a little bit of a dope sometimes, and she could be overbearing when it came to Mel's mental health… but, even with all that considered, Junie's heart was just so pure. Who could ever be mad at her? Not Mel—not Mel, who owed her infinitely.

After all…when Mel had come out of prison with no place to go but a halfway house, who had taken her in without question? Junie. Who let Mel say whatever she wanted and took it all without complaint? Junie. Who was the only tangibly real person who told Mel "I love you" these days?

And who was going to walk in on that wild-ass scene in a few hours, finding a body in the bathtub and a shitload of bugs crawling all over Mel's abandoned, opened, rifled suitcase?

"Sorry, Junie," said Mel to the open air, grimly turning on the radio's classic rock station to give a little weight to the air and keep her from sorrowful thoughts. Maybe Mel would leave a note…Junie deserved some kind of explanation, even if it would mean nothing to her in this life.

The night drive was smooth and tranquil, with few if any cars still traveling through the dark hours. Cruising along to "American Pie" filled Mel with an unexpected peace—and an abundance of unwelcome emotion. The peace itself was a thing that she might not feel the same way anymore once Rexie made her his wife.

Things would be different. She would be different.

Wouldn't she?

How many times she'd thought about this night! How

different this night already was from the way she'd thought it would be.

For one thing, well—it had been cleaner somehow. Simpler. Restoring her one true love's memory had worked out with a naive silliness in her imagination.

SCENE:
Lakeside resort.

CHARACTERS:
Rex Virgil (A handsome movie star)
Melba Daniels (A desperate girl haunted by telepathy)

[REX reclines in his lakeside lounge,
looking singularly cool in his
sunglasses mid-tan]

MELBA
(approaching)
Mr. Virgil?

Melba grinned at her own silliness. She pulled into the parking lot of the liquor store while, on the stage of her imagination, Rexie turned his head from his lake reading and lowered his sunglasses.

But it hadn't been so predictable in real life. In fact, it had been very strange. She hadn't been ready for it. In her version, she had all this time to get her nerves up. To brace herself against the hard reality of finally having another chance to talk to Rex in the flesh.

This time, he would listen.

The clerk at the liquor store was very helpful and, from the sounds of it, fairly used to people from the resort coming to avail themselves of his selection. It wasn't long before Mel had a surplus of fancy liquors loaded into the trunk of the car. Feeling generous, Mel tipped the guy the twenty she had intended to spend on cigarettes (she had bundled a carton into the liquor purchase), bid him a good night, and hit the road again.

HE KNOWS ABOUT TAYLOR'S BODY

THE POLICE ASKED HIM

TO LOOK FOR YOU

HE'S ON THE PHONE

WITH THEM

RIGHT NOW

Melba's hands tightened on the wheel. She turned down the radio and exhaled when this abated the voices. It was much better when they linked themselves to some feature of her environment…although removing one conduit sometimes just opened another. When she turned down the radio, her phone buzzed in the seat beside her.

Mouth twisted in annoyance, eyeing the road as long as she could, Mel reached over, plucked up the device and glanced at it sidelong.

DADDY
You're a stupid little piece of shit, you know that?

Mel's eyes bugged. She flung the phone from her hand and focused on the black road bathed in her headlights. Daddy hadn't even been alive for smartphones! Yet there was the text, plain as day. A transmission from another dimension.

"Don't let me see him when I go there, Rex." Melba chanted the words to herself, rocking a little in her seat. Leaning toward the wheel, she peered across the headlights and begged, "Please, please don't make me see him."

Daddy's nasty words had already leapt from the phone to her ears, repeated ad nauseum as though from somewhere within the car. That was fine. She preferred him invisible. After his death, he had appeared before her only a few times—rancid, bloated, crusty as he'd been in life—but each instance had been more upsetting than the last. Thankfully, Rexie was usually there to keep the lesser beings away; and, when he wasn't, the Gray Man preferred to look in on her personally, without sending an emissary.

What was it going to be like without all these creatures oppressing her? She had turned it over in her head a hundred thousand times since she was old enough to think, but her mind had still never settled on a satisfactory model for what seemed likely to happen to her in the afterlife. What it would be like to have a clear mind.

"I know," Rexie always said in her greatest moments of distress. "I know what it'll be like so well that you don't *have* to know, sugar. You just have to trust me. Do you trust me?"

"Of course, Rexie."

"Then don't worry about it. All you gotta know is that I'm gonna take good care of you, angel. You and me, we're gonna see the world—do a million things. Be a million things. Whatever you want. We can dance all night and watch the sunrise. We can take a plane to the moon. I can show you the future. It'll all be so beautiful, Melba…you won't even think to miss this place."

He had a way of telling her these things when she was lying beside Junie in a vain effort at sleep, or thinking of a departed pet, or enduring some other depressing aspect of her deeply troubled reality. When he granted these gentle reassurances in such situations, she just wasn't sure if it was truth or placation.

But now, driving to meet him, her hands trembling with adrenaline on the wheel as she pulled through a hall of trees that led to the resort, she fully believed every word he had said. Everything was working out too elegantly to be anything but truth.

After taking a left to the private drive that permitted her to miss the resort in favor of Rex's house, Mel pulled quietly to the edge of the road, shut off her lights, and reached into the purse beside her.

The box of foil-packed Rohypnol rattled in her hand.

This stuff was only a precaution, so she didn't want to give into her temptation to pre-drug any of the drinks while in the car. However, she was going to have to be very careful. There were probably a few internal security cameras if there were two visible from the street. After thinking it over, she took the pills out of their box, stuffed the abandoned cardboard sleeve under her seat, and zipped the foils into the inner pocket of her purse.

Then, she was ready.

Exhaling, inhaling, steadying her focus, Mel marveled to think this moment would only come once. The universe might run itself over again. Entropy might reverse so the Big Bang could perform another explosion: another production of the same old show. But, in Melba's perception, there was only time she would be able to savor this moment. Maybe all eternity would just be this moment, this anticipation, over and over. Maybe. Maybe.

But, so far as she knew for sure, she could only have this experience the once.

She dedicated herself to savoring every second.

A breathless moment later, Melba's car trembled before the little black gate. She but glanced at the building while leaning out the window to pound the entry code. 1974 opened the way, and, with a giddy laugh as abrupt and bold as a crack of thunder, Mel pulled her car in beside Rex Virgil's.

Hands still on the wheel, Melba shut her eyes to stave off a panic attack.

Why was she even worried about it? He would know. Rexie knew everything she thought and felt all the time, even though, when he was in his physical form, he pretended he couldn't. That was just it, though…he was the best actor in the world, the smartest and most creative man that had or would ever exist. It was nothing for him to flip a switch and pretend this or that thing, whatever served his purposes.

And his purposes? His purposes…

More than once she had asked herself about Rexie's goals. When she was first learning the identity of the male voice who had distinguished himself from the rest and taken a sympathetic, often romantic attitude toward her, Mel made the terrible mistake of telling one or two people about it. Some told her to quit letting her imagination run wild; some recommended she seek medical help.

June's parents, however, Melba's aunt and uncle, had decided to take it upon themselves to bring Mel into church to have a long, frustrating talk with the pastor.

Mel didn't like to think about it. She had been 14 and he had been trying to look down her blouse every chance he got, but that isn't what really bothered her. What really bothered her was the way he listened with a grim affect to everything she said before folding his hands and regarding her for a few long, blood-boiling seconds.

"Melba, I'm afraid this is a very serious condition. It sounds to me like you may be facing the early stages of demonic possession."

No shit, she was facing a case of demonic possession… but Rexie wasn't the demon. It was the Gray Man, whose hideousness was beyond any expression. The Gray Man had come first—had been there ever since she was a little girl.

She had almost appreciated its presence at first. It had given her something to look at while Daddy was giving her too much attention. Then, though, it started coming around any old time. Then it was hovering over her, watching her sleep. Then it was conducting a choir of voices, some of whom she knew and most of whom she didn't, to make her suffer with painful, shameful thoughts and intrusive horrors that made her mind a living hell.

So, yes. She was certainly dealing with a demon of some kind, whatever it was. But, from the evils that demon conspired to produce for her torment, something beautiful had happened. A luscious red rose blossomed from all the mire, and that rose was Mel's one single treasure in the world. It was her one relief; her one reassurance that there was something good to all this. Some purpose for being here.

Without Rexie, everything was just shit.

Her breath hitched as the front door of the extraordinary house opened to reveal the tall, toned shape of the man who owned it. Mel swallowed sharply and, ducking her head, gathered her purse, shoved the rope in a little more, fixed the gun in the back of her waistband, and let herself out of the car as Rex came to greet her.

"I knew I had a good feeling about you! Here, let me help you haul it in…you want to just pop your trunk for me—"

It was unnerving to hear Rexie speak like somebody from a big city instead of somebody from Mel's family. She caught the edge of one wide-flashing smile and, blushing furiously, produced a stupid little grin of her own while hitting the button of her keys. The car's trunk popped open while Rexie hurried to it, clasping his hands and exclaiming in pleasure.

"Nectar of the gods! I should have figured out where the movers put that dolly…"

It wasn't being in Rexie's presence that made Mel so nervous. In addition to being super casual and very down-to-earth, Rex Virgil's linear self had interacted with Mel on three separate occasions. She was used to being near him. It was natural. It was meant to be.

What made her nervous was the deeper meaning of what it meant to be with him now. It was the true end of Mel's time on Earth. No backsies. No changes or do-overs. No second drafts.

Junie was gonna be so sad.

"There we go!" After about four minutes of hustling back and forth through a sublime foyer with vaulted wood ceilings and an open flow to the living and sun rooms that overlooked the lake, Rex smiled at the collection of hard liquor arranged across the bar of the brightly decorated kitchen. "Looks like a party for sure! What a relief…I thought I was going to be in for a boring night. Thanks again, Gwen…"

Smiling, taking her hand to shake, Rexie stared into her face for the first time all night.

Time slowed. This was really happening. From this second on, Melba had no fucking idea what she was going to do or say. She could only hope her hand wasn't too sweaty. Fuck, oh, he smelled so good! Just like she remembered.

Still shaking her hand, his face searching hers, Rex said, "Now that the libations are here, what do you say to…calling your friends—up."

His hand froze, still clasping hers.

Every miniscule facet of his features changed. A microscopic parting of his lips; the urgent shrinking of his pupils.

Rex released her hand so quickly he might as well have been bitten by a snake.

He stepped back, looked her up and down one more, sharp time, and said in a stern tone, "You shouldn't be here."

And, with that incredible ventriloquist's skill that allowed him to speak without moving his mouth, he added in the rural voice that Melba better knew, "But I'm sure as shit glad you is, baby girl."

SEVEN

MELBA WRANG HER hands for only a few seconds before, realizing the way the gesture made her purse sag open to reveal its contents, she stopped to yank it up her shoulder again. "I'm sorry," she stammered, "I know—I know I might get you into trouble, but—"

"*You're* the one with the restraining order," Rex reminded her gruffly, backing another step in the direction of the living room. "I'm not the one liable to get into trouble here."

"It was an honest coincidence," Mel continued, barreling through the fear she knew she'd cause him. "Really, Rex. I was just going down to the store to buy cigarettes—*you* talked to *me*. I just thought—"

"Thought you had a way to sneak into my house like you did my hotel room…"

Unable to help herself, Mel giggled. "You're a real kidder, baby—I sure do wish you woulda stood up for me in court, though."

Rex ground his teeth.

"Melba," he said, his measured tone not unkind despite its tension, "I know it seems to you like you know me very well through all my movies…but I'm a real person. I meet a lot of people all the time. Just because we meet each other—even if we've had sex—that doesn't mean we're friends. You know that, don't you?"

"Oh, sure. I have sex with people I don't like all the time. But it's not about the sex, Rexie! You know you mean more to me than that." While, running his hand over his face, Rexie produced a sigh, Mel assured him tenderly, "I know you gotta run all around with these girls to protect your image—to be Rex Virgil. And that's fine. I understand it. That's all fine to me. Just as long as you come home when I'm too lonesome. Or…will you still need to do all that when we're together?"

"You need serious help," said Rex, shaking his head and turning away. "Come hold my hand and let's talk a little while, angel."

Beaming to be so invited by his sudden turn to that country twang, Mel hurried after him and snatched up his hand while he jumped in surprise. Looking as frozen in shock to touch her as she was to touch him, Rex just stood there with his eyes fixed on her face.

"I knew you cared about me, Rexie. You and your games!"

"This isn't a game." City voice again. He jerked out of her grasp and flexed his hand as though hurt by the force she'd used. "This is my career we're talking about! Look—Melba. What do you want? Why did you come here today? Is this a money thing? Do you want money?"

Her brow furrowed.

"No, baby, I don't care about your money. I mean, it's nice, but—you *know* why I'm here. I'm here to make you remember."

Rex shut his eyes.

He inhaled, gathered himself, then refocused those piercing blue eyes that made her want to scream with pleasure.

"So this is some #metoo thing," he said, arms crossing. "I get it. You're here to teach me some kind of lesson, right? To get me to apologize to you?"

Mel wrinkled her nose. "Apologize for what, Rexie? Not defending me in court? I already said I understand—you don't have to apologize for anything."

"I can't imagine you'd be here if it wasn't still on your mind. I mean, come on—if it's not money or an apology you're after, then what do you want from me?"

"I just want to talk. I just want you to remember about yourself…about us."

"Look—Melba—"

With another sigh, Rexie took her unready hands. She gasped, her fingers pulsing with the delight of his contact. He looked earnestly into her, those great big hands tightening around Mel's.

"I really am sorry, okay? Jesus. You're right. The least I owe you is an apology. I was younger and stupider, and I had no business taking advantage of a sixteen-year-old trying to get my autograph. I—I don't know. I don't have an excuse. You were just—I…I made a mistake in the heat of the moment."

"Don't contradict me," he added in her Daddy's tone while taking a deep breath.

She had just about to point out that there weren't no heat-of-the-moment about it. Fact was, Rexie had personally invited her to meet him when, in the romantic comedy *Love Lorne*, he stopped addressing the somewhat goofy title nerd-turned-cheerleading queen to instead pour his heart out to Melba. She had been stunned, then moved to tears, and had wholeheartedly accepted his invitation to come meet him while he was doing a one-man-show in Memphis.

He had known what he was doing when he invited her, in other words…but it wasn't lascivious. She still remembered everything he said when revealing that he was the male voice so tenderly watching out for her. "I have loved you since before there were stars in the sky," he told her, a mist in his eye. "Since way back when we were both the same person."

It was a warm, gallant love, Rexie's. That was why he felt bad about fuckin' her the first time they met, she was sure. He had been so busy at the time that he couldn't stick around Tennessee to be with her. Had to ditch her. Besides, she was a teenager then.

But she understood. Of course, she understood.

While, overwhelmed by memory, she stared into space and Rexie's face at the same time, he was still busy trying to say he was sorry.

"I hope you don't feel like I forced you to do something truly against your will. I know that a sixteen-year-old can't *legally* consent in America, of course, but I just mean to say, I hope that at the time—ah, fuck. Listen to me. There's no excuse. I'm really sorry. I really, truly appreciate you choosing to keep everything about that time to yourself when we were dealing with the courts."

"Who on earth could I tell, silly?" She laughed and shrugged. "Nobody would ever believe me."

Rex's perfect brow furrowed. A slight mist wobbled before his eyes.

"My God," he murmured, releasing her. "I'm an awful person."

Mel's heart broke while he made his way back to the living room's sitting area. Melba joined him, hurrying along behind to perch upon the couch where he cradled his face in his hand.

"I knew I was doing something cruel when my agent said I needed to file a criminal complaint. I know, but—"

"It was what you needed to do," she said, daring to touch his bicep. "For your career. To be Rex Virgil. I understand, Rex, I don't blame you. That's why I went down."

Nodding mutely, Rex averted his gaze to the floor. His eye was snagged by the tattoo on Melba's calf.

He hesitated.

"That's a beautiful tattoo," he said in an absent tone. "Is that from something?"

"From a dream. Do you recognize it?"

His lips pursed and he studied it, a slight furrow to his brow as he did. The crease was ironed back to perfection when, suddenly snapped out of his thought and into his present reality, he shook his head.

"Sorry. Look. This is all just really unexpected. I don't know what to say. I guess I appreciate that you didn't break in this time, but—I don't know. I wish you had approached me differently, or that I hadn't approached you, or…fuck. Ah!"

With a noise of supreme angst, Rex leaned his head back against the couch and pinched the bridge of his nose. "You spend so much of your adult life trying to avoid responsibility for mistakes that, even when you have a chance to accept them—even when one's standing before you—you can't let honesty into your heart…pathetic. You know, Melba—I'm glad you're here."

While Mel perked, he once more took her hands in his.

"Let me make it up to you. My girlfriend is coming tomorrow afternoon, so I'd like it if everybody could clear out by then—but, if you still want to have your friends over for a little party, I wouldn't say 'no.' It's the least I could do. And… what do they call it, parole? Probation? Whatever it is, I'll write to your officer if you get into trouble. Just—thank you, thank you for coming and talking to me face-to-face instead of—I don't know, posting something on Twitter or writing to the *Times*."

"Rexie! I wouldn't dream of it, silly."

"Then you're truly a generous-hearted person. Hey, come on!" Beaming, a new vigor to his motions, Rex sprang from the couch and strode to the kitchen. Melba straightened a little, walking the fine line between casual observation and physical readiness for action. "Let's have a drink together before we get the rest of the party over here. I know that I panicked last time—you *did* surprise the shit out of me—but the first time we met you seemed like a nice girl. What have you been doing since then?"

Blushing, rolling her eyes, waving a hand, Mel pushed hair back from her face. "Just workin'. I am—was—an esthetician, but I do tarot and horoscope readings online these days. It's a little hard findin' work since the arrest and everythin'."

He cringed. "Sorry about that. Daquiri?"

"Sure! Not too strong, if you please. Anyway, don't worry about it…since I got out, I've been using the time to write a script!"

Rex lifted his eyebrows while taking mixer from the fridge. "No kidding! What's it about?"

Nothing in his tone seemed to indicate anything patronizing or derisive, so she answered. "It's a horror movie," she explained, her prideful grin a mile wide. "I think it could be pretty good! I'm still tryin' to get the current draft a little tighter, though."

"You mean you actually finished it?"

"Yessir, I did."

"No kidding! Can I read it?"

Bringing it had been purposeful—she had intended to get Rexie to read it as though that were the only reason she wanted his time—but now that he offered, the tips of her ears burned like her cheeks. She shook her head rapidly, laughing as she told him, "Oh, no, no! I can't."

"No, no, hey, come on. I'd love to read it! What if I'm passing up the next Citizen Kane? Come on. Let me read it. It's the least I can do."

With a flourish, Rex picked up the two cocktail glasses and returned to her.

"I'd love to read your script, Melba," he said earnestly, presenting her with one of the daquiris. "I want to prove that I mean what I say, and that I'm grateful for your…discretion.

What happened between us before is water under the bridge to me if it is to you."

Poor Rexie! If only he remembered. The material world really had done a number on him.

Well…that, or he was acting.

Maybe it was a little of both.

Rex Virgil was known these days for his method acting, often going for entire shoots without once breaking character. He had described it in interviews as an effort to forget that he was acting. And that, Melba suspected, was what living in linear time was really like for him. It was more that Rexie was so good at pretending to be a mortal, petty celebrity that he had forgotten he wasn't really those things. He was such a talented actor that he even fooled himself. He thought he had different priorities than his soul knew he did.

And that was part of the game.

In this instance, Rexie thought his job was to keep Melba pacified until he could get her out of his house. Melba's job was to avoid getting thrown out at all costs: to stay there until he remembered who he really was. When he remembered, he would be able to exhibit all his phenomenal powers.

When he remembered, they would be liberated from the Gray Man together.

"Melba?"

Melba blinked to be snapped from her thoughts. She looked blankly into Rexie's face before, smiling just to see him, she asked, "Yessir?"

"You just looked distracted."

"I am, a little bit. I—"

Mel had leaned back against the couch and glanced casually to the side, but the word she had been on the cusp of forming stuck in her throat.

The elongated gray head of her specter slowly leaned around the living room's corner.

For the first time in Melba's life, the Gray Man was

adorned with something akin to eyes. Two ringed black circles around murky pools. The eyes of a spoiled fish.

It stared into her as she sat frozen in absolute terror.

"So, Melba? How about that script?" Looking at her in genuine curiosity, Rexie rested his glass on his knee. "I'd love to read it. Or is it in the car?"

"I—uh—no—I— It's actually here—"

Her eyelids fluttered beneath the oppressive burden of organizing her thoughts. With a glance back to the corner where nothing out of place could now be seen, Melba bent toward her purse and rifled through it for the script.

The rope coiled within spilled out at Rex's feet.

EIGHT

MELBA'S BLOOD TURNED to ice.

Mouth agape, Rex stared at the rope that had sprung across his floor.

With little more than a quick glance at Mel, Rexie threw down his glass and leapt from the couch while it shattered. He sprinted across the living room floor in seconds, leaving Mel to gasp and spring from her seat. A shard of glass sank straight through the soft foam of her flipflop; she barely felt it while, still fleeing, he called without looking over his shoulder, "I like it rough, angel. You know I ain't gonna letcha get me that easy!"

Laughing, a sigh of relief soothing the edge of her fright to see him running from her, Mel drew the gun from her waistband and experimentally pointed it at Rex before he could get out of sight. She pulled the hammer back until it clicked.

He stopped there at the edge of the living room, looked over his shoulder with a pair of chilled eyes, and finally raised his hands to either side of his head.

"How rough do you like it, baby? This rough?"

"Please." His eyes flickered between her face and the gun, the tip of his tongue darting sexily across his lower lip. "Don't hurt me, Mel. We're friends now, remember?"

"Of course we're *friends*, Rexie…we were always friends, even though you forgot all about it on the day you was born. Come on! Don't be so scareda me…unless you *want* me to scare you, of course."

"No! No, please. I'll do whatever you want. Just—don't hurt me."

"Rexie, baby…" She felt a little bad for scaring him like this, but Melba knew Rexie better than he knew himself. She knew what he really wanted. When, edging nearer to her again, he warned, "If you kill me, you'll go to jail for a long time," Melba knew his human shell was worried about things irrelevant to the soul matter at-hand.

"I'm not fixinta be *that* rough, Rexie…but I do wanna play a little before we get all serious."

Awash with bliss as he was at last within arm's reach, Mel grabbed him with one hand and dragged him close by the shirt. He yelped while she pressed the pistol up against his face, enthusing as she did, "Is this what you like? A little spice, a little spook…maybe you really *will* like my movie, Rexie."

"Please, God—"

While his watering eyes rolled toward the ceiling, his lips motionlessly produced the words, "God, God, give it to me, Mel…don't hold back. Whip me, beat me…let's do bondage, baby."

Laughing, Mel told him, "Now you're talkin' my language," and grabbed him by the back of the head to hold him still. Flinging herself high upon her toes, Melba clamped her mouth over his for an eager kiss that made her melt into a moan from the first contact. His unready tongue stiffened, then relaxed against hers as he eased into the true devotion shown by her caress. Whispering his name, Mel slid against his body—

And jerked away, laughing, when one sneaky hand bumped the gun.

"Nice try," she said, waving it like a finger in the face of a naughty kid. "All right, enough's enough…bondage, really? You're so kinky, Rexie."

Feeling inspired as he stammered out, "Wh—what," Mel waved the gun toward the coil of rope spilled upon the floor. "Go on, babe. Go get it and bring it to, oh…how 'bout that chair?"

The black-and-silver modernist monstrosity caught her eye at the edge of the living room, set so as to allow a nice view of the outside without having to exit to the sunroom on a hot day. Keeping an eye on him, she dragged it toward the center of the living room and waved the gun toward its seat.

"All right, Rexie, come on…let me show you a real good time after all you've done for me."

Tears rolling down his cheek for as high as the emotions of their impending union were, Rex made his slow way toward her with the ropes still in his hands.

YOU ARE WRONG

YOU WILL DIE

THERE WILL BE NOTHING

Could they not show her even one shred of privacy?

"Fer Chrissakes— Will you *please* tell them to shut up?"

Was there not one moment in her life that could ever be hers?

THIS IS NOT LIFE

THIS IS DEATH

YOU ARE ALREADY DEAD

HE IS ALREADY DEAD

THIS IS ALL

YOUR LIVES

WILL EVER

BE

"Shut the fuck up! That ain't fuckin' true. Please, baby, make them stop."

Something breathed in her ear.

She glanced sharply around in search of the Gray Man. Nothing.

Would he disappear forever if she put a bullet through his head? She ain't never thought to try it, to be honest.

Rexie didn't reply to her requests. He stopped before her, his hands trembling, his face pale. Staring at that gun, he extended the ropes. Mel sighed heftily and took them from his hand.

"Thank you," she said. "Fuck, oh, keep him *away*, please…I really hate his guts. We won't have to deal with him when we're free of this place, will we?"

"I don't know what you're talking about," he whispered before going on in his thick accent, "I told you before, baby, you ain't got to worry none about him. He's just a fact of life. When it's time for him to go away, he will."

Rexie stared into her eyes while he spoke, his lips firm. As though he waited for a response. Melba sighed when he finished his thought.

"I guess that's true. Still, wouldn't mind if he left right now. Go ahead and sit down, baby…or should I call you somethin' mean right now? 'Motherfucker'—no, 'slave!'" Tipping back her head to laugh, Mel blushed. "I could never do that, oh hell…"

But she did like the thought of Rex tied up. With one more glance at the gun, he slowly did as she bade him and lowered into the seat before which they conversed. With a grim stare through her, he waited.

"Don't you get too fresh now," she warned him, wagging the gun before tying him up.

One-handed bondage was actually pretty tough when you got right down to it, but that was why Mel took care of binding his wrists to the chair first. With those under control, he couldn't monkey around—free himself or none of that nonsense. He could have his damn game, and she could celebrate the joy it brought her just to be close to him. Rexie!

"I'm so happy we're finally together," she said when she was able to put the gun down and work on his ankles. "Rex, oh, honey, I've been waitin' since I's a kid…I used to be so afraid of this day, but as soon as I understood what you were trying to tell me—"

"I wasn't trying to tell you anything."

"Of course. You're right. You don't have to try…whatever you do, it just comes together for you. Your lessons are everywhere. Ain't you proud I learned how to listen?"

He stared on, his unmoving mouth enthusing, "I sure am, baby. Damn! Sure am. Melba, Melba. Daddy loves you, angel."

Blushing, giggling like the schoolgirl she never really felt herself to be even as a child, Melba leaned against his knee. "I love you, too, Rexie."

Her heart hammered at the contact with the fabric stretched over his leg. His *warm* leg…oh, Rexie really was such a warm man. Exhaling to touch him, Melba looked over every inch of his body: from his gray trousers to his pinstripe shirt of brown and cream.

Her trembling fingertips extended to trail over the front of his shirt. The fabric was so smooth, so expensive, that she almost felt bad for touching it. His stomach tightened beneath her caress, though, so she kept at it, trailing up over his chest and then down along his ribs.

"You're so beautiful, Rex," she murmured, gazing into his face while a smile grew across hers. Her lower lip disappeared shyly between her teeth while she glanced down at his lap. "I'm glad you made me a pretty girl. Lots of awful things have happened to me because of it, but at least it means I'm good enough for you now that we're together."

"Sure does, baby," he said while staring grimly on.

So in-character! Laughing softly, Melba leaned up and pressed a kiss to his still mouth. Then, leaning back down and squatting upon her heels, Melba trailed her hand down the buttons leading toward his pants.

"You don't think I'm easy, do you, Rex? I mean…I know I gave it to you the first time we met…but you're, like, a fairy tale prince…"

"Please," his city voice softly uttered while she unzipped his pants.

"Oh!"

Thrill surged through Melba to reach in and blindly touch him. With a moan of desire, she gingerly drew him from his pants. To see him elicited memories that made her gasp.

"God *damn*, Rexie! Look at that thing…you really are the king, you know…"

He cried out from the second her lips touched him. As her tongue explored along the surface of his flesh, no contour going untouched, Rex murmured in a low, desperate tone of voice.

"Please, Melba—don't do this. Whatever you think you—you want from me, you could get from anybody else. You could—oh, oh, let me give you money…you can get any man you want, just, please—stop—"

Melba moaned, the shape and feeling of him divine. A fire burned between her thighs, its only fuel the scent and heat of him while her head bobbed.

It was too easy to tell when men were just playing around…he was hard as a rock in no time. Couldn't fake that.

Mel chuckled with him in her throat and, driven to ever-higher states of desire to feel how aroused he was by her, she reached between her own legs and pushed a hand into her shorts.

Damn…no real sense in waiting when she felt like this.

Her body dissolved of identity and reduced to pure, unadulterated yearning, Melba released him from her mouth to stand upright. Though at first he gasped as if in relief, his body soon re-tensed within his bindings.

Sensually as she could stand to make herself, Melba stripped off her clothes.

"Remember my body, Rexie?" Smiling, her panties around her ankles, Melba ran her hands over herself before she straddled his lap. "You don't remember the tattoos, of course…I didn't have 'em yet."

"Oh, God…"

He gasped sharply, shocked by the same tsunami of exposure, astonishment, knowingness that rocked her when she lowered herself upon him.

Rex's eyes shut and he whispered to himself again, "Oh, God," while the captivated woman cried out.

"Oh, Rexie! At last—oh, honey, I've wanted to be with you for so long. Thank you for keeping your promise to me."

"Anything for you, angel." His second voice twanged above the inaudible, frightened murmur that passed through his mouth like a babbling brook. "You're so good at doin' everything I ask you. Least I can do is reward you."

"Yes! Oh! Fuck, oh, Rexie, oh—"

"Tell me you would do anything for me, Melba."

"I'd do anything! Anything for you! Rex, Rexie, oh, Rex Virgil! Yes! I'd do anything, anything you asked. I'd kill myself for you right now, Rex!"

"Please don't," he whimpered, his throat tightening with the swallow that bobbed his Adam's apple and ended in a pitiful gasp. While she cooed and kissed his mouth, he murmured insistently against her, "Please, please—you don't have to hurt me, or yourself, or anyone. You could just stop— you could just go. Please."

"Oh, Rexie, baby, I would never leave you behind…never, ever—ah!"

Crying out, her back arching, Melba moaned into the heights of pleasure. Blood ran from the arch of her foot down to her toes while she bounced in his lap, but she forgot all about it—forgot every last sensation but Rexie, Rexie's body. Rexie's fine, kissable mouth that whined so pitifully while she guided them both to orgasm.

"That's good, Rexie," she whispered as he at least gave up and released himself in her. "That's real good—oh, baby, that's right. Doesn't that feel nice?"

While she stroked his face, his heaving breath reached a pitch like a drowning man breaking the surface. Tears threatened to brim over his eyes. Damn, he was beautiful.

"Okay," he said, his tone unsteady with its desperation, "now, will you please—please, just leave. Just leave. Maybe even call the cops on the way out so they'll find me and let me go. I won't even ask you to do that much for me."

"Poor Rexie! Why are you so sad? It's nice that we're together…you've been so fucked up by this awful place that you can't even remember that much. Poor angel."

Sighing in sadness for him, Mel straightened up and cradled his head to her bosom. She rocked with him in her arms, her eyes fluttering closed while she hummed his name, basked in the Armani cloud of cologne, kissed his warm scalp through his dark, gelled hair.

"Don't worry," Mel summarized, dismounting him and reaching down to untie one of his wrist bindings. "Just like you've taken care of me all this time, I'll take care of you now, too."

A slow, steady exhalation slid past his lips to feel the rope loosen beneath her tug.

She only stopped when the house's doorbell rang.

NINE

WHILE MELBA WINCED, startled by the intrusive noise echoing ominously through the otherwise empty home, Rexie's pocket buzzed an accompanying warning. She glanced down at it, then grimaced to see the mess of red on the floor.

"Shit, baby! Hell, I'm sorry!"

Springing up, wincing at the pool of blood that the white carpet further wicked from her foot when she stood, Mel pushed her hair back from her face and reached around the pockets of his trousers to find his phone. After finding it was in his front pocket, she shook her head with a noise of genuine envy and couldn't help her laugh.

"Damn, what big pockets! Must be nice. So much room… here we go."

With a few contortions, she managed to get the device (the *ritzy* device—newer than any model of phone she'd ever even held) out of his pocket to find it aglow with an alert from the predicted digital doorbell. Blowing her hair from her eyes, Melba selected the prompt to view the visitor at the door and was briefly confronted by a demand for the phone's password.

"What's your password, honey?" When he didn't speak, she asked, "1974 again?"

His lips tightened. She laughed, tried it, and was immediately greeted with a live video stream that churned her stomach.

June's face was distorted by the angle and the quality, but her knitting eyebrows were unmistakable…as was the furiously arranged expression of the clown behind her. Rolling her eyes to see that Taylor had come along—and even brought Candy and Daisy, by the looks of it—Mel looked over at Rexie.

"You know what'd be really kinky, sugar," he said as she bent to pick up her panties, "is if you kept me all tied up while they were here and didn't know."

"Sounds fun…but what am I supposed to tell them when I'm here and you're not?"

"Any old thing. Tell 'em we're getting' married and I'm takin' a shower before we get on a plane to the Bahamas."

Laughing and rolling her eyes, amazed that he could laugh without smiling, Mel propped her fist against one hip and demanded, "But what if you change your mind and start hollerin' up a storm?"

"That's where the kinky part comes in," said Rexie.

Mel realized what he was getting at after only a few seconds. Then, grinning down at the panties in her hand, she filled his mouth with the lacy scrap and, amid his protestations and attempts to spit them out, slid his belt from his waist.

"Now hold on to your horses, Rexie…gosh, just relax… stay quiet or we can't have any fun. If they find you too soon…"

Or at all, for that matter. Mel had absolutely no idea how this was going to develop. There were so many things wrong from the outsider perspective that there was no way Junie'd abide much before calling the cops.

Thankfully, babe was an actor.

After grabbing the gun again, Melba asked, "If I take off your gag for a few seconds, will you tell them to wait at the door?"

Nodding urgently, Rex stared with some real cute puppydog peepers until she removed the impromptu gag and gave him a chance to gasp. He caught his breath while, gun in one hand and phone in the other, Melba hit 'talk' as the faces on the screen turned to reconvene.

Clearing his throat, Rex looked twice up at Mel before saying to the phone, "Hello?"

June whipped around and leaned down into the camera. "Hello! Um, hello, sir, uh—I'm so sorry, I don't know where to start—"

"You're looking for Melba, right?"

Her voice and manner overflowing with anxiety, Junie managed, "Well—well, yes."

"She's in here," said Rex, staring into Melba's face, adding to top it all off, "We're having a great time."

Melba beamed to hear him say such a thing and said to the phone, "I'll be right there, Junie, just wait!"

"Mel—"

She closed the app without another word.

Grinning, Melba, kissed Rexie before shoving his gag back into his mouth. He protested, his muffled grunts and cries a noble match for the struggle he put up against the chair to which he'd been bound. Laughing, Mel shook her head and looked around for someplace to take him. Soon, she found it: an adjoining game room that was easy enough a location to drag his chair.

"You just wait right there," she said with a wink and another kiss, sliding the tall door shut behind her and turning around with a wince.

The pain in her foot was great, but the pain of the blood trail left behind her was greater. Good thing they weren't long for this world—or she wasn't, anyway. Awful to think of his house looking like this because of her. And such a nice place, too! Didn't even want to contemplate the cost of these carpets.

Hopping on one foot rather than fucking up the carpet even worse for now, Mel returned to her pile of clothes, dressed, and considered her wounded foot. A few seconds later she had her flipflop back on, got the glass removed, and had wrapped a wad of paper towels around her foot so that the sandal held it in place. Then, feeling pretty good about the mobility afforded by her contrivance, Mel made her way back to the grand foyer's front door.

"Mel!" June didn't hesitate to dash across the threshold and throw her arms around her cousin. "Oh, Mel, I've been so worried—"

"You better stay worried," said Taylor, whose name Mel still only barely retained when the word 'dumbass' was the natural substitute. Gesturing to the blackened nose that was stuffed with bloody tissues, he demanded, "You see what you did to me, Melba? *And* stole my gun. Where the fuck is it?"

Under her hoodie, currently, in the back of her shorts. Good thing Junie didn't feel it on her during their embrace.

"I threw it in the fuckin' lake," lied Mel, limping into the house. "Come on in, this makes my life easier. Rexie was gonna have me call y'all up on account of his wantin' a party, but I'd just as soon keep thing restrained to present company."

"A party?" June's head whipped around and, pressing closer to Mel's side, she bent to whisper. "Melba, what's going on? Wasn't that Rex Virgil?"

"Hell yeah, it's Rex! He's just takin' a shower upstairs, said he'll join us shortly. For now—hold on—there's a cool room this way, I think…aha!"

The theatre room had a fabulous glass wall that permitted a view of the lake if one could tear one's eyes from the oversized television taking up most of the wall. What wasn't television was covered in bookshelves of scripts, with the furnishings arranged to allow guests to admire both.

"How'd you find me," asked Mel, gesturing to the couches.

"I ain't a total mor-on," groused Taylor, his concussed eyes blearily tracing the contents of the room. "Will say, though—this is one hell of a fuckin' house."

"Ain't it? Sit tight and I'll go get us some drinks."

Gasping before Mel left, Junie rushed up. "Melba! What happened to your foot?"

Shit. Paper towels were already soaking through to leave her standing on a bloody tatter. Sucking a tooth in displeasure, Mel said, "Oh, that? Uh—it's nothin', really. Stepped on a sharp rock. I'll be back."

Breathless with a kind of deception that, under normal circumstances, would have meant nothing to her, Melba hustled back to the kitchen and looked around. Her purse still sat on the floor of the adjacent living room; she dashed over to remove the foil-packed Rohypnol and, one blister at a time, popped the pills out into her palm. After frantically crushing them with her fingers, she tossed them into the rum bottle Rexie had opened and just barely had it shaken up by the time Junie called her name from down the hall.

"This way," called Mel, playing it cool while she looked around for glasses. The cabinets were plentiful to such an extent that a few were empty but rubber shelf liner, and a number of them had various collections of devices—pasta makers, sausage grinders—that had either never been used, or used once and put away forever. Rexie needed a more creative chef! But, well—with Mel, he could just fire the whole staff. She would take care of him. She'd show him he didn't need anybody else when he had her.

"Melba," said Junie while emerging in the kitchen, one helpless hand on her forehead to see her cousin, "Melba, what's going on? Where is he? Does he remember who you are?"

"'Course he remembers! We've been hangin' out and havin' a nice discussion before you all interrupted it. Aha! Come here, Junie."

While Junie trotted over to bring down a few glasses, she asked, "And he's *okay* with it? He can't be okay with it. Doesn't he have security here?"

"Hell no! He comes to this place to escape. Who'd own a cabin in the woods and then bring regular staff around to know every damn thing you did with your time off?"

"But—but after everything with the restraining order, I mean—"

"His *agent* made him get the restraining order!" Her mouth shaped in a vindicated smile, Mel set her glasses down upon the island and watched approvingly as Junie did the same. Then, one at a time, Mel filled all five glasses with daquiri mixer. "He was just tellin' me all about it. Said he knew it was cruel at the time. Even apologized to me!"

"But that's not enough drinks," said Junie while Mel turned to grab the tainted bottle of rum. "What about for Mr. Virgil?"

"He's already had one," said Mel smoothly, nodding toward the living room.

Junie followed her gaze and, rather than stopping at the drink, gasped and rushed toward the unnerving red pool. "Mel! Mel, is this blood from your foot? Melba, what on earth is going *on*?"

"I told you," she said while Junie's back was turned, hastily pouring Rohypnol rum into three of the glasses before setting it aside for a different bottle of a darker, sweeter Caribbean rum. Quickly cracking it open, she had one drink poured by the time Junie turned to face her. Her cousin was so distressed by the blood and broken glass that she must not have realized the bottle was different, because she said nothing on the matter.

"But you told me you hurt your foot on a rock."

"So?"

"So—so, that isn't what happened at all! Look at all that broken glass. Melba—oh, Melba—"

Mel jumped in surprise when, rushing up to her, June grabbed her by the shoulders and looked wildly into her face. "You haven't hurt him, have you? Where is he? Please, Melba—just talk to me."

The pain in June's face was so obvious that a rare pang of guilt twisted Mel's stomach. She longed for a way to tell her cousin, person she most loved in the whole linear world, what was really happening. This was a celebration. A honeymoon, a good-bye party. A graduation.

"I told you, Junie, he's in the shower." Shoving the untainted drinks into Becky June's hands, Melba took up the three for the others and made sure to push past her cousin in the hallway. "Now, come on…let's hurry up and play "hostesses" before what's-his-face pockets a paperweight or something."

"Taylor's *real* mad at you, Mel."

"Well, fuck him. I'm pretty sure his instinct back there was to rape me."

Wide-eyed June got out almost all of the word, "What," before Mel barreled into the sitting room with smiles and drinks for everyone.

"Here we go! No hard feelings about before."

Mel passed the first glass to Taylor before presenting his women with the other two.

Nobody thought twice—just hooted and drank on. Especially Candy, who exclaimed, "This shit is about to get wild, let's get wasted! We gotta get everybody else up here before they, like, pass out by the lake."

"Just a minute," said the clown—Taylor, that was—who took a pensive sip while watching Mel move across the room. "What are we gonna do about my gun?"

Mel shrugged her slim shoulders, grateful for the bulk of the hoodie in which she fairly well swam. "Hell, I don't know. I'll ask Rexie. He's probably got enough cash lyin' around here to buy you twenty fuckin' guns, if it's that important."

"I can't believe you threw it in the lake."

"I didn't want you coming after me, did I?"

Mel stared hard into Taylor, who scowled before taking another mouthful of tainted daquiri. As predicted, he did not want to reiterate the details of their fight in present company. Instead, he let it go with a long sigh and a thump back into the red leather armchair across from the television.

"I must admit," he said, contemplating the drink before admiring the television, "a man could get used to this life."

After locating the remote in a compartment beneath the coffee table, he kicked up his feet and hit a button on the television remote. The sleek glass panel that was nicer than anything Mel had even seen on sale in a department store clicked on without hesitation, its crisp image blazing forth to flood the room with the light of a smiling woman who stroked the phallic bottle of her preferred shampoo.

"Get your fuckin' feet off the table," Mel commanded, but the asshat didn't hear her over the sound of the television.

"So how is it you know Rex Virgil, exactly? I thought Junie here said you broke into his hotel room."

"That was a misunderstandin'." Mel took her drink to sit at the piano gathering dust in the corner of the room. "I met Rex for the first time when I was sixteen, and we've been friends ever since."

With a couple of astonished gasps, Candy and Daisy looked at one another before regarding Mel with new awe.

"No *way*," enthused young Daisy in particular, her eyes aglow with delight. "Are you for real?"

"Sure I am. We fucked the night we met and really liked each other, but a couple years later, the second time we met up, his agent told him to say I'd broken into his hotel room and press charges on account of they didn't want our story to hurt his career."

Junie looked physically pained, her drink forgotten in her hand and her jaw tight. It always bothered Junie to hear Mel insist on the truth, but Mel was tired of bowing to a world that wanted her to lie.

Rexie was right. It was time to take some goddamn responsibility for her life.

"I love Rexie," said Mel, shrugging her shoulders, "so I went up the river for him. Now that I'm back, we decided to meet up here and figure out how to, you know, move forward an' all that shit."

"That's *amazing*," Daisy continued, her eyes rolling in her head and her hands clasping with delight. "Oh-m'God, Rex Virgil is, like, my *favorite* actor in the world."

"There ain't none better," agreed Mel, annoyed by the girl's excitement and silently willing her to drink more. To encourage them, Mel sipped her own beverage. It at least got Taylor and Candy to follow suit, but Daisy resisted the urge.

Damn! If this bitch didn't keep up, the other two were going to pass out in front of her. And how would that end? Mel shuddered to think.

"Aren't you so freaking excited for the Valentino biopic? Did you already see it? What did you think?"

"Court says I'm not allowed to buy my own tickets to his movies, which of course he will rectify for me as soon as he can. Probably has a big ol' collection of 'em upstairs. Dunno, I've never seen this place with my own two eyes...only talked to him about it a little."

"Mel," said Junie, looking significantly at Taylor, "do you really think Rex would want you sharing all this stuff with them?"

"Why the fuck not? Truth's gotta come out eventually."

With a harsh laugh and a slap of his knee, Taylor leaned forward.

The asshole looked at her in the mocking, patronizing way so many had before. People at school, people at jobs. They loved to gas her up and giggle about it because they didn't understand what she was talking about, and their lack of understanding made her reality deeply untrue to them. She had his number in a second, Taylor; but Mel let him mock on, because the drug was working and he already sounded absolutely fucking slammed. Between that, his head injury, and libations consumed at the bonfire, he was not long for this period of consciousness.

"Well hell, Junie, sounds like she knows the score! We're here in Rex's house, ain't we? She can't be that delusional, then."

"She's *obviously* not fucking delusional, Taylor," said Daisy in the snotty tone of someone who had not been told relevant details of the situation. "Like you just said—how else would we be here right now?"

"That is a good question," agreed Taylor, taking another mouthful of his daquiri and furrowing his brow with an appreciative sucking of his cheeks. "Damn! This shit is delicious. Little bitter, but smooth. What is it?"

"Pineapple daquiri," said Mel, throwing back a mouthful that at last encouraged Daisy to suck on her drink. Even as she did, the young woman's admiring—some might say "scheming"—eyes stayed fixed upon Mel's face. When the drink lowered, her mouth was arranged in a petite little painting of a smile.

"When do we get to meet him?"

"Soon, I think."

"Are you really sure Rex *wants* to meet new people on short notice, Mel?" Junie, nervous as a bird in a house, fluttered over to take Melba's free hand. "I mean, it's already pretty late, and—"

Candy lowered her drink just long enough to boo. "Come on! The night is *young*."

For her part, Mel smiled patiently at her cousin...no matter how much she felt like smacking her across the head.

"Hell yeah, Junie, it's barely nine! Let's hang out with Rexie and figure the rest when we get to it."

"Sounds good to me," said Taylor with a belch into his empty glass. After setting it down without a coaster between it and that nice-ass coffee table, he leaned back in his seat. A sudden frown twisted his mouth along with his disoriented look around.

"Fuckin' hell," he said, looking over at Mel, "goddamn! That was one stiff drink."

His frown deepened and his gaze unfocused into strained thought. While Daisy ignored him and continued asking of Mel, "So…how *big* is it," Taylor leaned at the waist. His expression grew deeply uneasy.

Ignore him. Melba grinned at the younger woman and threw her a wink. "Big enough that I know better than to spread that info around. Can't have you ladies tryinta steal him out from under me, now."

While Daisy covered her comic pout with another sip of the drink, Candy wandered to the nearest shelf of scripts. "Damn! Has he been in *all* these?"

"Nah," said Mel, who had glimpsed a bound copy of *The Big Lebowski*'s script. "I think he just collects 'em. You don't want to keep your valuable scripts in this room, anyway… the sun'll come through the window and fuck 'em up. You all right, Taylor?"

He had leaned forward a little more, his knees slightly spread and his hands balled into fists between them.

"Uh-huh."

The grunt was intended to be a positive noise, but it sounded so breathless that it could have easily been taken for the opposite.

"Mel," tried Junie again, glancing down at Melba's paper toweled foot, "maybe you shouldn't be drinkin' with your cut, honey…"

"Ah, it's fine. You girls are gonna see my script on that shelf soon," said Mel, taking another sip of the drink after using it to gesture. The smooth, bright pineapple rolled over her palate, deepened by the richness of the rum, to act as balm to her slightly annoyed nerves. Would these fuckers pass out, or what? Real life really wasn't like the movies.

"Nu-uh," enthused Daisy, her sparkling eyes on Mel again. "Are you, like, a writer?"

Mel blew a raspberry. "Hell fuckin' no! I couldn't stand it. I'd blow my brains out sittin' still all day—bad enough doin' readin's for three or four hours every morning. Nah, I don't know…somebody told me I should do a project to keep myself busy when I was out of prison, and I got this idea for a movie and it just kind of—fell outta me, I don't know."

Looking suitably impressed, Candy turned from her study of the bound scripts. "What's it about?" Her words had taken on a slur.

"It's still kinda missin' a twist, but it's about a couplea girls who kidnap their favorite actor to make him star in a snuff film."

While Candy and Daisy laughed together, Daisy enthused, "Right on! That sounds fucked up. Like Rob Zombie or something."

"Oh," said Mel, "shit, I fucking love Rob Zombie! Y'all like—"

Taylor's retching interrupted the first moment of genuine bonding Melba had experienced with the other women. By the time everybody had turned to see the source of the gross noise, Taylor had staggered up and barely made it to the nearby potted fern before projecting a spray of thick orangish vomit that made Melba nauseous to observe. Her nose and lips screwing in disgust, she turned away while washing the imaginary taste from her mouth with a sip of untainted daquiri.

"Taylor," remonstrated Daisy, shocked and horrified by her brother, "what the fuck is *wrong* with you? Oh my God! You're so embarrassing, I wish I could kill myself right now—"

"What a fuggin' lightweight," agreed Candy thickly, shaking her head before taking one final swig of her daquiri. As she set it on the nearby end table, a little sway in her step made her laugh and catch herself against the wall. "Some people jes can't hold their liquor…I thought you were *better* than this, Taylor."

"I—I don't know why—what—"

Another wave of vomit erupted from the idiot's mouth. Junie looked on the verge of a panic attack.

"Does he have alcohol poisoning?"

"He's fine," insisted Mel. "Just a little drunk. You're fine, aintcha, big boy? You ain't needta go to the hospital or nothin', do you?"

"No, no, fuck, no—"

"See," said Mel, turning to June as a third wave of spasms took control of his esophagus, "he's fine."

After the third wave, gasping, panting, Taylor lay his cheek against the edge of the potted plant. A trickle of neon puke idled down his lip while Daisy, tears in her eyes, set her drink beside Candy's.

"Fuck, dude! I'm so sorry—oh, man, please, don't think badly of my brother, he's just a total idiot—"

"I get it," said Mel, adding, "and he definitely is an idiot."

While Candy laughed stupidly, Taylor's eyes slid closed. "Yeah," said the party girl, slapping Daisy on the shoulder. "*And* he can't hold his liquor. What a drunk bitch! Drunk *bitch*," she sang, extending 'bitch' for a few bars.

"I want to go back to our cabin," said Junie, looking around for either a place to set her drink or for somebody to come barging in to place them under arrest. "I get the feeling we should call it a night now, Mel. Don't you think?"

"Fuck no! We're just gettin' started."

Candy cackled, stumbling back from Daisy with a clap of her hands. "Fuck yeah we are," she shouted, continuing to stumble until she fell back into the bookshelves. "Yeah, let's *party!* Let's get the rest of the resort up here, come on. O-oh, shit—betcha somebody'll have *coke*. Does Rex have coke? Fuck, I want coke—"

Daisy, however, had taken notice of her brother's abrupt silence and hurried over to him.

"Fuck," Daisy said, giving him a shake and leaning down to listen to his breathing. "Shit, he's *out*. Ugh…what a fucking embarrassment. I'm really sorry, Melba—"

"Shit, girl, it's all right, you ain't your brother's keeper."

"Maybe not, but—"

A great clatter erupted from where Candy had tried to straighten up but had sunk her hand upon a row of scripts rather than the in-built bookshelf. In pulling herself upright, she had succeeded in knocking about five of the bound scripts out of place. As they triggered a cascade of others to slide out or flop along the shelf, Candy slid down with a terrible slam and soon groaned in a disordered pile.

"Candy!" Daisy's eyes widened in horror and, stepping up from her brother, she stumbled toward her friend. Mel sighed in annoyance and studied the drink in her hand.

Damn…now it was going to be a pain in the ass.

Seeing the direction of Melba's gaze, then taking new stock of the friends passed out around her, horror widened all the feature of Daisy's dainty face. "Did you *drug* us?"

June gasped sharply and looked at her own drink. "Melba!"

"Oh, Junie, relax! You know I'd never do something like that to you…hey—"

Daisy hadn't drunk enough, the little bitch, and accordingly darted out past Mel and June while wailing along the hall like an ambulance siren. "He-lp! Help! Somebody *help* us!"

Her screams echoed through the empty house and landed on no one's ears but Mel and June's and Rexie's.

Even so, Mel gritted her teeth.

Wrenching June's drink from her hand amid screams of "He-lp! Hell-lp! Someone," Melba jerked her head in the hall's direction.

"Don't just *stand* there," she told her cousin sharply, "go get her!"

June's lips parted in greater shock than they had at the drugging. "You want *me* to—"

"You can't very well fuckin' expect *me* to do it." Nodding down at her bleeding foot and the flipflop that had taken on a nasty scarlet stain, Mel shoved her cousin toward the door. "Go, go, hurry up and fuckin' go! She'll put me back in jail, June!"

Panicked by the thought, June did what Melba most loved her for: she turned off her brain and did what she'd been told. Fueled by the hope of making things right, she sprang off like a deer at the hunter's starting gun.

Damn! June had always been a solid runner but, in the urgent situation, Mel had to wonder if she'd ever seen her cousin run half so fast.

After assessing the scene, Mel set the two untainted drinks down, limped over to Candy, and knelt to turn her over. Her slim bosom heaved beneath her glittery pink t-shirt far more comfortably upon her side. Nodding in satisfaction, she glanced only fleetingly at Taylor before rising to her feet.

The Gray Man towered on the other side of the room when she turned around, shivering in place while regarding her with its new eyes.

Melba averted her gaze, her focus fixed somewhere around its waist while she edged around the room's perimeter. Daisy's tainted glass still sat on the end table; Mel took it with her and, breathing again only when free of the Gray Man's observation, half-hopped her way after June and the girl taken down mere feet before the front door.

"I'm sorry," Junie was saying rapidly, "I'm really sorry, it's just that we have to keep you here until things get straightened out, because otherwise—"

"Keep her held down," Mel ordered, kneeling beside them.

June had, quite wisely, clasped the front of the girl's t-shirt and dragged it up over her mouth rather than holding her jaw shut and leaving herself vulnerable to direct bites. Consequently, Daisy was reduced to a pair of aptly named shorts, a tightly trembling stomach, and a pair of watery, terrified eyes that looked six times bigger due to the mascara rushing down her face.

"Okay," said Mel, straddling the young woman's thigh to keep her in place when Junie shifted over. "On three, pinch her nose shut. You ready?"

Taking her meaning with a glance at the liquor, Junie said, "Oh, Mel, please, I don't know. What if we just—"

"One," Mel began.

June's her eyes averted down to the girl in her arms. "Two."

Daisy squealed out a vague protest.

On "Three," Becky June did as she'd been told.

This next sharp plea for "Help!" was Daisy's last and most regrettable. She had no breath when Junie clasped her nose shut. Her mouth gasped open to collect what her body was being denied and, in exchange, she got a big jawful of Rohypnol cocktail—half of which, Mel had a feeling, she literally inhaled, because Daisy put up a big show of choking and puking and coughing. Grimacing, Mel repeated June's solution of using the girl's shirt to cover her mouth just before a bit of daquiri splattered against the fabric.

"Bitch, if you don't take your medicine I'm gonna get the whole bottle of rum and a goddamn funnel! Drink, slut, drink!"

Sobbing, coughing, barely able to get a lungful of air for all her efforts, Daisy shook her head as much as she could in the grip June had locked around her. Mel grit her teeth and used her free hand to prise open her jaw—

And the little slut snapped her teeth over the tip of Melba's finger.

"Fuck!"

Sharply withdrawing her hand, her eyes blazing with

rage, Melba examined her bloody finger with disgust before waving it in June's face.

"Look what that little bitch did to me!"

"Maybe if we just calmed— Melba!"

June cradled the girl a little tighter while, quickly standing, Mel stomped her good foot down on the cunt's diaphragm. The weight this placed on her bad foot made her cry out in pain, but her cry was not near as sharp as Daisy's. Taylor's sister gagged and heaved—and, as she gasped for air, was once more met with a river of drugged liquor.

At last, the glass was empty, and that suited Melba just fine. Settling back down to straddle the bitch's waist and keep her in place while the drug took full effect, Mel set the glass aside.

"There," she said to Junie as much as Daisy. "Was that so damn hard?"

TEN

THE NICEST THING about Junie was that, ultimately, she could be relied upon. She had a natural, irresistible urge to care for things, and Melba was by far and away the thing—the person—about whom she cared the most.

So far as Melba felt, that was how it should have been. She felt a little bad about that right now, of course, because Junie looked real upset while moving Daisy's body…but it wasn't like they could just keep her there on the foyer floor, ready to wake up and run for the cops.

"Why did you *do* this, Melba?"

It was the only thing June could ask. All questions of Rexie disappeared while beholding three unconscious bodies. When they finished dragging Daisy back to the television room, Mel straightened up with a sigh and an appreciative stretch of her lower back, then shut the television off.

"Because! They shouldn'ta been here in the first place… and, anyway, I didn't want them to find out I had this."

Melba drew the gun from her shorts and merited another, sharper gasp from Junie, whose face seemed to age at once.

"*Melba!* What are you doing with that? I thought you said you threw it in the lake."

"Well, hell! Like I said. Didn't want him comin' after me...I really meant that part. But what was I going to tell him when he asked—that I had it on me? No way in hell I'm throwin' a gun in the lake! This is a valuable commodity. We've got a civil right to this—it's home de-fense."

Shaking her head, anxiously running her hand over her cheek, June said, "I don't think there's anything defensive about this. Oh—oh, Mel, what are we going to *do*?"

"Well, first thing is we need to get some rope or some such. Hey!"

Joy glowed through her, pristine and absolute: the perfect glory of the universe bleeding into her. Yes, her. Living hyperspace, thinking hyperspace, which had made itself this world and now had this sweet opportunity for the created, causal world and the unmanifest, miraculous world to intersect.

For Junie to meet the man Melba loved.

"Let's go ask the owner of the house," said Mel with a laugh and a slap of her cousin's arm. "Come on!"

June paled even further as she was dragged toward the kitchen. "Where is he? He's not showering?"

"Nah, he had this idea for a sexy game. It was *supposed* to be sexy, anyway, but it's hard to be sexy and deal with guests. If I'm bein' perfectly honest with you, Junie, that's the real reason I wanted them outta my fuckin' way...this is time I'm supposed to be spending with *Rexie*."

At the door to the game room, Melba felt she might explode from the sheer excitement. Grinning ear-to-ear, she gripped her cousin's hand.

"Are you ready? Oh, shit, Junie! I'm more nervous for you to meet him than I was to bump into him tonight...would you believe *he* was the one who noticed *me*?"

While recalling this with delight, Melba rolled open the tall door. As Mel cried, "Ta-da," Junie threw a hand over her gasping mouth.

"Mr. Virgil," she whimpered behind it, her face written with misplaced terror.

"Ah, hell"—Melba darted in to her beloved with an almost childlike happiness—"he's just playing!"

"My hands," said Rex, "thank God you're back—I can't feel my hands. Who is this?"

Ignoring his question for a few seconds, Mel bent to examine the swollen purple flesh of his perfect hands. "I guess these are a little tight…" After loosening the knot of one wrist until he gasped with pain for the blood rushing in, she smiled into his face.

"I'm sorry, baby. What'd you ask me, now?"

"He asked—about me. I'm June, Mr. Virgil…I'm Mel's caregiver."

"Then you need to do a better fucking job. She's crazy, she—"

Mel laughed after fixing the other wrist, having noted the panties that had fallen to his lap and the belt that was loose around his neck. "You're too damn good at this game, Rexie! You oughta take it easier on me…I ain't never made a gag before. Next time I'll find something better."

"Listen," he told her coldly, "please, *please* listen to me."

She did.

"I thought being cooperative would help me out here, but I was obviously wrong. If something happens to me, you are *both* going to prison, so please"—he looked imploringly at June, who winced down at her feet—"please, let me go before this situation gets any worse."

"I'm ready to fuck you again," he added in that twang.

Mel giggled and pinched his cheek.

"You randy dog! Junie's my *cousin*—you can't say somethin' like that in front of her. Anyway, baby, we was just wonderin', you got some more ropes around here? Some electrical cords, maybe, or somethin' like that? Laundry line…"

String, jump rope, hopscotch, girlhood, rite of passage, passage, train, a field, open sky, space, peace, no Gray Man. Rexie drew her from her rapid-fire thought process by asking, "Why do you need *more* rope?"

"When we're on our honeymoon, Rexie, will you really take me to the moon? That'd sure be nice. I've always wanted to go to space."

"What the hell are you—"

"The rope," Junie explained in a numb tone, "is for, uh—the people I came here with, sir." Her eyes wide, as though she tried to express something Mel was too busy dreaming to analyze, June continued, "Mel—Mel drugged 'em."

"Excellent," said Rex in his accent while his mouth opened wide in shock. "You *drugged* them! Were you planning to do that to me?"

"Take you to space?"

"No!" Looking on the verge of insanity, Rex shut his eyes. "No, Mel. Drug me. Were you planning to drug *me?*"

"Oh! Well, I mean, we can later if you want. Anyway, where are the extension cords?"

His eyes still shut, Rex gave her the information. "And come get me when you're through," he commanded while doing deep breathing exercises, amazingly able to produce these words without once interrupting the rhythm of his respiration. "I want to see your handiwork."

"I will, baby! Oh, I love you…"

Her bosom burning with love, Mel bent to cradle his head toward her heart. He jerked away a bit at first, embarrassed to show affection in front of Junie, but while she kissed his head he held still for her to pet him.

"I love you so goddamn much," she reiterated, gazing down into his blue eyes and interrupting something he had been mouthing silently to June. "Oh! Rexie! You're so important to me."

"Then please let me go," he said softly, making her laugh.

"You goofball…nice try, honey. You're not winning the game that easy. But, since you got the gag off, I suppose you can leave it off. Come on, Junie."

Free to leave the door open, Mel gestured for her cousin to follow her and led the way to the extension cords. About thirteen minutes, the collection of three cell phones, and some discussion later, the decision had been made to arrange everyone in the living room. There were just more solo chairs, and aside from that, there was that much more distance between everybody and the front door.

Anyway, Mel didn't like the idea of dragging Rexie and his chair all that way. Seemed much more respectful to bring him the rabble he wished to observe.

The girls proved easy to move, but Taylor was a fucking mess. His whole front half was covered in vomit and when they got up close it smelled like he may have shit himself. Junie looked horrified at Mel but ultimately helped roll his body onto the nearby blanket, a revamp of the rug trick Mel related to her on the way to the living room.

"That's sure some quick thinking," said June in her most anxious tone—and most distracted. "Say, Mel—"

"You weren't listenin' to a word I just said, were yeh."

"No, no, I heard. About the rug and the deer head and all. It's just—I mean, what are we going to do?"

"When?"

"I don't know. When they wake up? When somebody comes lookin' for Rex? Tomorrow, or the next day, or the day after that?"

"It's no wonder you're such an anxious fuckin' mess, Junie, thinkin' like that. Christ! Let tomorrow's problems be tomorrow's problems, baby. I'm livin' in today!"

"But these are *real* problems, Mel! Don't you understand that you're going back to prison?"

"I ain't gointa prison, Junie."

"You *are*! Of course you are. And you don't even understand it."

Stopping to roll her eyes at the sound of Junie's hiccupping sob, Mel set down the rug and pushed her cousin to where she could weep in peace.

"Here's the score, Junie," Mel said with one hand on her shoulder. "I hate for you to be upset, so I'm gonna do my best to explain some things…hold on, stick with me here…fact is, I understand that if the police walked in here right now, Rexie would tell 'em I broke into his house, and Patty would see me thrown back in jail for the resta my goddamn natural life. But that won't happen. You heard him! We're having a good time."

"He sounded very scared to me."

"He's just pretending. We're celebratin' our relationship in the open for the first time! And I swear, Junie—it'll all be okay."

Her eyes ringed with terror, her gaze jumping toward Mel's waist and prompting a glance down at herself to see if she'd gotten some of Jackass's vomit on her, Junie asked, "How can that be true?"

"It will be. I can't say how. But I promise, Junie, it will all work out. You believe me?"

Hesitation. Infinity in three seconds. What if she put her foot down?

Instead, Becky June's trembling voice sought for steadiness.

"Yes. Yes, it'll be okay. We'll find a way to make it okay. Okay. Okay."

Mel always knew she could trust her cousin.

Nodding herself into agreement, Junie went back to the blanket and, holding her breath, dragged it on. Melba smiled in approval and hurried to help her, the two of them making quick work of the rest of the transportation.

Another ten minutes passed, more time than Mel would have expected—but she didn't have a whole hell of a lot of experience tying people up. What'd she look like, a dominatrix? Fuck no. Being an esthetician was gross e-fucking-nough.

Still, she had to note that by their final set of knots she had become, if nothing else, a bit more proficient in the process. Junie was useless and only helped in arranging chairs, then arranging people in said chairs. When it came to actually restraining them, she mostly watched.

"Are you sure they can all breathe, Mel?"

"Well Jesus, I didn't *ask* 'em…but they sound fine to me."

One person at a time, Mel listened for respiration. Everybody sounded a little bit soggy—at least, Daisy and Taylor did, accounting to all the vomit and all—but after inspection Melba was satisfied and nodded to her cousin.

"Nah," she concluded, "they're breathin' fine. Let's get Rexie out here now…"

With pursed lips, Junie accompanied her back to the game room and helped her drag him out. Rexie regarded them both with silent eyes and an animated voice chiming, "Brava, ladies. That was a hell of a lot faster than expected! So glad to finally meet Miss Becky June in the flesh."

"I'm real sorry if you're uncomfortable, Mr. Virgil," said Junie, dragging him to the door while Melba pushed. His mouth remained unmoving. "I'll see if Mel can let you out soon—don't you think he'd be more comfortable?"

"Sorry, cuz. I don't want to traumatize you, but he and I were just, you know—*en flagrante delicto* as the preacher usedta say about Mary Katherine and Lester Hudgeons gettin' busted durin' the tour that time." Melba chuckled at the memory, then glanced down at Rexie to see if he had anything to say before she went on, "Anyway, proceedin's were supposed to continue, but then y'all showed up so we decidedta change it up a bit. He just wanted me to take him out here, so that's what I'm doing."

"That's right, and you'll see why in a second, sugar…damn, smells terrible! Put me nearer to the couch, would you…"

"Come on, Junie, don't stop there! Go on, go on…"

Soon the room was arranged. Rex stared at her in dry expectation. "Just what are you expecting to do here, Melba?"

"Oh, Rexie, that's all up to you. You know I don't really care how this happens. As long as I get to be with you, that's all I care about."

While he looked up at the ceiling, his jaw clamping shut to the grinding of his teeth, Rex continued in a merrier tone, "I sure do love your devoted spirit. Rest assured, you certainly *will* be with me. We just have to get a certain monkey off our backs."

THERE IS NO ESCAPE

YOU ARE ALREADY DEAD

DEATH IS ETERNAL

THIS IS NOTHING

THERE IS NOTHING

YOU ARE NOTHING

Melba clutched Junie, the nearest person in the room. For the voices to rise in the midst of so many people—before Rexie, even—was almost unfair. It certainly didn't comfort her to think about, although Rex took it in stride.

"Now, sugar, don't panic. You know that's what ol' Gray Man wants. Just relax. Breathe deep with me, now."

"What's going on?" Junie's was tearful with misplaced fear. "Melba—what's happening to you?"

"Well…"

Steadying herself as much as she could for her cousin's sake, Melba vacillated before deciding there were scant details that could illustrate a little of what she was experiencing.

"I'm thinkin' some things are really gonna change with me, Junie," she summarized, looking her cousin earnestly in the eye. "I think I need to—to move on from here and start again. This place that I'm in, this situation…I can do better, don't you think? Don't I deserve better?"

"Well of course, Melba. But that's why you have to take care of yourself. You can't just—just do things like this!"

"I'm not doing anything! I just wanted these three dopes out of the way so I could be with Rexie. He was the one who wanted to see 'em."

"And you did a good job arranging them for me," he agreed while adding with his mouth, "I didn't."

"Well, sure, baby, but you didn't have to."

"And that's why I'm so glad to have you around, Melba. Why I'm so excited for our future together. Melba—angel, I love you. Will you kiss me?"

Smiling, forgetting all about Junie, Melba bent to take her lover's face in her hands. His nostrils flared with a sharp inhalation as she pressed her lips to his taut ones. Junie gasped, uttering her cousin's name before Mel pulled away.

"Now, what did you need them out here for, Rexie?"

"Well, sugar, because they are a vital component of our exit operation."

"How so?"

"We can't have the Gray Man followin' us on our honeymoon. If we're gonna get him to stay behind, we're gonna haveta trade him somethin'. Somethin' that isn't you."

"What the fuck would he take, though? The only thing that bastard wants is me afraid—afraid, or dead, or both."

BECAUSE YOU ARE DEAD

REALIZE IT

While Mel screwed up her face and covered her eyes with one hand, Rexie told her softly, "Now, angel, don't worry."

"I sure do wish these fucking voices would shut up! Just shut the fuck up sometimes."

"And they will. They will."

WE WILL BE PACIFIED

WHEN YOU ARE DEAD

"All they want is me dead," she echoed.

"Then we need to give them death." His head turned toward Junie. "Is she always like this?"

"I think she must be havin' a real bad episode—she hasn't been taking her medication for weeks now. Melba, oh, honey, you never *told* me the voices were back."

"Because only Rexie knows how to deal with 'em," she explained with a shrug. "And he told me to keep 'em to myself, because otherwise everybody'd freak out."

Rex scoffed, looking between the women. "Me? Why would I know anything?"

"You kidder." Melba laughed and nudged him.

Junie said something, but it were as though the volume on her speech got turned down way, way low because Rexie was also speaking.

"No, baby, you're right." His tone was gentle and warm as the afternoon sunshine. "You're absolutely right. I do know how to deal with it all. It's very easy. All you have to do is kill these three, and you'll be able to leave with me forever. Free. No more Gray Man."

Mel's heart sped. She bent before him, touching his chest. "Really?"

Rex regarded her impatiently and she felt terrible to have even minorly displeased him. "What are you *talking* about? What is even going *on?*"

Again, though, this was a distant sentence at the end of a tunnel. A spark formed on his mouth but not touching the volume of his true voice. It spoke from his eyes and out of his mind when Mel stroked her hand along the collar of his shirt.

"Sure enough, Melba, that's all that's required. And since

they're the *real* ones who are already dead, there ain't even nothinta feel bad about."

The breath seemed stolen from Mel's lungs. All three victims were still well blacked out, their heads toward their chests and occasional snores drifting from their struggling sinuses.

Mel bit her lip.

"I don't know if I can do that, Rexie."

"Do what?" Junie's muffled voice produced the words while he went on, still tender.

"Now, there's nothing to get upset about. It's easy. You can even let Junie live! All you need is three to replace the one. Three lives to replace yours. Then, we'll be free to move on. We can leave all this behind. Won't that be nice?"

Mel said nothing, afraid for a few seconds that she was somehow misunderstanding him. In her hesitation, he reminded her with force, "These are people who have already left all this behind. The left it behind in another place, at another time. Here? These are just shadows here, baby. These three are not their real selves. They are the clones of people very far away."

Slowly, carefully, Melba nodded. "Like what Junie'll see left behind."

A shadow crossed his face. His features did two things at once in a strange and beautiful way: a fluttering, dreamlike effect in which a faint smile touched his lips and pride exuded from eyes that otherwise looked simply exhausted.

June, hearing this without context, looked at her cousin in some alarm. "What do you mean? Left behind where, Mel?"

YOU ARE WRONG

YOU ARE DELUDED

YOU ARE THE CLONE

WHEN YOU DIE

THERE WILL BE NOTHING

Mel shut her eyes, her body heaving with a great breath she had to take to steady herself. Her father's voice was preeminent among the choir and, forgetting Junie's question altogether, Mel pressed the heel of her palm to the temple of her forehead.

"You're right, Rexie," she said sharply. Her tone warbled and she laughed at herself, wondering why she was so afraid of the lies she had been told a hundred million, billion, *trillion* fucking times. "You're right, you're right. We can't be happy with all these bullshit lies followin' us. I'd do anything to be free forever. Oh, Rex!"

It would be so nice. With Rexie, everything would be perfect. The whole experience of reality would be so blissful, so exquisite, that there would be no *room* for the Gray Man. It was going to be quiet in her head, finally. Finally, she would turn on a radio and hear music every time without fail—but she wouldn't need the music to think straight. She would be able to go out any time of day or night and feel confident that no monsters would crawl out of the darkness. No otherworldly monsters, anyway.

But the question of getting to that place had seemed so impossible that this price was small. A purgative she had never recognized was all around her: blood. Of course! Blood.

Good damn thing she didn't have to feel bad about anything that was going to happen tonight.

Junie would, though. Junie was going to spend the rest of her life hardcore fucked up, and it would be Melba's fault. But that was what Rexie wanted, right? Well…it must have been. The question was how she would convince Junie to either help her, or let her do the work herself.

Then Melba thought about the format of the guests. Two women, one man.

Rexie suggested the answer to the dilemma just as she realized it herself.

"Just record a performance of the script and make one

kill the other. That leaves only two for you to worry about, and maybe you could set Junie loose before you do one or both. Doesn't matter how it happens, so long as blood is spilled."

Guessed that was true. Mel nodded, reflected that the Gray Man was a real sick bastard, and turned to Becky June.

"Junie, I need you to go back to the cabin we rented and pick up the camera—oh! But that reminds me—"

"What? What do you need the camera for, Mel?"

"—I'm surprised those fuckin' bugs didn't *eat* his ass," Mel continued without missing a beat, waving toward Taylor's unmoving body. "What the hell were you thinking? I thought I told you to keep the bag off the damn floor."

"I'm sorry, Mel. But I don't—I didn't see any bugs. What bugs?"

"Ugh! Guess they escaped…he got fuckin' lucky. Anyway, go on. I can't walk or drive. Not with my foot like this."

Rex, who had been looking at June intently, now nodded at a fast clip. "That's right," he said with his mouth, "Of course, Melba can't walk like this."

"Mel—"

June pursed her lips and looked harder at her cousin. She said again, softer, "Mel."

"Just go, Junie! Hurry on back. Rex and I wanna direct our first picture together! He's gonna show me how the big names do it, and then we'll have, you know, like a proof of concept for my script! All we need's three actors. You could be one, and then there's that dipshit, and Candy or Daisy could play the third role. But to film all that, we need my camera."

"Maybe Rex has a—"

"No," Rex said firmly, looking June in the eyes. "No. I don't have a camera. You have to go and get the one you guys brought. Okay?"

After returning his stare for a few seconds, June nodded.

"Okay," she said softly. "But, Mel…I'm afraid to leave you alone."

Junie's eyes watered. She took her cousin's hand, saying hoarsely, "I don't want you to go back to prison. How can I leave you alone? How can I think of you going back to prison?"

Sighing slightly, Melba drew her cousin close. "Oh, Junie…come here."

As Junie lowered her head to Melba's shoulder, the younger woman burst into a torrent of tears that were accompanied by snotty, toddler-like gasps for air. "Melba! oh, Melba—"

"Now, Junie, angel, I keep tellin' you! Ain't nothin' like that gonna happen, okay? All you gotta do is get that camera and be right back. It'll take you five minutes if you drive. You want the car keys?"

She shook her head, wiping the heel of her palm against her cheek and flicking a glance at Rex. He looked quickly at the ceiling as June said, "No. I need to walk. I need to think. I—I need to calm down. Please, oh, Melba— Please don't do anything *drastic* while I'm gone, Melba."

"You know damn well I can't do a thing in this world without your help, Junie. Go on! We'll be here waiting for you. Show can't start without the camera—this ain't a play."

Stifling another sob and nodding instead, Junie straightened up, wiped the back of her hand across her cheeks, and got while the getting was good.

Mel waited until the front door shut.

Praise the Lord.

ELEVEN

MEL WAS TEMPTED to get it over with and kill these three all at once, while Junie was gone. But there were two problems with that. One, well…Mel had done a lot in her life, but she wasn't sure how she'd fare when it came to committing murder. Three murders? That seemed like an awful lot for her last day in the world.

Then, of course, there was her simple desire to peacefully see Junie again, even if only for a few more minutes. The idea of their most recent embrace being their last came upon Mel now as a choice she could potentially make, and it was one that was so sad she lay a hand upon her heart.

"Hell, Rexie. How can I do this?"

Rex stared into her with eyes that saw everything.

"You don't have to do anything, Melba," he said calmly, his unaccented city voice so much colder than the one she knew.

On he went, his every word concise and soft.

"If you untie me and leave right now, I won't tell anybody what happened. If I never see you again, nobody will ever have to know about tonight. I'll even pay them off"—jerking his head toward the sacrifices—"and we can all go our merry ways. Just like you never said anything about what went on between us the first time we met, I'll never tell anybody about what's happened here. In fact—so far as I can tell, nothing's happened. And that's the way it could be forever."

Nice try, Rexie. Melba would never dream of something so foolish. The idea of changing her mind now, now that she and Rex were together—now that he had given her a solution to the Gray Man? Turning away from that made her sick to her stomach in the most literal sense.

"If nothing happens tonight, baby, then *I'm* nothing. Will there ever be another chance for us to leave together? Doubt it. Not in a way that makes sense, anyhow…and if it's not in a way that makes sense, it can't happen in this world." She smiled wider at him. "See how well I listen to you?"

"Melba"—his hands closed into fists and opened again to keep the blood flowing—"then listen to me now. Right now. What you're doing is wrong. What happened earlier—that was rape. You raped me, Melba. Now you've drugged three people. What's going to happen next? What if the police come?"

Melba thought of Tibetan monks coming to join a Zen practice and being repeatedly refused by the Master before proving their devotion; of the space monkeys made to stand outside the Paper Street house in *Fight Club*. Melba loved *Fight Club*. Would she ever watch it again?

"If the police show up, then I'll be dead." Melba shrugged, answering her love and master in metaphysical arts, "Therefore, since this is the universe where I'm alive forever—alive at all—the police won't come."

"Very good," he said in his normal Southern drawl while his eyes gently closed. "I'm damn glad you take my teachings to heart, angel."

"I love you, Rexie." Melba genuflected before him again, folding her hands upon his knee and gazing up into his face. Could he feel the full power of her devotion? Could he *really* understand how sweetly it pained her to look at him? How much she loved him? How her love truly was like a fever?

"Of course, I understand…it's how I feel about you, too."

"I just want to make you proud of me, Rexie," she said, gazing into his eyes. "I'm so happy to be close to you."

"This isn't the way to get close to somebody, Melba."

"You're right." Mel glanced at the unconscious guests before sliding up into his lap. While he exhaled, she asked, "How's that for you? This is much closer…I like being this close, Rexie…"

"That's not what I meant," he said, cut off when she cupped his face in her hands and bent to kiss him. His lips parted with a noise like a scoff; her tongue slipped in, probing excitedly against—

"Ow!"

Melba jerked back from him, the tips of her fingers pressing to her bitten tongue.

One small dot of blood.

With another, giddier spate of laughter, Melba ground against him.

"You bad boy," she teased, laying a slap across his face. The sharp noise echoed through the house along with his cry— and Melba's light hiss for the sore fingertip that little bitch had managed to sink her teeth into. Poor Melba was getting all bit up her last night on Earth!

She stroked her burning fingers down his chest while he leveled his gaze with hers once again. Rex's lower lip drooped with the split formed by a well-placed knuckle.

"I'm going to see you rot in prison," he told her.

"Oh, Rexie, what a mean thing to say…you love scaring me, huh…"

She was leaning down for another kiss, her good hand trailed toward his trousers.

"No," he begged against her, "Melba, stop, wait—"

"What—what the—fuck—"

At the sound of an idiot waking up, Melba's caresses paused. Taylor looked with appropriate dumbness at his surroundings, his jaw practically on his chest as he peered at his sister through unevenly open eyes. "Fuck! What the fuck is this—what is this?"

"Oh, you're awake! That's good. You're gonna be the star in a movie, so we'll have to get you some coffee or somethin'… otherwise, you won't be able to deliver your lines."

"I'm tied up?" Still unable to process—looking fucked-up, to put it casually—Taylor twisted to the left, made a noise like a stabbed goat, and wrenched his hands in his electrical cord bindings. Melba had tied him and his friends into a far more uncomfortable position than Rexie's privileged monarch pose, which was of course on purpose. Taylor practically dislocated his shoulder in his efforts to wrench his wrists free, a task soon dropped in favor of whipping his head toward Melba.

"The fuck is wrong with you, you psycho? You gettin' off on this, or what?"

"Don't flatter yourself, you redneck piecea shit. I just do what Rexie tells me."

"*You* told her to do this? Are you nuts?"

Rex rolled his eyes and looked sternly at the younger man. "Oh, my God. What are you, stupid?"

While Mel laughed at Rex's question, he nodded at her and said, "She's clearly insane. There's nothing normal about the way she thinks or speaks. You ask her a question, and if you get an answer at all it won't come for at least five seconds… and when it does, it won't make sense."

Mel giggled at his assessment of her. "Damn, baby, you're roastin' me. It's true though…you're always distractin' my ass." With a grin, she flicked Rex's ear. He sighed while going on with the cover story.

"She's delusional. She broke into my hotel room a few

years ago and she's obviously still obsessed with me. I don't know what she thinks I'm telling her, but I barely even know she exists!"

A likely story. Mel chuckled to herself while turning back toward Taylor. "Y'all know I exist now, for sure…not for long, though."

Taylor scoffed. "What does that mean?"

"It means you are contributin' somethin' very valuable to the workings of the universe, so just sit there quietly and we'll finish what your daddy started."

"Jesus." Taylor shook his head. "Either I'm high, or you really are crazy…both, most likely. I got no idea what you're saying."

"She means," explained Rex, his voice still draped with that stern, cold affectation that got Mel's blood runnin' like fire, "that she's going to kill us."

"Not *you* baby! We don't have to kill you when there's threea them here, remember what you just told me."

"What the *fuck*, man!" His head whipping back and forth between Mel and Rex, Taylor said in a tone of sharp desperation, "I can't die now! I'm only twenty-four!"

"Holy Jesus! You're *twenty-four?*" Howling with laughter, Mel nudged her mid-forties lover in the shoulder. "Like them billboards usedta say…"Meth: Not Even Once." Only reason I paid attention to 'em is 'causea that time you did them ads, Rexie."

Turning her attention back to the task, Mel regarded Taylor with more open coldness than she had ever regarded a human being. The truth was that she really wasn't a 'people' person, mostly because the vast majority of people weren't real. Not in her universe, anyway, where Rexie was trying to teach her to be more than human.

Still, Mel *tried* to like people. She tried to be friendly. She got out there in her early life. Made friends at school. Worked like a team player. Even gave boys a try a time or two before

Rexie stole her heart. Daddy had been dead four, oh, four years before then, and of all her many harried first handjobs (not *her* first, obviously) and collected virginities, only her one perfect night with Rexie had washed away the dead weight of her father's bloated corpse.

Weren't her fault people turned out to be so damn hard to like.

"Hel-*lo?* Holy shit! Is she *deaf,* too?"

Mel stirred from her thoughts to recognize a conversation in the works around her. She stared between the two and only managed to blink when Rexie answered, "She's schizophrenic."

"That's what they call me! Easier that way."

Taylor scoffed. "I thought schizophrenics were just, like, quiet people who hear voices and live with their moms their whole lives! Homeless people, you know. Syd Barrett. Not this *horror movie* shit! Not in real life!"

Mel laughed. "I thought so, too—but you never know how life is going to work out, I guess. I've always wanted to be in a movie, anyway…and I guess, since this is my universe, it's my movie, in a way."

"What in the fuck are you talking about?"

While Taylor made his exasperated demand, Mel slid the gun from the back of her shorts and brandished it for effect.

"I mean," she said, "this is all proof that I have the right to kill you with perfect impunity. My *God*-given right. But lucky for you, I'm going to hold off on it, and I'm gonna let onea *them* do it—so I guess it'd be mighty decenta me to let you decide who'd you rather do the killin'. Your sister, or her drunk-ass friend? Not that they aren't both wasted now, of course."

"You're completely fuckin' crazy! Where's my—did you take my phone?" Taylor's eyes widened and he wiggled in his seat, cursing to feel the absence of the device in his back pocket. "Sonofabitch! Where is that fucking thing?"

"Hm," said Mel, nodding. "That's probably a good idea. Hold on here…"

Her tongue darting across her dry lips, Mel told Rexie, "You holler if they manage to wiggle free—or wake up," and exited to the television room.

Yeah, the phones. That was a dilemma. What was she going to do? If they were going to film the movie long enough to have one kill the other before Junie realized what was what, then these assholes were going to be released from their bindings. That meant Mel would have to be prepared for an escape attempt…even if a disorganized, roofie-laden one.

Walking into the sitting room instantly erased all thoughts of phones from her mind as the scripts in the bookshelf caught her eye. She would have been sucked into this vast store of information contained in perfect hyperspace grids… had the Gray Man not been rocking like a too-tall redwood over the phones on the coffee table. Junie had dumped them there unceremoniously and now, with equal neglect, Mel cast a furtive look up at the entity while scooping the devices. Least he kept her on-track.

In the kitchen, she turned on the sink and looked around for a plug. Eventually she discovered some little mechanism that just twisted the drain shut, which was some wild shit and made her laugh. Every tiny little thing was just better in Rex's house! Shaking her head, vaguely aware of the protests leveled from the adjacent living room, Mel dumped the phones into the sink one device at a time.

"Now let's see…" She searched for the first power button and shut it off while saying, "one, that's Taylor…"

Taylor groaned with the hard 'plop' of his device into the sink, the water not yet deep enough for a full splash. It was by the time she found the power button of the next device, saying, "Two, that's Daisy…"

By three, the phones were fully submerged. Then, apologetically, she said, "Sorry, Rexie," and removed her lover's device from her pocket to condemn it along with the others. "All accounted for!"

Not all, though. Melba paused. After a few contemplative seconds, she hurried over to the couch where she'd left her purse. Carefully claiming her bag from the area of broken glass, she sighed at the device, turned it over in her hands, and shook her head.

"Sure is hard to let go of something that contains so much—stuff, you know."

"You're doin' the right thing, baby," said Rexie in one voice, while his other reminded her, "You don't have to destroy your own phone, you know."

"You're right…doin' the right thing when you don't have to makes it all the more meaningful."

Nodding, Mel limped back into the kitchen, tossed her phone into the mostly full sink, and shut the water off.

A great weight lifted from her shoulders.

There! It was done. Like nothing. That was half the battle right there. Everything was being left behind. She was making the choice to walk away from everything now, before the final event had clicked into place and jettisoned her from reality and samsara—what the Buddhists called the cycle of suffering and reincarnation. She read that in one of the spiritual books Rexie had started to recommend three or four years prior.

Before leaving the kitchen, Rexie's drawl came to Melba in a whisper. He had to whisper, since he was also whispering to Taylor at the same time.

"Hide that gun real quick, sugar," he said. "Don't worry, we ain't lookin'."

Hide it? Well…she didn't like the thought of letting it go for any reason, but if Rexie thought she needed to do it, then she needed to do it. With a quick scan of the area, Melba slipped the pistol out from her backside and hid it in the drawer of the island, which came up to her waist and was sufficiently tall to hide the activity. When she made her way back down to the living room, both men looked sharply her way.

Rexie was the only one who wore a smile.

"Hey, Mel," he said in a croon that, while not his Southern drawl, was still sexy and sweet. "I was thinking—before we get on to the, uh, you know…serious killing stuff…why don't you and I take a few minutes upstairs? You got me so turned on just now, baby—but with this guy awake, we can't very well do anything here."

Flush with desire, now understanding why Rexie had suggested she get rid of the gun for the moment, Mel giggled and fanned herself. "Normally I'd give you a nice slap for talkin' that way in fronta mixed company, but I reckon it don't matter since they're on a tight schedule…you really mean it?"

"Hell yeah, Mel—come here. Kiss me. I'll show you how much I want you."

Her heart pounding in her mouth might not allow that, but she'd try anyway…and boy, was she glad she did. Rexie tipped his head back and regarded her through the sexiest pair of bedroom eyes she'd ever seen. Gasping softly, she bent over him and—wow!

Suffice it to say, Mel had never been kissed like that. Sighing, she wilted to the floor before him with her lips glued to his all the while. When at last he lifted his head away, she swayed.

You can bet your ass she smiled.

"Hell," she said, more to herself than to him, then laughing, then saying again, "hell!"

While, with trembling fingers, Mel unbound his wrists, she could hardly form a thought; could hardly do more than giggle like a sixteen-year-old.

"Why didn't you say so," she finally managed to say with another, slightly weaker and sillier spate of giggles, dealing with his left hand while he experimented with the rotation of his freed-up right.

Part of her had expected Rexie, who of course still did not consciously remember the truth, to put up some kind of challenge to heighten the stakes. She figured he'd knock her over, or in some way attack her, or try to find the gun.

Instead, he waited with a patient, regal air as she unbound his ankles, one firm hand rubbing the opposite wrist and vicing the versa. When she finished, he smiled fondly, rose from his seat, and offered her one beautiful, big hand up from where she knelt.

"Excuse us for a few minutes," said Rex with a nod at Taylor. Taylor looked at him through hazy eyes, but only lowered his head and continued futile struggles against his bindings.

With a whisper of a smile that excited her beyond all measure, Rex squeezed Melba's hand and drew her in the direction of the foyer.

"Why don't we go see my bedroom, Melba," he told her, his city voice husky with desire that made her body tremble all the more sharply—especially with her hand in his. "You and me. We can have a drink, maybe smoke a little pot. Do you like pot?"

"You know I ain't supposedta, baby." Sighing with desire, Melba permitted herself to be guided down the long hallway and across the foyer. It was split into several axes rather than one like the traditional foyer, on account of the stairs winding up through the house; the interior above the first floor was somehow more modern than she had expected. "You change this place recently?"

"I had a few rooms renovated a couple of years ago. I guess you read the thing in *AD*, huh? You really do like to follow my exploits…I wonder how many people there are like you out there, Melba. People reading about my every move without the bravery to even write to me."

"However many there are," said Melba, feeling again that cold detachment from humanity or whatever was pretending to be humanity all around her, "not a one of 'em matters."

"I suppose that's true," said Rex, guiding her up their

gentle golden spiral. On the second floor was another sitting area, plus rooms beyond for guests; but the third floor to which they ascended was Rexie's private quarters. A short hallway with a few rooms and then, at the end, a breathtaking suite with another pristine wall of glass to reveal the finest view of any lake Melba had ever seen. The moon hung bright in the sky, and the water beneath quivered with a doppelgänger of it all: one duplicate for each object God had set upon the Earth.

"Isn't it a beautiful view," remarked Rexie from behind her, flicking on the light and banishing the image at once. Now it was his reflection that stood in the window, off in the distance, carefully regarding her image—or the real her. Maybe it was the real Rexie that looked at her reflection, and his reflection that saw the real her. Hard to tell which it was. Hard to tell what it meant.

"Which one is the real 'me,' Rexie?" She looked at herself, at the strangeness of herself. She was thirty-five and had been to prison, but had fiercely gripped her youth in spite of it all. The only proof of aging was a single forehead line provoked by a stressful sentence away from tretinoin. Melba touched that line and ran her fingers over her face. The reflection followed suit over its identical map.

Rex watched from over her left shoulder, still across the room. Behind her. Both.

Her own voice rose in her ears like a stranger's.

"Is the real me the 'me' that's going to die? Is that really me?"

Melba breath hitched. She reached toward that self, that body-self in the reflective window. Her fingers pressed against it and she marveled at the sight of herself—at the theatrical, psychedelic strangeness of the human eye with its swirling iris and great black dot drawing in and in and in

LIKE THE BLACK HOLE

THAT NOTHINGNESS

TO WHICH ALL THINGS

WILL BE REDUCED

EVEN IF YOU

MANAGE TO LEARN

WHAT HEAVEN IS

"Melba."

Rex's hand on her shoulder, paired with his voice, drew her out of terrible reverie. She snapped back and looked up at him, her unblinking eyes fixed on his face to drink in every second she could of this wonderful vision. Of being alive.

"Is that dead thing the real me, Rexie? It's not, right? There really must be two of me. Tell me there's two of me, Rexie, please—"

Grief overwhelmed her. She clutched his shirt with a sob.

His stern affectation giving away to a look of slight pity, Rex folded her in his arms.

"Hey," he said softly, leaning her head to his shoulder and patting her back, then stroking her from shoulder to the waistband of her shorts. "There, there…it's all right. I know. It's hard to think too much about—life."

"It sure fuckin' is," she said, catching her breath, forcing her tears to stop as best she could. While he released her from his embrace with a strange look of slight frustration, which she accounted to the same tears she was trying to rid herself of in the first place, Mel rested a hand upon his chest. She tried to smile.

"But at least you're with me. That makes it easier, Rex."

"I'll tell you what," said Rexie, "how about we put on a little music. Relax before we…you know." He nodded toward the floor, indicating the people below. "You sure you can't smoke?"

Damn tempting. "I suppose since it won't really matter soon," she admitted.

Mel had been so taken with the view that she hadn't even really seen the room. Not until Rex patted her hand and left to remove a cigar box from his nightstand. It was pretty comfortable, with a big bed and a painting of *Leda and the Swan* that she knew hid a television. A little more stuff here and there, too, since he must've had it cleaned up before the *AD* photo shoot. Statues, snow globes, a row of glowing gold awards.

In the same drawer, he saw something else. He laughed.

With a doggish grin, he removed the fuzzy handcuffs from the drawer.

"In case you feel like continuing our proceedings from earlier…I wouldn't mind something a little softer."

"Maybe…but we're going to have to keep you walkin' around if you're gonna help me with the movie. You really don't think Junie'll know what's what?"

With a serious look, Rex said in a strange city tone, "No, I don't."

While Mel nodded, Rex's mouth started to say something else—but his normal, Southern voice overlapped it.

It was increasingly difficult for Melba to keep track of which Rexie was speaking as the night wore on. He was going back and forth between his two voices so much, and sometimes they overlapped. Often the message seemed to be not so much in one or the other but instead in their careful collage. Not even matching lips to sound revealed the reality of the situation, because his mouth visibly crossfaded in that odd way. First into a smile, then into shaping the sounds of his Southern voice.

"Now that we're alone, sugar, what do you say we drop the pretense."

Of all the interactions she had ever had with Rex, none had put her into such an immediate state of insane, heart-throbbing excitement as this moment. This—this was the *true* first moment they were alone together.

A great light shone from her chest. It warmed and purified her soul with love as she threw her arms around his neck.

"Rexie," she cried, nearly knocking the cigar box and cuffs from his hand, "oh, yes, please, I'd love that."

"I sure do love you, Melba."

His head ducked over hers and, sighing, Melba received his kiss as she had downstairs. The absolute rhapsody of sensation sent her melting backward upon the bed. While setting the cigar box aside, he looked earnestly down at her and caught her hands in his. Rex looked like a gallant knight speaking to some refined lady—moreover, he made Melba feel like that lady.

"You trust me, don't you, babydoll?"

"Of course I do, Rexie…oh, I love you! I trust you with all my heart."

"That's good. That's real good…"

His arms slid around her waist and he embraced her, kissing her stomach through the fabric of the sweatshirt he pushed up over her head. When it was gone, they kissed again. The fierceness of this kiss soon had her pushed down into the pillows.

"Oh, Rexie! I'm so happy to be with you—"

"You can't imagine how happy I am, Melba, and how proud…you just have to hold on a little longer for me, angelbaby. Just keep doin' what I say. I'll make damn sure that you and me shake off that Gray Man and have one sweet, sexy honeymoon."

Laughing shyly, her hair blooming against her cheek with the giddy push of her shoulder up toward her ear, Mel took his next kiss with a moan. Her hand had latched to his shirt again and now ran up into his hair. One of his hands, meanwhile, explored her body. The other reached around to the side of the bed.

Something snapped around the wrist of the hand she used to stroke his hair.

Melba looked up at the fuzzy handcuffs with a moan. "I sure do like a man who knows how to have fun. Oh!"

The electric thrill of pleasure-pain as he roughly jerked her arm up to be secured to the bars of the headboard was second only to the masochistic desire inspired by his hard blue eyes.

"Where's the gun?"

His demand was calm, but he was not. Something in his eyes had the thunder of victory and Melba laughed to see it. Poor baby! He was so brainwashed that he couldn't even hear himself speak.

"I hid it," she said while he pawed her, patting her down for the weapon one last time before gritting his teeth in a fury.

"Where," he demanded of her again, catching her face in his big hands. She moaned, wiggling her legs in giddy anticipation.

"You gonna whip it outta me, baby? I think we left your belt downstairs…"

Nostrils flaring, Rex left the room without another word.

"Real funny," she said, tugging at the handcuffs to find them surprisingly sturdy for a cheap sex store prop. "Get back here and let me out, you goofball! I gotta be back when Junie gets here. If not, she'll end up cold feet."

The house echoed its master's feet as he hurried down the three flights of stairs.

"Don't take too long," she called, listening.

Waiting.

Waiting.

Waiting.

"Fuck," Mel said sharply, whipping around and jerking harder against the handcuff. Fuck! This thing was really strong.

So were the iron bars of the headboard.

Teeth bared, Mel wiggled as far as she could to the side of the bed. Just barely, she could reach a corner of the nightstand.

Fuck yeah. She always watched horror movies and rolled her eyes at scenes where something vital—a key, usually, just as in this situation—was millimeters out of the protagonist's reach. Mel always felt that, in such a scenario, she would be able to stretch the additional .02 inches required to reach a MacGuffin.

Now was her chance to prove it, she guessed.

Tongue set firmly in her teeth, Mel stretched as close as she could to the nightstand. The tips of her fingers brushed one wooden corner and, exhaling, she told herself that if she could touch that much she could touch more.

Just barely, she did. With a careful pinch of her thumb and forefinger, Melba relied on the mighty leverage of the human machine to give her two digits the strength to scoot the nightstand just a little. Just a little. Just a little more.

Then it was three fingers. Then it was five.

Then, with a triumphant laugh, Melba reached the tip of the drawer's knob.

She jerked it open and, when it did not come out of the nightstand, used it to drag the entire piece of furniture over to the bed. The awkward angle made her arm feel like it was going to dislocate, but it was worth it. Amid business cards removed from wallets, condoms that made her envious, and Viagra that made her excited, Melba discovered a tiny key about the size of her fingertip and practically made out of posterboard for how malleable the metal seemed to be.

"If that ain't a handcuff key," she said to herself out loud, twisting to manipulate it into the lock at her other wrist, "I don't know what is."

She shouldn't have spoken that thought aloud, however. Speaking the thought aloud—uttering any kind of noise with her mouth—made her realize she was alone in a room without music.

She wasn't safe.

Her heart hammered with her increasing anxiety. Lips

pressed in a thin line, Melba tried to jam the key inside its lock.

A piece of fuzz barred its entry, caught its tooth, and bounced it from her hand.

As Melba's heart sank and the tiny key dropped into the darkness behind the headboard, Taylor's scream filled the house.

TWELVE

MELBA BARELY REGISTERED the cry aside from the focus required to attribute the sound to Taylor. She was busy producing her own agonized moan, a low tone of frustration that echoed the key's descent into nothing.

"No," she whispered sharply, jerking the handcuffs again, her voice raising more with each word. "No! Shit, fuck, no—Rex? Rex! Rex-ie!"

No response.

Breathless with terror, Mel shoved her hand into the darkness between the iron rails of the headboard and the wall.

Even her slim wrist barely contorted through the maze. Her fingers didn't reach the floor where the pitiful key now lay, too small and perhaps too flat to easily acquire even if she could touch it.

And that was all before the cold thing slithered against her hand.

Melba nearly pissed herself. She jerked her hand back with a yelp and a subsequent hiss as her fist banged straight into one of those bars. As the pain throbbed through her, nausea taking hold along with the sharpness, she examined her fingers.

No trace of moisture.

That was almost worse than seeing something. A presence felt but not evidenced could only mean one thing. She looked around the room, braced to see the Gray Man.

Instead, her fat father stood in the silence. Naked as the day he died; the curly gray hair that ought to have been allocated over his head dispersed thickly along his chest and stomach, his shoulders and back, his legs and arms and groin, his gross beard that hurt when he kissed her. Seeing him made the nausea revolve into something dangerously close to actual vomiting.

She shut her eyes.

"Rexie," she screamed without looking. "Rexie, baby, help me! Help me! He found us—Daddy found us—"

Worse, that more expected pursuer now hovered by the bedside. She didn't need to look to feel the faceless entity whose new eyes bored ceaselessly into her skull. As always, the presence was palpable behind her closed lids. The Gray Man produced a choir of soft whispers in the top of her head, amplified by the hideous presence of her father. His mouth didn't move, but, as usual, he was calling her a stupid, crazy slut who would never amount to anything more than a walking glory hole.

Her breast heaving, tears pooling between her closed lids, Mel bit her lip to contain the fear and the helplessness.

None of this mattered. By the end of the night, she and Rexie would be married. They would be off on their honeymoon. They would be peaceful and happy and she would live forever with him. The Gray Man would not be there; her father would not be there. There would be a perfect escape from everything. From herself and all the anxieties that filled her muscles with tension from the moment she awoke to the moment she finally caught a few hours of beneath the gravity of the Gray Man's stare.

It was just life to her. That life was soon to be shuffled off. She just had to remember that, after tonight, she would never see the Gray Man again.

Exhaling slowly, Melba forced herself to open her eyes.

The Gray Man's empty visage hung half an inch from hers.

Usually he'd disappear when she opened her eyes, but that terrible energy would remain even when nothing was visible to her. Now, the vision and energy remained intermingled. The Gray Man peered with black eyes that curled merrily along with the suddenly appearing, sickly smile that opened a black slit across a formless jaw.

Melba made a strangled crying noise, like the bleat of a sheep about to be slaughtered, but the Gray Man lifted a finger to this new mouth. She regarded the seven knuckles of its long index finger with cold fear, afraid it might try to touch her—and, as it happened, it reached up as though to pat her on the head.

She winced away from its slow-moving palm, begging, "Hey, now, please don't—please, don't touch me—"

But the long hand of the Gray Man continued past her, above her, down into the space between the wall and the bed.

Melba could barely understand what was happening. Her body released another noise, one that was half a laugh and half a gasp of absolute relief.

Slowly, inch by inch, the arm withdrew again.

Then, the hand.

The fingers.

The key, pinched between one long digit and an uncanny thumb.

Her voices grew quiet for the moment; not stopped forever, but hushed as at the behest of a conductor.

The Gray Man set the key upon the pillow beside her head, still refraining from physical contact.

Without a sound, never breaking eye contact, the being took its new face and quietly withdrew beneath the bed.

Melba trembled, unable to wrap her head around what had just happened. The implications. The bevy of questions.

There was no time to ponder. Her father had disappeared, too, and who knew when he'd be back? She had to get the hell out of Dodge.

Melba made sure she had a firm hold of the little key this time. With a steady hand and a snapping open of the rudimentary lock, she jettisoned herself from the fuzzy handcuffs.

And, though she was momentarily grateful to the Gray Man, she still found herself leaping a little farther from the bedside than most adults would have.

A hard landing upon one bloody foot made her hiss, but she didn't stop to think about it. She only limped on downstairs, following the sounds emanating from the sitting room. As she emerged into the kitchen, her weight still almost entirely on her good foot, Melba breathed a sigh of relief to see all heads accounted for—albeit, not exactly as she'd left them.

"She's dead, ain't she?" Tears poured down Taylor's reddened cheeks while he watched Rex perform CPR on Daisy, having valiantly delayed his own escape to prolong the girl's life when paramedics were unreachable. "Oh, Jesus—"

"What happened?" Mel looked over the scene from where she stood behind the island, discretely removing the gun from the drawer where Rexie had urged her to hide it.

Taylor's breath hitched. "She started to puke, and then she started to choke, and—"

"Gross! Rex is givin' CPR to puke-mouth? Rexie, don't do that to yourself."

He kept at it while Melba's lip curled. Blech! She'd have

to make him brush his teeth before the next time he kissed her.

Ah...who was she kidding. Even tasting of some sorority girl's puke, he could make Melba do whatever he wanted.

"This is good though, right?" Wandering into the living room with the gun openly in her hand, Melba stood over Rex while he blew air into Daisy's lungs. "I mean—if she dies, then we only have to kill two."

"It's a terrible thing, baby," Rexie told her in his Southern voice while his mouth went down to deliver another too-good breath to the girl. "An awful thing."

"But why is that?"

"Who the fuck are you talking to?"

Melba wanted to smack Taylor upside the head for interrupting, but she lost interest as Rexie lifted his head for a set of rapid chest-pumps. "I told you before. Blood must be spilled. You, or me—even Junie. Don't matter who, but *somebody* has to spill the blood. This chick chokin' on her own puke ain't blood spilled. Three lives are required to be offered up as sacrifice and keep the Gray Man from following you. Sacrifice can't be an accident."

"But—but the Gray Man was good to me just now, Rexie. He helped me up there."

"And that means you want to spend eternity with him looking at you?"

"Well—no. No. I only want you."

"So, we gotta get rid of him. And if this girl dies by any means other than mindful, purposeful slaughter, then you'll have to find somebody else to be your third sacrifice."

She didn't like the implication.

Just that quick, the panic set in.

"Rexie—please, save her! Save her, Rex."

"I'm trying," he said in his city voice, his tone of gruff annoyance. "But I'm not a fucking paramedic! Fuck, ah—maybe you could go get my iPad and call—"

And lose her life?

"No," said Mel sharply, snapped out of the tricky tactic to win the game. "No—I ain't lettin' you get one over on me like that."

"We won't say a fuckin' thing if you call the cops for us, Melba." Taylor pleaded to her with desperation in his reddened eyes. "Please! Don't let my baby sister die."

"Fuck it," said Rex, pushing himself to his feet to make his way to the hall, "I'll do it."

Melba laughed. "Where you think you're goin', sweetie? We ain't even half-done yet! Sit down."

Rex broke into a sprint.

Cursing, Melba dashed after him, almost gagging with the fiery pain that pulsed through her foot every time she put weight on it. The paper towel looked like a two-day-old menstrual pad, absolutely soaked through with blood and shriveled from constant friction between her foot and the foam sandal.

Sweat dotted her forehead.

She stopped at the hall's entrance, raised the gun, and fired. Once. Twice.

She had intended to fire a couple of warning shots in hopes that he would drop to the ground or duck into the television room, where he would be cornered; but, since Melba had little to no practice firing guns, she nailed Rex Virgil right in the calf.

"Fuck!"

"Rexie!"

Gasping at herself in shame and horror, her brow furrowed, Melba hurried to his fallen body and winced to see his trousers shining wet with a developing pool of blood. She crouched over him, almost touching the wound but not quite able to bring herself to do it.

"Oh, Rexie! Baby, I'm sorry—"

"You shot me," he hissed while the real Rexie said in a

cheerful, laughing tone, "I'm damn impressed. That's a good idea! Keep me in one place, for sure…"

"You really don't mind?"

His face reddened as if in anger, oddly, but he didn't get a chance to say whatever it was he'd meant to.

The doorbell's ring echoed through the house again.

He looked sharply at Melba, wild animal hope lighting his eyes.

When Melba answered to find Junie there, completely alone and dutifully carrying the camera bag, he released a groan of absolute suffering.

"Why did you come *back*?"

"Well, because—because I can't let Melba go back to jail. I'm sure that there's some way we can—"

Junie had been watching her cousin shut the front door— but now, turning to find Rexie bleeding from a bullet wound on the hallway floor, her mouth fell open. She recoiled a step.

"I know," Melba said with a shake of her head, "I feel like a total fuckin' imbecile. I's tryinta get him to duck into a room or somethin', and instead—well, I don't need to tell you."

"Why—what's happened—"

"What's happened is that Melba never should have been sent to prison. She should have been sent to a mental hospital, and permanently."

Rexie was such an incredible actor. Melba smiled at his performance, then remembered she should probably hide the mirth so as not to rub their special connection in Junie's face. Gritting his teeth, he went on, "That girl, Daisy, is dying— she's choking on her vomit, or was. She might already be dead."

"What? No!"

"You want to try CPR, be my guest. My mouth tastes enough like vomit already, and besides—what am I going to do, walk in there? Ah, Christ—"

Almost throwing the camera into Melba's hands, Junie

sprinted down the hall into the kitchen. Grinning, Melba opened the bag and removed the camera to admire it in the light.

"Look at this thing, Rexie! Isn't it great? I know it's not a big ol' fancy pro-fessional model or nothin' like that, but I think it's pretty slick! Takes a pretty picture, anyway."

With an increasingly practiced hand, Melba flipped the lens cap down, turned the device on, and focused the recorder's eye on Rex's gasping face.

"Damn, baby…you really do look extra-good on camera."

"Melba"—fire burned in Rex's eyes while pain contorted his mouth amid shallow breaths—"please, please stop. You can still stop. There's still time."

She echoed a few bars of the Led Zeppelin classic, singing about paths and still being able to pick a new one. His face fell while a blissful smile expanded across her mouth. "Oh, baby…when I think about all you've done for me, all the songs you've written to say you love me or all the movies you've inspired—movies you helped create even before I was *born*, or you were—that have secret messages to me, I get so emotional. It's such a sweet gift. You're too good to me, Rexie."

Rex, saying nothing, lowered his head upon the floor.

Beaming at him and then at the camera, Melba said compassionately, "Yeah, you're right. It's gettin' late—we should start filmin'. Lemme get the script!"

Mel turned toward the door, joy in her heart, anticipation of perfect fulfillment in her mind and soul. She was only stopped by Rex's Southern tone of uncharacteristic seriousness.

"What about the third life?"

Mel paused, her teeth sinking into her lower lip.

"Maybe she'll live," Mel said optimistically, stepping out into the night and shutting the door behind her.

"Stairway to Heaven" whistled from her lips as she made her limping way down the path and to the right, where the driveway sat with her car parked by his. Like husband and wife. She giggled to herself, wishing her foot were better so she could hop and click her heels like they did in movies.

But Rexie would heal her soon. Yes! Soon everything, mind and body, would be better. Soon there would be nothing standing in the way between her and Rex and perfect union.

AND NOTHING

NOTHING AT ALL

UNION WITH REX IS NOTHING

YOU ARE A FOOL

HE WANTS YOU TO DIE

HE WANTS TO CORRUPT YOUR SOUL

That was a short-lived reprieve! Shaking her head, eyes squeezing shut as the chorus receded again to the usual series of rumbling, rambling demands—as though she were a little kid listening to party guests talk about mysterious adult things in another room that allowed the escape of only the occasional scandalous word—Melba leaned into the car and reached for the script.

When her hand rested upon it, a black centipede scuttled up her wrist.

Melba's scream must have pierced every ear in the resort. That was the first moment it occurred to her that interlopers might really catch wind of the happenings in Virgil's cabin. Could come looking for a juicy story to sell to gossip tabloids or slap on Youtube. Frowning, Mel quickly assessed which parts of the house she could reasonably see from the street. Then, throwing open the front door just as—having managed hobble up and over to it on his bad leg—Rex reached for the knob, Melba smiled. She pushed him in and said while shutting the door after herself, "Good thing I went out there. Although…"

She shuddered, holding the script out from herself. The black centipede had been flung from her hand with a sudden wild gesture and scuttled under the seat of the car she no longer needed, (poor Junie!), but who knew if there were more hidden in these pages. Probably left a few eggs nestled in there. Shuddering, Mel held the script out from herself before pushing it into Rexie's hands. "You hold it, please. That motherfucker was the biggest centipede I ever seen in my damn life! I don't want to risk one leaping out and—ugh!" Another shudder, more violent.

"Listen, Melba." Rex threw the script down and didn't look as it dropped into his thin trail of blood. "Listen—this is *wrong*, do you understand me? Do you understand that what you're doing, what you're about to do, isn't just criminal? That it's immoral, that it's sick? Do you understand you're *sick*, Melba?"

Melba, who had been lost in thought, grinned at the romantic notion her mind had concocted and said warmly to her darling, "Look, baby! We got matchin' blood trails. What I get you in, right leg? I got left! Foot, anyway."

While Rex shook his head, picking up the script and shuffling off with it, another series of Taylor's low wails emanated from the living room. Junie's sob soon followed; Mel's heart just about broke.

Especially because the death was useless to her.

"Shoulda cut her open while she was suffocatin' to death on the floor," Mel muttered to herself, earning a glance from Rexie and a soft Southern chuckle.

"Angel, you know as well as I do that such loopholes are matters of the letter of the law versus the spirit of the law… the spirit is always more real than the letter."

"That's why I've always preferred movies to readin', but then again I sure like the books you been talkin' about in interviews. Kabbalah and Hermeticism and all."

"A lot of good they've done," said Rex with a slow shake of his head. Shuffling into the kitchen, he perched on a stool at the island bearing the cornucopia of liquors. Rohypnol spirits: a suitable concession for the audience to such a sordid play.

The show unfurled with four actors, three still living. Melba's sweating forehead grew all the hotter as she considered the number; as she regarded limp Daisy there on the floor, her mouth slack and her eyes shut.

Junie stopped the process of untying Taylor and looked up at Melba with big, watery eyes.

"She's dead, Mel," Junie said miserably.

"I can see that," said Mel, glancing at the corpse before jerking her chin at June. "Whatchu up to back there, cuz?"

"Oh, Mel, I can't—I can't just make him sit there looking at his sister's body! I have to—"

"Fuck that, you ain't have to do nothin'. Put a blindfold on 'im like they do with horses. I don't want to see you helping them again, Junie…I find it mighty discouragin'."

"But Mel—"

A rage unlike any Mel had felt for June—and she'd had quite a few outbursts toward her cousin over the years—came erupting from her eyes and mouth and clenched fists. The thought of her beloved Junie being the reason Melba missed her chance to have Rexie forever was too overwhelming to consider, and the impotence that plagued her when it came to explaining it all sufficiently pushed her over the edge.

"God damn it, Junie! God damn you—don't make me pull this gun on you."

Junie's tears overflowed from her wide eyes. Mel looked away. Seeing that Rexie actually skimmed through her script, which made her intensely self-conscious, she found it preferable to look back at crying June.

"You wouldn't do that, would you, Mel? Really—you wouldn't."

"If you make me, I'll do anything. I don't want to, Junie, but I might have to. And if I have to, well…then I don't know what'll happen."

Then she'd get her three deaths, but it wouldn't be right.

It wouldn't be glorious or liberating; it would be horrific and suffocating. Horrific to think she couldn't escape the world and be with Rexie without the death of her best friend.

"Junie is just another attachment, baby," said Rexie in that gentle drawl, "but you got it right. All that unfinished business stuff, ghosts and ghouls and nasty business…you know those stories."

"Yeah," she said quietly, "I do. But—heaven with you is better than any happiness here, Rex. Get away from him, Junie. Please." Melba stepped toward the cousin she now addressed. "Let's stay close forever."

With a wet little sob, Junie nodded.

She backed away from the weeping sacrifice.

Meanwhile, beneath shallow gasps of air, Candy began to stir.

While little groans emanated from the third sacrifice, Taylor raised his red eyes to Mel and thrashed in his seat.

"You *killed* her, you bitch!"

"If I'd been the one to kill her, it would have been bloody, but never you mind that. We need to talk about the script!"

Mel grinned and waved the camera in her nondominant hand, then aimed the lens at the two people in their chairs. "Castin' should be easy—and we'll need you, too, Junie."

"But—but Mel—we can't keep playing around with that body here. A girl died." Growing very quiet, Junie suggested, "Maybe we really should call the police."

The temperature of the room dropped in an instant. Each word was like another stab right through Melba's heart.

"Told you she's another attachment," said Rex without looking up from the script. "Don't forget, Mel…this is *your* universe, not hers. No matter how similar your two universes are until this night, well…this is a point of divergence."

"I guess so."

"She's not real, Mel. Somewhere out there, there's another Junie livin' this moment; and she'll live past this moment.

Maybe even this Junie will seem to live past this moment tonight, but the truth is that nothing of this world—your world, Mel—will ultimately survive you. The world as it seems to be will vanish."

"And then someone else's real universe will be the movie you're directin' and actin' in?"

"That's right."

"That thought makes me so fuckin' sad," said Melba, miserably pressing her free hand to her eye. "Ah, fuck—"

"Are you okay, Melba? Who are you talking to?"

June stepped toward her just as Candy managed to lift her head. She was infinitely less coherent than Taylor, who was experienced enough with hard drugs to navigate through the thick of Rohypnol thanks to all the pukin' he did. Candy may have been a drinker and an occasional cokehead, but a lack of experimentation with opiates or benzos meant that she was easily overwhelmed by the downers.

That seemed ideal.

Junie's voice again. "Mel? Hello?"

Melba sniffed. Junie approached her with slow, steady caution.

"Nothin', Junie, never you mind. Just talkin' to Rexie."

Eyes flicking to him at the kitchen island, Junie asked, "What about?"

"Haven't quite figured that out yet," he answered for both of them, flipping to the next page of the script. "But I will admit while I have the floor—this script is a lot more lucid than I expected of you, Melba."

She beamed. "Thank you, baby! I'm pretty happy with it, but I think it might be missing a little somethin'. Not sure what, precisely. Lemme know if you figure it out…until then, well—first, what if we shot it in that sunroom over there? Rexie? What do you think?"

"At this time of night? Lighting might not be great."

Frowning, Melba wandered to the windows and peered

across the lake. Got more beautiful by the damn minute! While she gazed across it—wowed and disappointed that she couldn't find a way to incorporate the exquisite mountain, the tree-covered hills, the vast, dark waters—Candy asked ditzily, "We're gonna make a *movie?*"

"What the hell else are we supposed to do at Rex Virgil's house," asked Mel, considering the private dock accessible through the door to her left. The path down to it was sort of treacherous, but in addition to the boat that might as well have been a luxury yacht, a happy rowboat bobbed placidly in the waves against which it stood its ground.

"Maybe we could go upstairs to that nice landin' I saw while you took me to your room, Rex. The second floor one?"

"Knock yourself out," said Rex above the tinkling sound of a drink being made.

"Thank you! Easier'n movin' the body and cleanin' all that broken glass to film down here…come on, Junie. Let's get these two upstairs."

They succeeded in getting Taylor as far as the kitchen before Melba noticed just what drink Rexie had fixed himself. She dropped her half of the wiggling chair; when, surprised, June followed suit and Taylor fell backward, his cracked sharply against the floor. The sound was no match for Rex's profanity as Mel slammed his hand, and the daquiri within it, against the edge of the island.

An easier tactic than trying to yank it from his hand, perhaps, but Mel felt the horror of the gunshot all over again to hear his cry and see the instant discoloration of a hand cut to ribbons by broken glass.

"That rum was drugged," said Mel, gesturing to the bottle. "How much did you drink?"

"Shit, ah—a mouthful—"

Holding his wounded hand at the wrist, Rex squeezed his eyes shut and maintained just enough presence of mind to ask, "How—how much did you put in?"

"Like a whole package of Rohypnol. Fuck! Well, at least we stopped you at one. It's okay, baby. Let's get this train movin' upstairs. If I needta, I can keep you awake."

Sighing through his teeth, Rex tried the fingers of his hand, grabbed a kitchen towel to wrap around his cuts, and took the hint that he was to go ahead of the other two.

"This reminds me of that riddle," said Mel cheerily when they had, a few minutes later, succeeded in dragging Taylor every one of twenty-six thumping steps to the second floor and its little guest sitting room. "You know the one, Junie—about leavin' a fox with a chicken and some corn or whatever. The wrong combination could really fuck me up here!"

Laughing to herself, Melba coaxed Rexie toward the stairs. "Come on, sexy…let's go help Candy up and grab the camera while we're at it."

Setting down the script, Rex obeyed in silence. They descended the stairs and Junie's heart throbbed with joy just to bask in his shadow—but better still was the way he pushed her against the nearby wall and kissed her in the first-floor hallway.

Mel moaned, capturing his hands as they moved over her breasts. "Now hold your horses," she cooed, pushing the greedy man away. "We gotta get our last actor! Not to mention a few props. You know what—oh! That's it."

Slapping Rexie in the arm with a great big smile, she told him, "I've been thinkin' too small! Oh, man, the whole scale of the movie has been fucked up! There's too much emphasis on the first act…you know what I really ought to do?"

"What's that, baby?"

"I'm thinking we should build out the heart of the movie. The third-act torture scene."

THIRTEEN

TOOK A LONG damn time to get started filming. Maybe it was because Mel insisted on wandering through all the rooms in the house, studying items of inspiration.

Mel meant what she said. She wasn't a writer by any means. Hell! She could hardly spell without a computer to help her; and, if she was being honest, she didn't have much in the way of imagination.

But Rexie *was* her imagination—had been her imagination even before she knew he was Rexie. She had therefore relied on his expertise in matters of writing, much as she intended to in matters of directing.

"What do you think, baby?" Mel frowned while peering around the garage, pausing to take note of the beer fridge and have a little peek in. "Shit, babe, there's cookies in here? I eat about six meals a week some months, but I'll never say "no" to a cookie."

"They're—"

His voice was staggered by hesitation before, in a self-correction, he said, "Go on."

Mel kept one hand in his to keep him from getting wise. Though he looked with sincere and obvious lust at the array of barely-used tools hanging along the wall and organized in boxes too neat for anyone with real handyman experience, his attention drifted back to her questioning eyes.

"They for later? I can leave 'em, but it's not like—"

"No," he said in that crisp, clean city voice, flashing her an equally pristine smile and squeezing her hand. "Go ahead! Take two or three if you want."

"Tryinta fatten me up so nobody wantsta steal me, huh…" With a grin and a wink, Melba nabbed a pair of cookies from the plastic bag and continued her study of the garage amid her munching.

"You know, honey"—she smacked her lips at the unpleasant experience of the treat—"I think I see your hesitation…tastes like dirt. This some kinda Californian wheatgrass cookie or some shit?"

"Something like that," he said as she stuffed the remainder into her mouth to get it over with. "I'll take the other if you don't want it."

After freeing up her hand, Mel dusted her fingers off on her shorts and studied a hammer arranged on the dusty worktable.

"Torture seems so hard to depict in fiction," said Melba idly, putting down the hammer before studying the nail gun and the fire axe mounted to the wall above it. "Seems to me that just near about anything that could be done with violence *has* been done—or, at the very least, that the effort to depict the "most violent" act of violence is futile. Every time somebody's made the darkest movie or written the most fucked-up book, that's just fuel for the fire of somebody else's imagination."

"You know, Melba," observed Rexie, turning half-eaten

cookie for investigation, "all this is really a shame. You've got an artistic mind…I wish you had gone into something like writing or painting earlier in life. Might have given you something to do."

"Maybe," she agreed, putting down the nail gun and settling on a simple pair of pliers she slid into her pocket, "but, if that *were* the case, you and me might nota been able to come together like this."

"You're right," he said, dusting off his fingers. "We wouldn't have."

He made a quick move toward her and she jerked away, laughing to draw the same gun for which he'd made a fast but useless grab.

"That was a nice try, sweetheart, but I don't feel much like fuckin' around. Let's head on in and check for somethin' else. Pliers are a good start, but I feel like I need something more *innerestin'*, you know?"

Following her back into the house with a sigh, Rex said, "I hope you realize that the things happening in movies are *fake*."

"Which is what makes this a rare artistic opportunity! Just think about it, baby—why, hell! Mosta the time, when murder's on tape, it's for sexu'l gratification. Snuff films, or rape on tape. If it ain't that then it's just war footage and gore shit like car accidents or whatever. This, though! This would be the one and only genu-ine murder on film for the sake of *art*—at least, that we know of. That was filmed with the involvement of a real Hollywood hero. Rexie!" Melba kissed the corner of his frowning mouth. "We'll be in history books, baby! Cary Grant ain't a goddamn thing next to you."

Judging by the cast of his face, Rexie seemed ready to produce a harsh response when his step down into the foyer instead elicited a soft cry of pain.

"Fuck! Ah, Melba—"

Wincing, Mel glanced down at his bullet wound and the blood still flowing from it.

"I reckon we oughta patch ourselves up," she decided with a glance at her own wound, throbbing with each step but so far away in the back of her consciousness that she barely felt the pain.

Rexie, on the other hand, had started to look pretty pale… though she wasn't sure if it was the pain or the blood loss or the drugs or all of the above.

"There's a medical kit upstairs," he told her through clenched teeth, his voice faint.

"Then come on, baby," she said, the gun still in her hand as it slipped around his waist. With her other hand, she guided his grip around her shoulders and smiled. "Lookie here! Two good feet between us. Like a couplea Siamese twins."

"Conjoined," he corrected through gritted teeth and eyes scrunched shut against the pain.

"What a time to act like you're really from California," she chastised him with a playful laugh and shake of her head. "Come on, come on…"

They paused only on the second-floor landing, where Junie rushed up to them and clutched Mel's hand.

"Melba, um—Mel—it occurs to me—"

"Yeah, Junie?"

"Well, I was thinkin' that I really can't afford to go to jail because—because, well, what if my kitty comes back while I'm gone?"

A great black shadow fell across Melba's soul, enfolding the words of their conversation with a terrible shroud. Mel tightened her arm around Rexie and glanced in an obvious way to the flight of stairs before them.

"Then he's probably been hangin' out near the apartment the whole time, and he'll still be there when you're able to take care of him," Melba answered.

"But—Melba, that could be a long time. If we go to prison, it could be—"

"Look, Junie! Me and Rexie really gotta take carea our

injuries for a minute or two before we can film that movie. I been coverin' every last damn thing with blood and he's got a bullet in his leg. You and I both know I ain't no surgeon, but we gotta figure something out, so just keep watch on these two. Hey!"

Realizing the quiet and doing a double-take, Melba laughed to recognize the two victims had been gagged using a set of neckties probably taken from a wardrobe upstairs. She raised her freer hand for Junie to high-five, saying, "That's the spirit, June! I'm glad to see you have the attitude I need in a friend."

"What—the gags? Oh." Slightly pale, as though she were horrified to be praised for such a thing (and, sensitive as Junie could be, she probably was), June recoiled from the high-five and looked at her hand like she had absorbed some sort of burning acid. Chagrined, she shook her head and pressed the same hand to her heart.

"I just couldn't listen to them, Melba…not to him, anyway. She's real messed up"—Mel noticed Candy had passed out again, so Rex's gimpy ass got dragged over while she made sure the girl was still breathing—"but I just figured I'd ought to take care of 'em both in case she sobered up a little and started…askin' for things."

"Good thinking," agreed Mel, glancing briefly at struggling, muffled Taylor. Looking less and less high all the time. "Make sure she doesn't die like the other girl, all right, baby?"

"Of course not," Junie said, nodding while Mel kissed her cheek and dragged Rexie toward the stairs. "Um—but, Mel—"

Melba paused, tried not to look annoyed, and turned to her cousin with her eyebrows expectantly lifted.

"Just—just do you think—uh—"

Junie's eyes, which had been red and shining with the struggle against tears for the whole night, lost their struggle and once again overflowed. Melba tutted, glancing sidelong at Rexie while Junie wailed like a kid lost in the mall.

"Do—do you think I'm gonna get—get to go home?"

"Sure you will," said Melba sternly, looking her in the eye. "Hell *yes* you will, Becky June. I won't let it be any other way. I would do anythin' to see you survive."

With a soft gasp of relief through the waterfall of her tears, Junie nodded rapidly.

"Okay! Okay, Mel—okay. Thank you."

"You know I love you, Becky June," said Melba, leading Rexie up the next flight of stairs before Junie could continue fussing. "Now, mind you just wait a few more minutes. We'll be back. Make sure that camera's charged up…"

Poor Junie! She was so sensitive. Melba couldn't help the pain that arose at the thought of leaving her cousin alone in the world—but, somehow, Junie would make new friends. Without Mel to worry about she'd probably find a better place to live! Maybe even have the courage to get a better-paying job. She could fall in love and start the family she'd always wanted. Get herself another cat.

Sighing, shaking her head, Mel told Rexie as they made it to the solitude of the bedroom, "I sure do regret havinta deal with that cat. Junie's so sensitive…wish I could find a way to tell her without her spendin' the rest of her life all traumatized and shit."

Spotting her hooded sweatshirt lying on the bed, Mel pulled it on over her tank top. She grinned to find her pack of cigarettes and, upon fishing her lighter out of her shorts, lit one while walking into the bathroom.

"First aid, first aid…aha!" Head under the sink, Melba blew a triumphant column of smoke at the small plastic box. "There it is! First aid. Let's see what we got."

The case resting on the counter, Melba flipped open the latch and lifted the lid.

Damn! Now that was some pitiful horseshit right there. A box of bandages, some burn ointment, a roll of medical tape and a wrap for sprains. Liquid stitches, at least. She'd need that for herself, for sure.

But what about him? The shit in there wasn't exactly conducive to digging a bullet out of a human leg—especially not when there was a strong possibility that said bullet had embedded itself into bone, judging from the dead-center hole.

"Wish you had some sutures or some shit like that around here," Melba said idly, opening another cabinet to find a pair of tweezers small enough for digging into a bullet hole. At least she might not have to damage him with the pliers…

Still, this was gonna suck. Guess she'd have to hope the roofies would kick in soon…maybe it would help if she tied him down. Good thing those handcuffs were still lyin' around.

"All right, angel," she called, striding from the bathroom with a bottle of peroxide and the pair of tweezers, "let me take carea you, first, since I think this son of a bitch on my foot has finally started to scab—"

Rex nailed her over the head with an object that would later turn out to be an antique snow globe. It shattered, fluid spilling everywhere as it got in on the theme of the night by leaving a bunch of glass across the floor. Sorta seemed like what Mr. Carl Jung would have called a 'synchronicity.'

Sorry. Dr, not Mr.

Melba never was very good at being polite.

"What in the ever-loving fuck," she cried, hissing in pain as a combination of tiny glass shards and snow globe fluid splattered over her face and eyes. Jesus, shit! Whatever the fuck it was, it was greasy and burned like an absolute bitch. "Ah! Fuck—"

There wasn't even time to remonstrate her lover for the low blow: he was busy grabbing her by the back of the sweatshirt and yanking the gun out of her drawers. Gasping, grabbing blindly, Melba got ahold of his elbow and then, twisting back against him, his wrist. While the elbow hand switched to the task of trying to extricate the gun from his grip, Rexie swore.

His other hand got into the fray. First, he tried tearing or crushing her hand away; soon he was just pulling at her hair or trying to stab a thumb up into her already blinded eyes. Melba grimaced, struggling to throw him off.

The gun discharged through the floor.

"Damn, baby! Don't waste the ammo—"

Slamming her skull back against Rexie's face yielded a crack and a pop and a scream so terrible that Melba regretted it hadn't been recorded. Would have made a very fine sound effect for future generations. Wilhelm, move over.

As the pain of a broken nose incapacitated him, Rexie fell backward and dragged Mel with him—but he maintained a grip of the gun all the same, sending an additional bullet flying into the ceiling. Cursing, Melba looked down at sexy, disheveled Rex, his hair in disarray and a curtain of blood now pouring across his mouth and jaw. His trembling hands struggled to maintain hold of the gun much longer, and tears poured from his eyes as he gasped for air.

Melba pitied him while he wept on the floor, stroking his face and tutting as he slapped her hand away.

Junie finally made it into the room, her eyes wide with terror.

"What's happening? Are you okay, Melba?"

"Sure, baby, I'm okay—Rexie's not, though. Check out his nose!"

"Oh, Mel!"

"Please," sobbed Rexie, his voice affected by the hollowness associated with a stuffy cold, "please, please just stop. Just leave."

"Oh, come on…you know you don't want that! You only think you do…but deep down inside, Rexie, you know just the same things I do."

"Melba, he doesn't. He—"

"Mind your business and go get that rope I left downstairs." Melba commanded her cousin with an imperious wave. "I'm gonna need it for his ankles when we're gettin' that bullet out."

"You don't have to," whispered Rex against the crimson downpour. "You really don't have to. I've got a great doctor. Just great. I can go to him."

"But I don't want to wait any longer before we go away, baby…"

Lips pursing into a small frown, Melba ran her hand over his chest and gazed into the pools of those crystal blue eyes. "I sure am sorry about your nose. Just like me to injure you while tryinta fix the bullet hole I gave you. Between you and me, you look pretty fuckin' foxy all covered with blood…but I feel awful bad about your nose. Guess it'll heal crooked, huh?"

Rex shut his eyes, saying only, "I'm so tired," as his Southern voice crooned on in a merrier way.

"Now don't you worry about my nose, angelbaby…it'll come back straight as a new highway when we're on the other side. But I sure would appreciate it if you got that bullet out at any cost."

"Of course, baby! Oh, poor thing…here, come on. What am I doin' on topa you? Let's get you in the bed…"

With a truly grateful noise that reminded Melba of a helpless child, she set the world's greatest actor reverently upon the edge of the mattress. His trembling hands were covered in blood, and not just from his nose or Melba's injuries. The snapped snow globe glass had lacerated him in a places, leaving his left hand bruised, bloody and fairly well crippled.

"You might wanna lie down—I heard that'll make the blood run into your stomach when you're havin' a nosebleed, but—"

"No, no—I do. I want to lie down."

While, still crying like a boy, Rexie crawled up toward the head of his bed and curled into a fetal ball, Mel regarded him with a few seconds of surprise. Then, around the same time she noticed a little fly buzzing around the handcuffs on the nightstand, an interesting thought occurred to her.

She was really taking it for granted that Rexie's physical embodiment was Rexie through and through. But didn't Rexie's being embodied make this man, Rex Virgil, also a simple mortal?

Damn! Now how was that for some shit. So that was what they meant about all that Jesus stuff…God and also fully human.

It was natural for a mortal to have moments of weakness. Maybe if Junie's universe would go on and permit her recovery, Rexie's universe might permit the same before his gradual ascendance to the absolute truth.

Junie's return to the room with the cry, "Mel?" drew her back to earth. She had been swaying in silence, lost in her thoughts while Rex wept on the bed. At Junie's return, Rexie's tears quieted somewhat; Mel hurried over to grab the handcuffs.

"Help me get him still," she implored, waving toward Rex as he raised his head. While Junie hurried over, he started to push himself up.

He made it halfway before wincing back down.

"Dizzy," was all he managed to say, his eyes remaining shut.

"Poor baby." Shaking her head, Melba grabbed his wrist and jerked his arm up. While he groaned in pain, she chastised him. "I'm glad I managed to get that drink out of your hand before you had much more of it…though now, since we're lookin' at surgery, maybe I should have."

"Are you sure about this, Mel? I really, really think—"

"Junie, I know what you think by now. How about you just zip it shut and get his legs down with some neckties or somethin'? Help me turn him over, first…"

Squeezing her eyes shut so sharply that it looked like she had been slapped, Junie obeyed. Mel looked at her with satisfaction and continued locking Rexie in the cuffs—a mite more effectively than he locked her, might she add. Rather than cuffing him to the bed she did the smart thing and looped the chain around one of the headboard's bars. The vertical iron held strong against Rex, who barely had the strength to fight between the pain and the Rohypnol.

"We'll just get this mean little bastard out and patch you up—maybe stick a little gauze in, or somethin'. Hey, Junie, go pick up that medical kit. Make sure nothin' broke…"

In the passage of a few minutes, Rex had been secured face-down and spread-eagle to the bed. Melba straddled his waist to tear away the leg of his trousers. "All right, angel, let's see…ah! Jesus—"

The vile black hole in Rexie's leg had, without immediate attention, begun to take on a certain lividity that would have concerned any doctor. Her tongue in her cheek, Melba examined it and said, "Too bad you went to rehab that seven or eight years ago, baby…even a little bita coke to numb this bastard'd be better than nothing. No pain pills? Nothin' but pot?"

"Just liquor," he said with a sob. "Don't—ow! Oh, Christ, please don't—"

"Sh, sh, don't kick—"

He couldn't kick, not really, but he could bend his knee enough to aggravate the wound and send another flow of blood blooming down his calf.

While Junie cried out to see her do such a thing, Melba raised the tweezers she had taken from the bathroom medicine cabinet.

"Mel, oh, you can't really be about to do this—"

"You're right," Mel agreed, examining the tweezers and leaning over for the brown bottle of peroxide. After dipping the former into the latter and shaking the equipment off with a smile, she bent down and, tweezers pinched shut, slid the tips of their prongs into the little bullet hole.

"Oh, fuck," he screamed into the pillow, "fuck, oh—stop!"

His knee jerked again. The tweezers tilted inside of him, twisting at such an odd angle Melba had a sympathy pain.

"Don't fuckin' fidget so much, baby! Junie—June, come here, do a better—thank you—"

Grimacing, her eyes fixed to the scene, flicking away from it, alternately drawn back again, Junie threw her weight down on Rexie's feet to keep him from moving his leg. Together the women restrained him like a wild animal enduring an extremely inept veterinary surgery and, as he forced himself to still with a sob, Melba shushed him.

"That's it, that's it…that's right, baby, just relax…"

Speaking gently to him all the while, Melba dug the tweezers down into the bullet hole and found the situation was exactly as she had feared. The slug was buried deep—very deep. The tweezers could try but, between the depth of the hole and the blood flowing around them, extracting the bullet would prove impossible without first widening the hole.

"You got a sewing kit around here, sugar?"

"Wh—no—no—I just buy new clothes—ah! Jesus!"

Mel yanked the tweezers out of him as quick as she could so as not to prolong the agony. While a new torrent of blood flowed from the wound, she looked up to find Junie as white as a fresh-cut line.

"You okay, cuz?"

Gagging, Junie flew off in the direction of the bathroom.

Seemed to make it to the toilet just before puking, at least.

Shaking her head, Mel said, "That girl could never be a surgeon…you wait here, Rexie. Junie?"

Between the sobs and bursts vomit, Junie managed an almost coherent, "Unngh?"

"Keep an eye on Rex here and make sure that he doesn't do anything silly. I'm going to go get something to get that bullet out for sure."

"Mel, wait—"

Disinterested in negotiation, Mel made her way into the hall, shut the bedroom door after her, and rolled up her sleeves with a sigh.

You want a job done right, you gotta do it yourself. That's what Mel was learning tonight. If she told Junie to go get the knife, June'd probably come back with some kind of little paring knife. Mel needed something that could go deep in one cut, and therefore fully intended to look for a big-ass boning knife—

But every idea of it flew from her head at the second-floor landing.

The chairs sat empty, the cords on the floor.

The sacrifices were nowhere to be seen.

FOURTEEN

"NOW YOU SEE why I made you shoot me," Rexie informed her solemnly.

Amid a cry of frustration and fear, she hurried down the stairs with her slit foot bleeding anew.

"Where are they? What happened?"

"Not far—hurry."

Mel dashed to the stairs and, seeing nothing, rushed down the flights between her and the ground floor. From her waistband, she withdrew the gun.

Two shots left, right? Did clips have six rounds, or was that only six-shooters? Maybe it was ten in a clip. Mel didn't know a goddamn practical thing about guns, and she didn't know how to check the clip, either—so, she supposed she was just going to have to get lucky.

When she reached the bottom of the stairs, it was just as Taylor was trying to negotiate the front door lock around the drunk girl draped in his arms.

"Look at you, up and about! Shit, brother…I knew you did a lot of drugs just to look at you, but you must do a *lot* to be capablea all this. That, or you puked out all the Rohypnol into Rexie's plant."

Melba fired the gun without warning and missed, but at least the idiot dropped Candy to flee down the hallway.

Limping after, Melba after him and fired another shot.

This was the same area where she had shot Rexie, and it seemed to be good luck: she nailed Taylor right in the side, producing a terrific cry but failing to slow him down all that much. Hand over the wound, he kept on running.

Melba rushed into the kitchen just after he'd swept through it. Teeth grit, she drew a knife from the butcher block.

If she had to personally kill anybody tonight, it might as well have been this fuckhead.

Rushing through the house, Melba reached Taylor just as he passed through the back door while screaming, "Help! Help!"

She sliced through the air and got a nice cut deep into the meat of his back, inspiring a wail and a fast instinctive response. Taylor turned and, with his hand still on the slider, slammed the door shut as fast and as hard upon Melba's wrist as he could.

Melba snatched her hand out of the gap and almost lost the knife in the process. Luckily, the chimp was too busy trying to get away. After spending little more than a second to examine her wrist for breakages, she threw the door wide again and pursued Taylor down the rocky terrain to the dock.

His instincts were all right, but his delivery sucked. Melba had to laugh when, halfway down, his ill-fated flight through the dark proved the cause of his undoing.

Unable to see, Taylor managed to snag his foot in a crooked step, twist his ankle, and take a dive.

He collapsed with his arms thrust out ahead of him, braced to catch any measure of stability while he tumbled down the jagged steps made crooked after years of erosion. He groaned, uttering one more helpless scream before using his bruised and scraped hands to drag himself down the remainder of the slope.

Melba took her time, negotiated down with great care, and met him five yards from the lapping lake.

"I do apologize," she told him, dragging him back by the shirt a few feet before rolling him onto his back. While he cried out and raised his hands, she lifted the knife.

"I'd drown you like you seem to want, but Rexie says blood's gotta be drawn. Blood it is—but, between you and me…this is gonna be mighty satisfyin' on a personal level."

Taylor's cries as Melba slashed the knife down through his hand were somehow very exciting. Not in a sexual way, (well, maybe in a somewhat sexual way…sorry, Rexie), but in a way that was somehow related to her anticipation of her beautiful fate.

It was a grand gesture. An act of pure devotion to Rex Virgil.

Now there was really no going back.

She would free herself of the Gray Man, that sordid entity that stood upon the waters of the lake to watch through the darkness.

As if Rexie weren't motivation enough.

Melba hacked the knife into Taylor's hands until his only defense dropped away; then it was his face, his neck, his chest and shoulders. Blood splattered across her cheeks as she jerked the knife from his sternum. Laughing, Melba plunged it back into his throat and twisted it in his windpipe until black blood erupted from his throat like Satan's bile.

The levity she felt was a signal of what this event, this sacrifice, truly was. It was an initiation ceremony. It was changing her.

When her arm ached, she realized Taylor was dead in a pool of mud and blood and probably his final shit. Wrinkling her nose, Mel dismounted the dead body and looked around for witnesses.

Amazing. All that screaming and nobody really seemed to care. Maybe it was just because everybody hated rich folks… or maybe they assumed it was a weird sex thing.

As she gripped the body by the collar and dragged it down to the lake, the wind kicked up. All the rattling leaves spoke in Rex's voice.

"The first blood has been spilled," he pronounced. "Now we will require the second sacrifice for your safe passage."

"Whatever you say, baby." Melba slid the corpse into the water, giving it a kick when it didn't drift off right away. Maybe she ought to have tossed it off the end of the dock but, well—it didn't really matter. "Thanks for makin' me shoot you…I never would have caught those two otherwise."

The night seemed darker than before. Mel thought it was a figment of her imagination until she looked up. The stars had disappeared from the sky, and the moon wobbled as it had upon the waters. Her eyes ached to be closed, but she refused to surrender to this passive drive to rest and give up the most important task of her life.

Carefully, Melba made her way back up the crooked stairs. She almost slipped more than once and marveled upon reaching the top. It was only by Rexie's grace that she had engaged in successful pursuit of her first sacrifice.

The second sacrifice lay in the foyer, still slipping in and out of consciousness from her high level of intoxication. Melba discovered her after shutting the back door and making her way through the house, a journey that felt somehow strange. For a second, Melba had the impression that she had entered the wrong house; only Candy there on the floor confirmed it was right.

Right?

Melba tried to get her bearings back, but somehow it was difficult. The house, like the night sky, had darkened in some way. She frowned, leaning into the television room to try a light and make sure they were on.

SOMEONE IS IN HERE

YOU LEFT THE DOOR OPEN

AND SOMEONE CAME IN

WHILE YOU WERE GONE

AND THEY ARE GOING TO

KILL

YOU

AND YOUR BODY

WILL BE EATEN

BECAUSE

YOU ARE NOTHING

Melba's eyes whipped rapidly around as the forceful unification of the chorus broke through her thoughts. Breath hitching, she touched the lamp a few times and then, upon stepping out of the hallway, checked every door she could find.

The voices' commands made her effort to reassure herself that no one was there far more difficult than it should have been. When Melba would begin to open one door, she would catch the sharp warning

HE'S IN THERE

and her heart would tighten in the anticipation of the Gray Man, or her father, or a stranger, or some other hideous monster.

But there would be nothing.

Then

YOU WERE TOO SLOW

HE LIKES TO GET BEHIND

HIS VICTIMS

LIKE YOU

VICTIM

and she would whip around to confirm there was only open hall behind her.

Then

THE PANTRY

THE PANTRY

IF YOU DON'T CHECK THE PANTRY

BEFORE YOU GO UPSTAIRS

HE'LL KILL YOU

BEFORE YOU KNOW

WHAT'S HAPPENED

This went on and on and on and on.

Melba was not permitted to proceed up the stairs until the voices were settled; until, at the very least, she could tell them that she had done everything she could to ensure her safety. After checking every room, closet, pantry, and fridge, Mel finally had no choice but to wash her hands of it.

"If," she said, dragging the stirring girl up the stairs by the back of her t-shirt, "after all that checkin', there's still somebody in this house fixinta kill me, they earned it."

One of the voices laughed. Melba grinned, herself. She

had always enjoyed making Daddy laugh, even if he had been a real asshole.

As far as folk that wanted her dead went, the Gray Man did turn out to be there on the way—but only to watch Melba struggle with the slight weight of the unhelpful girl she tried to encourage up the stairs. His head rotated because his eyes could not and, shuddering to think of the barn owl queerness of his unholy gaze, Melba turned her face away and hurried Candy toward her fate.

The nearer they drew, the clearer Melba heard a radio in Rexie's room uttering a series of ugly words that Mel could hardly stand to hear.

"…and I want you to understand that, no matter the form, idolatry means one pure and simple thing: the *rejection* of *God!* The condemnation of your soul to hell! All those alleged rewards, all the fruits of your chosen calf, will amount to *ash* in your *mouth*.

"Think about—I want you to think about Corinthians, Chapter 10, Verse 18 through 22: "Consider the people of Israel: Do not those who eat the sacrifices participate in the altar? Do I mean then that food sacrificed to an idol is anything, or that an idol is anything? No, but the sacrifices of pagans are offered to demons, not to God, and I do not want you to be participants with demons. You cannot drink the cup of the Lord and the cup of demons too; you cannot have a part in both the Lord's table and the table of demons. Are we trying to arouse the Lord's jealousy? Are we stronger than he?"

"Now, think about that. Think about the so-called rewards of—"

"Would you turn that shit off?" Bursting in amid Junie's cry of relief, Mel dumped Candy on the floor and locked the bedroom door. "You know this old dude's shrill-ass voice is like nails on the chalkboard to me. Sounds like that Heaven's Gate motherfucker—the eunuch, you know. And they call *me* nuts…"

As Junie hurried to the stereo built into a series of nooks opposite the windows, Melba caressed the back of Rexie's dark head.

"Hey, baby. How you holdin' up?"

"Been better," he said.

"Well, I finally got that knife—no thanks to our friends over here."

Blearily, Rex twisted his head and strained to focus his eyes. "What knife?"

"Damn, baby, you really did get pretty fucked up. You know! The knife to get that bullet outta your leg."

Edging reluctantly toward the bed as Lynyrd Skynyrd relieved them from the preacher's voice, Junie asked, "What took you so long downstairs, Mel? Where's Taylor?"

"Don't you worry about him."

"But—"

"I said not to worry," Mel repeated firmly but calmly, humming along with "Simple Man" while she resumed her position on Rexie's back. As he did as much struggling as he could, Melba patted his head.

"Just have patience, baby. We'll get that bullet right on out…get you taken care of."

"That's not what I—"

"Can you look in his closet for onea them belts? That door there. That's it—he's gonna need somethin' to bite down on."

"Please, God." Rexie sobbed, his arms straining against the handcuffs. "Please, please, oh, somebody save me. Please, God, please—"

Junie hurried back with a belt and a few extremely anxious glances toward Rexie's face. Poor thing was so damn sensitive that she couldn't even gag a man!

"Just hold down his foot like last time," said Mel, turning to slip the belt between his teeth and tie it behind his head. "We'll get this over as quick as we can."

"How are we gonna stitch it back up without sutures or thread, Mel?"

"Well there's liquid stitches in that kit right there—"

"Mel! That's not for surgery."

"Well, no, but if we wrap it up real tight and keep the two parts together then it'll probably be fine. For my part, Rexie can heal himself when he remembers one way or another, and for his part, he can get himself to a doctor when tonight's over. You just want that bullet out cause it's in so deep, huh, baby?"

While Rexie sobbed into the pillow, his smooth voice assured Mel, "Sure do, angel. Gotta get that shrapnel out if it's gonna heal right, right?"

"Right," she said, glancing up at Junie. "All right, ready? Here we go…"

Without much more warning, Melba cut into the wound on the back of Rex's leg.

As, gasping, Junie asked, "Mel, what's all that blood doing on that knife," Mel ignored her like she ignored Rexie's screaming. She sank the knife deeper. The sharp tip of the long blade slid into the tweezer-widened bullet wound. Blood flowed like magma from the earth as the red and white marble of his leg was bisected to access the bullet. While Rex screamed, his leg sometimes twitched. Junie would tense her weight upon him, her face as pale as their patient's blood was dark.

"Stop! Ah-ah stop! Puh-lease, please, stop!"

"I know it's hard to ignore what I seem to want," he added to her softly. "But you're doin' good, baby. Real, real good."

Nodding to herself, Melba gently slit the wound open from the other side. Soon she'd opened the angry mouth of a muscular vagina in the back of his leg.

"There," said Mel, turning away to exhale a sigh of relief. "There, the hardest part is over. Now—"

Now, feeling a little nervous about this part but trying to pretend that she wasn't, Melba very gently used the tip of the knife along with the tweezers to push his muscle fibers somewhat wider. As the wound reluctantly gaped with her pushing, she forced herself to peer into the evil red and black and white pool within.

Yes: in the center of the ugly little target was embedded the hateful black slug, contorted by the impact with Rexie's bone.

As Melba pushed open the wound, Rexie maybe a terrible gagging noise.

She cursed, glancing quickly up at Junie.

"Let's shift places on three so you can make sure he's not asphyxiatin' on his vomit."

"Oh, Melba—oh, God—"

"Three," Melba said, the women doing an awkward switcheroo around Rexie's open wound before he could bend his knee in a natural reaction to the pain.

Now perched upon his foot while Junie, at Rexie's waist, drew the belt from his mouth to help him breathe, Mel bent down to better vantage than before. She tucked a few dangling strands of hair behind her ear, then reached into the wound with the tweezers.

Rexie's violent scream as the tweezers slipped against the wet metal made her wince.

"I'll be damned if this ain't a dead ringer for that ol' Milton Bradley game," said Melba. "Always hated that damn thing."

"Me, too," agreed Junie, her tone wet with unproduced sobs. "Yeah, me too. I got so nervous. I was such a nervous kid. Oh! Melba. Melba, do you remember being a kid?"

"Yeah, and I fuckin' hated it. Lemme concentrate."

Better angle or no, the little tweezers were designed for picking hairs—not performing surgery. Definitely not for pulling bullets out of bone. To make matters worse, the wound desperately wanted to close around them. She had to work faster than this if she was going to help Rexie more than she hurt him.

That was when she remembered the pliers in her back pocket.

Exhaling slowly, Melba withdrew the industrial tools and studied them in the light. Yeah, there was the ticket—a little dirt on them from the garage, though. Turning away, Melba reached for the bottle of peroxide still beside the first-aid kit. After splashing its contents across the pliers, Melba looked up at Rexie and said, "You might wanna hold your breath, baby…"

Sobbing, Rex gasped enough air to obey—or to try, anyway. When the mean little needle nose sank into the wound, he released the most terrible scream Melba had ever heard.

"I know, baby," she whispered, understanding a little better why doctors were always asking nurses to wipe their brows. She could feel her own forehead with sweat, but it would all be over in a few seconds if she could just—

Yes.

The tips of the pliers closed around the bullet. Their textured surface held it tight.

Squeezing, Melba wiggled the slug as though it were a tooth.

After a few urges back and forth and a series of incoherent, screaming sobs from Rexie, the bullet popped out. It left a nasty, glistening pink glimpse of bone to make Melba's skin crawl, but son of a bitch! The little fucker was *out.*

"Fuck!" Examining the bullet that had been in Rexie and, after some thought, slipping the bloody little piece of lead (Were bullets still lead? Whatever…) into her pocket as the ultimate piece of fan memorabilia, Mel grinned somewhat sheepishly over at Junie. "I gave you a lotta hell for bein' too squeamish, but I will admit that this was some pretty harrowin' shit."

"I think he might be passing out, Melba."

"Keep him awake," Melba encouraged her cousin. "We're almost done…"

With the bottle in one hand and the other maintaining

the position of his leg, Melba splashed a fair amount of peroxide into Rexie's open wound.

That woke him up, for sure.

While, howling in pain, Rexie thrashed as much as the girls allowed, Melba worked fast. She daubed the excess peroxide and blood up with gauze, squeezed the wound shut as much as possible with a tourniquet improvised with the roll of athletic bandage, then tightened another layer of gauze along the outside when the liquid stitches proved, as Junie had advised, useless.

After wrapping his leg, Melba leaned back, nodded in satisfaction, and dismounted his ankle.

"That's about as good as it's gonna get," said Mel, rubbing her jaw to see the long slit of red oozing through the gauze each time the still-sobbing man twitched or thrashed. "But that bullet is gone! How 'bout that."

Smiling with pride, Melba put her hands on her hips. Her smile faded while Rex continued weeping softly, occasionally writhing, always looking miserable.

"You think you're gonna be able to stand up soon, baby? We got a movie to shoot, and we lost our male lead. I know you were gonna help me direct, but maybe you could act instead?"

As Rexie softly sobbed, Melba leaned down to kiss the top of his head.

And inspiration struck.

"Oh! Shit! Baby! That's it!"

Slapping his back, then pushing Junie with such excitement she actually fell off of Rexie, upon whose back she had continued to sit in a kind of hypnotic trance, Melba laughed.

"That's it, that's just it. Man, I knew this script was missin' something! What have I said? It needs a *turn*—a twist! You know. Somethin' unexpected. A shock. Somebody changin' sides. That sort of thing."

Melba hurried from the room, kicking Candy aside to

do so unobstructed. While the stupid girl laughed on the floor and Junie called her name, Melba flew down the stairs to snatch both script and camera from the second floor foyer. She didn't even realize the Gray Man hadn't been there until she was halfway up the stairs.

"Okay." Melba panted, scoping out the room. It was a miracle she was able to do any damn surgery at all—shit was dark, darker all the time. She sighed in exasperation. "Damn! How are we supposedta make a film in these conditions? The lightin' in here is piss-poor, baby."

"Your eyes look really red, Melba."

Junie frowned as her cousin thrust the script into her hand. As she leafed through its bloodstained pages without really reading any of their contents, Mel shrugged and said, "Probably 'cause babe smacked me upside the head with a damn snow globe, but it's all right."

"Oh, Mel! Is that what's all over the floor over there? Oh my God! Did you wash your eyes out?"

"No ma'am, I did not have time. As you have seen, the evening's schedule has been a bit harried."

"Melba!" Dropping the script and springing from the bed to grip her cousin by the wrist, Junie said, "Come on—we have to wash your eyes out! Snow globes have *antifreeze* in them. Does he have saline? Oh, God…"

It didn't really matter to Mel, but Junie was so worried that it seemed like something that needed doing. Shrugging—and figuring she couldn't film a movie with burning eyes—Melba followed her cousin to the bathroom, stepped carefully over the broken snow globe glass, and sat down on the shut lid of the toilet. There, Junie fussed over her: first washing her eyes with a bottle of contact lens saline solution, then checking on the slit in her foot.

For the most part the cut had stopped bleeding, though the thick layer of drying clot was easily disturbed. It occurred to Mel while Junie cleaned and wrapped it up that she would leave her body behind before the wound could clot. Indeed, one might say it would never clot. Her false body would bear the signs of a stigmata that would mean noting to her soon. Mel's real self would be safe and sound, having outgrown the world like a bird breaking from its shell. That must have felt like some scary shit to birds! Butterflies, too, all cozy in their cocoon. Imagine the caterpillars with no idea of the future that awaited them as they began, for reasons they could not explain, binding themselves in their own little threads.

Melba was just a caterpillar who knew, baby.

"There," said June, leaning back with a sigh of relief to study the bound foot. "How you feelin,' Mel? Your eyes better?"

"Stingin' way less, baby, thank you."

"Of course."

Junie smiled softly, tears filling her eyes again. She lifted a delicate hand to Mel's knee. Exhaling, Mel held it.

SHE IS NOT YOUR COUSIN

SHE IS IT

IT IS A CLONE

YOUR PATHS

HAVE DIVERGED

"That's just not true," Rexie told her lovingly, singing along with the Kansas song by then blasting through the speakers outside the bathroom. "I promised you that Junie would be with you to the end."

"Yes," whispered Mel. "Yes, you did."

"What's that, Mel?"

Melba shook her head at Junie's question, ignoring the voices.

"Nothin' baby, nothin'. I'm just so glad you're here with me, Junie—I'm glad you're real."

"Of course I'm real," said June with a soft laugh.

Melba laughed, too, softly; but her smile was weak, and she turned her face away while rising to limp from the bathroom.

What the fuck was she going to do? She owed three deaths, or her own…and if she died in the future, then she was already dead right now. Yes, then she was really nothing.

But Melba knew damn well she wasn't a nothing-clone, so she must have been the Melba that succeeded in freeing herself from the Gray Man and running away into immortal joy. A dead thing could not observe itself or the world, and Melba was observing plenty.

Of course…how many clones must have thought the exact same thing? How many were also certain they would be the real Melba, the immortal Melba, the Melba who would survive? How many selves out there in other universes made it this far, or even further, only to fail right before the end?

But how could Melba move on and avoid sacrificing Junie, a real and wonderful and lovable person?

Melba stepped into the bedroom, her eyes falling on Rexie. He had calmed down somewhat, just barely, probably through some kind of Tibetan meditation technique or some such business. He really was a man of the mind! Sighing in admiration, Melba strolled over to Rexie's side and touched his head.

"Let me go," was all he said.

Melba grinned down at him.

"Of course, baby. In a minute! I want to take advantage of this, though, because it's a rare opportunity. Hey—Candy! Candy—"

Melba marched over and slapped Candy in the back of the head before pulling her upright against the wall like an oversized, drunken doll.

"Wake the fuck up, bitch! Your services are needed—and I do not mean the services you seem used to providin'. You still wanna be in that movie?"

"Oh…fuck yeah…yeah, I wanna be in a *movie*…like, porn?"

"No, bitch, not porn! A bona fide Hollywood picture starring the one and only Rex Virgil!"

"Oh…h…h…shit, bitch, fuck yeah…yeah, I wanna be in a movie with Rex Virgil." Candy giggled in a singularly stupid way, then raised Mel's blood pressure by mumbling as her eyes slid shut, "Wanna make out with Rex Virgil…"

With a dark snort, Melba reminded herself that the girl was about to die and was therefore no threat to her. Strolling back to Rexie's side while the girl woke up, Melba stretched alongside her beloved to run her fingers through his sweat-dampened hair.

"So, you know how the script is about them two bad girls kidnappin' a man? Life emulates art, as they say…well, I was thinkin' the plot is just a little too straightforward. It needs somethin' to spice it up! So…what if…"

Melba bent and pressed her lips to Rexie's ear, where she whispered the words, "What if we have a twist where one of the girls secretly hates the other, and was in a relationship with the victim all along…all to let the oblivious girl's guard down and get her help in preparin' her own torture chamber."

Rexie's breathing changed in a manner perceptible only to someone who knew him as well as Melba did. Pleased to know he liked the idea, Mel ran her hand over his shoulders. "So just stay in there for a minute, okay, baby? We gotta get your release on camera for genuine effect."

After a few seconds of saying nothing, Rex turned his head slowly in Melba's direction. His bloodstained face was still tense with the pain—and now with the understanding coursing through him.

His bloodshot eyes found hers.

"What are my lines?"

FIFTEEN

SINCE THE SCRIPT was changing so much as a consequence of this creative decision, Melba threw out a whole ten pages from the middle. The rest of the changes were easy enough. Once the alleged victim was free and had revealed himself as one of the true torturers, it was just a matter of swapping lines and re-envisioning the genders of their speakers. So far as Melba saw it, torture was torture nobody who was doing it. All the same things could be said in the same contexts, more or less.

While Mel made a few notes on the script (mostly for her own benefit, since Rexie seemed perfectly capable of remembering even roughly improvised lines decided that very minute), Junie emerged from the bathroom with clean hands and a stressed face. She pondered Candy before busying herself by checking out the camera, whose lens she cleaned and whose battery she checked so many times she probably drained the damn thing 5 percent.

Didn't matter too much. What mattered was filming the climactic scene. What mattered was having this, this *real* tension documented. Then, when Mel was gone, somebody could use it as the heart of something else. Maybe, if Rexie's clone survived—and he would, of course, in his universe—he could build a movie around it starring lookalikes of Melba and Junie. Junie probably wouldn't be very interested in starring, after all.

Hell—she had to be sternly persuaded to star in even the scene where the wild twist was revealed. Junie looked grimly at the pages Melba showed her.

"I don't want to *torture* him, Mel," she said, regarding the old portions.

"You don't have to! The secret is that you've always hated Candy there. You two are supposed to be friends, but on account of some great betrayal—I don't know, that's for editin'—you hate her and have conspired with your boyfriend here to catch her unexpectin'. I'm thinkin' right now that early in the torture you'll get her help freeing him, like to move him from one location to another, and you'll accidentally let him get free—or so it would seem, until we determine that the real victim is Candy. Maybe. All I really want is the true footage, so it can be worked in once the resta the script is hashed out."

"I don't know about this, Mel," said Junie nervously, looking up at her cousin. "It says I'm supposed to have a gun?"

"Yes ma'am! Here's your prop right here."

Removing the gun from the back of her pants, Melba passed it handle-first to June. Junie gasped sharply and, lips thereafter pursed, accepted it to examine.

"Don't worry," lied Melba, "I'm pretty sure it's out of bullets."

"'Pretty sure!'"

"Well, hell, I don't know the first damn thing about guns. Do you, Junie?"

"No! Of course not."

"Rexie, sugar? How 'bout you?"

"I only pretend like I do for the movies," he said, his tone still tired but considerably more alert than before.

"See? So, I'm just goin' by what I know. Look, Junie, trust me! It's empty!"

"What if we try it?"

Melba shrugged. "Go ahead," she said, prompting Junie to stare uneasily at her. "*Shoot* the damn thing! Go on, go on."

Breath visibly held behind her pursed lips, Junie aimed the gun toward a nearby red lampshade with both hands. It looked like some dismembered organ found at a crime scene when the bullet had torn a hole through it.

"Mel!" Dropping the weapon and springing back as though it were a snake, Junie looked rapidly at Melba. "Mel, it really *was* loaded. If I had used that in the movie—Mel, something could have *happened*—"

Melba was quickly losing her patience here—least of all because Junie's life was at stake, and no clear alternative solution had yet to be presented.

"Then I'm sure it's empty now," Melba said.

"But—"

"Damn it, Junie, we can't stand around here yammerin' all night! Pick the gun back up and—Junie!"

Like an overwrought child who had spent far too long in the world's most hellish amusement park, Junie burst into violent tears. She looked like she was thinking of dashing from the room: at the very least, her gaze whipped between the bathroom and hallway doors about six or seven times before, through the contortions of her features and the tears pouring from her eyes, she found Melba.

"I just want to go 'home," she said miserably. "Melba, Mel—I don't want to do this. Why are we doing this? Why are *you* doing this? Why won't you just take your medication, Melba?"

Melba's lips pursed.

"Junie—"

"No! Stop! Stop! You think I'm stupid and weak and that—that you can push me around, can make me do whatever you want! I don't *want* this, Melba! I don't want to be a part of this! Oh, God!"

Poor Becky June covered her face with her hands. She sobbed, her shoulders heaving with each gasp for air.

"I just want to be at home. I want—want to be at home with my kitty in my lap—oh, I want my cat! Everything fell apart when he ran away—"

With a sigh down at her feet, Melba edged toward her cousin. She froze when, recoiling, Junie raised a hand between them.

"No! No. Just stop. What is all this about? Why are you doing all this, Melba? Why do you want to hurt Rex? I thought you loved him. Don't you want him to feel safe and happy? And me, too?"

"Well, of course, Junie. Of course! That's all I want for both of you."

"Then why?" Junie's voice arched up like a broken violin string at the end of the question, her lips trembling amid a glistening layer of tears and snot she wiped on the back of her hand. "Why? Tell me a reason that makes sense!"

"Tell her," Rexie said. "Go ahead, baby. I don't mind."

Melba looked over at the back of his head. "Do you mean it?"

"Of course. This is the eleventh hour. Tell her the truth now, and it will make things easier; before, it would have made everything far harder."

Her teeth ground. "Do you think I can really explain it?"

"To her, you're the only one who can."

Nodding to herself, letting her cousin weep for a moment, Melba made her way to the bathroom where she found a delicious bar of deodorant that smelled so much like Rexie she swiped a little of it on her neck so she could smell him whenever she moved her head. It wasn't exactly the same on her skin, of course; but it was like his ghost perched on her shoulder, whispering in her ear, kissing her cheek.

And didn't he always?

Rexie had a tall dressing mirror in the wardrobe, Mel had found, and she waved Junie in while saying, "Come on, Junie, let me show you something. I promise not to hurt you…"

While June uneasily edged into the room adjacent Rexie's sleeping quarters, Mel found that, amid the darkness of her damaged vision, a few of the hanging shirts seemed to twitch and quiver like the leaves of trees. Seeing that Junie paid the effect no mind, Mel focused on the music outside the room (Bad Company—the radio was really her friend tonight, baby) and sorted her thoughts.

The voices turned down a little as, newly calmed, she drew on the mirror with the deodorant. The left panel of the tall tri-fold quickly became dominated by her illustration, which was described as she drew it.

"So—damn, how do I explain this—"

She glanced down at her leg for whatever reason and, seeing the Tree of Life shape into which the molecular universe had been sculpted by the artist, Mel quickly slapped together a half-assed replication.

"So the Tree of Life here is a, uh, a model of reality and God. Like in science class, you know. When shit gets categorized? Taxonomy, and all, I think that's what they call it."

"Yes," said June softly, following the movements of Melba's hand.

"Well, this here's the taxonomy for the soul. So—so there's all these different levels to reality. This up here is the Big Guy what's too big to think about"—she tapped Keter, causing the deodorant to leave an extra spot there at the top of the tree—"and this one down here, Malkuth, is where we are."

"Okay."

"But, see, the thing is that it's only a model. God, and us, and everything in between?" She circled it all and said, "This is all present simultaneously. It's a singular experience. So the first thing you gotta know is that spiritual things *are* physical things, and vice-versa—but they're different, too."

Junie frowned. "I don't know if I rightly follow that."

"Well—like Jesus and God. Jesus *is* God, right? But also the Son."

"Oh," said Junie quickly, "well, yes, that's true. But—that's Him."

"No! That's all reality. See, that's what He really wanted us to see—the lesson we're supposed to learn. We are *also* simultaneously complete and incomplete. Here—"

Mel turned to the center panel of the mirror and drew a line going left to right. Throughout it she made dots while telling her cousin, "You know how time is the 4th dimension?"

Junie shook her head. "I can't believe you think about this stuff, Melba…it makes my head hurt."

"But you know what I'm talkin' about, right?"

"I reckon."

"So, when we're going through this dimension, we just experience things moment to moment in a—whatchacallit— linear fashion. We go from memory one to memory two to memory three. On and on. But, if we were able to observe the 4th dimension as a single object"—she tapped her first drawing before sweeping a similar circle around the timeline example—"we would see the time we experience as sequential for what it is: one singular, complete line that's already been drawn and is eternally present, but that we are experiencing in sequential order."

Her hands on either side of her cheeks, then lowering to fold across her ribs, Junie looked at the timeline for a few long seconds before shaking her head.

"What does this have to do with what's going on here?"

"I'm gettin' to that. So—"

Now, on the right mirror, Mel drew a perfect pair of intersecting lines. She made them exactly the same length, careful that Junie would not confuse it for a cross. All the same, she slapped 'God the Father' at the top, 'Jesus Christ' at the bottom, and then scribbled 'Mary' to the right and 'Magdalene' to the left.

"Consider this, like, the axis of a graph that changes as you move in the 4th dimension. Another way of looking at it is like—

Beside 'Jesus Christ' she scribbled 'Melba Age 0' and beside 'God' scribbled 'Melba Age ∞'. 'Magdalene' was paired with 'Gray Man' and 'Mary' was paired with 'Rexie,' and Melba smiled at the endorphins that rushed over a person who had just made an irrefutable point. She added a somewhat crooked dotted line to represent the X-axis, which she loosely labeled "space."

"The Tree of Life is about reality and kind of a "world-soul," but this graph here is like a map of the individual's soul, see, and the way their consciousness changes as they move through space and time. It's like a close-up of Malkuth. That Tree of Life, as you go down it, it represents the emergence of God's consciousness and its manifestation in the world as us—all of us. The idea is to raise your consciousness of God in life so that, when you die, your human ego and God-consciousness are propelled together into eternity and not crushed into nothingness, since consciousness is immortal but the ego ain't. Get it?"

June, who to her credit looked like she was genuinely giving this a listen and thinking about it as it went along, worried the fabric around the neck of her shirt. "If we're all God walkin' around in pieces, Melba, then how come you're hurtin' people? It's yourself you're doing all this to."

"Because"—Mel tried to keep the excitement from her tone but, because Junie had walked right back to her point, she couldn't help it—"to fully experience each and every individual human life as the humans experience it, God must embody every human in a sequential fashion. Consciousness is the awareness of God that navigates the 4th dimension and, like all things that navigate the 4th dimension, can go only in one direction while within it. However, when it is free from its physical form, it is liberated to explore other possible existences. The God-mind steps out of the mortal body and explores a new universe about a new person, see, Junie? And when that happens, *that* person is the immortal one who will be transcended outside of time along with the consciousness what's usin' it as a host. Everyone else in their world is mortal—and mortality is a lie, see, Junie, so mortal people can't be real. They're clones God makes for the person who's starring in the universe during that iteration, and they seem to die around that person while said person gradually reaches the point in their life when they will transcend the 4th dimension and explore higher realities at-will."

She once more used the deodorant to refer to the Tree of Life.

Taking all this in very quietly, June looked between the three diagrams and then looked at her cousin in a dazed way.

"Are you saying you think that I'm—I'm some kind of clone?"

"What! Junie, no. You're not a clone. Not yet, anyway."

Looking around for one last empty space, Melba knelt below the central image and drew three curving lines that intersected in the fashion of a rough braid before separating in separate directions. Left to right, she labeled their starting points J, M, and R.

"See, Junie," she said as she drew, "the way all these universes work, everybody on Earth is born their true self, and these true selves co-exist until they can't. Gradually, as life happens to these people, traumas happen. Some things are so bad that they keep people from fulfilling their highest potential, see, and in that case God don't wanna see that. Ain't no point in it. So that person unable to achieve their highest self is, in that universe, ineligible to be observed by the Good Lord. That'd be somebody like my Daddy from the perspective of this universe, but even then, he might have a universe way distant from ours"—she deigned to draw a curving line that floated by itself on the far side of the left panel—"where even he manages to achieve his highest potential. And maybe there he even deserves it."

A wave of sorrow washed over Mel, who was always surprised that she still felt anything about the evil bastard. June made a little pitiful noise of her own, but that drove Mel back into action. She tapped the central braid, explaining, "But sometimes traumas are successfully overcome, and in that case they're just a part of the true path because they may even contribute in some way to the future self-actualization of the true, God-observed individuals. However, when a person becomes ineligible for observation in a given universe, they are replaced by a clone. God cannot observe clones because they ain't got immortal souls."

"So you think other people are clones," June said carefully, "but I'm not. Yet."

"Exactly. Most other people in my life are clones, I reckon—most of society—but there's a lot of great artists and philanthropists and other good people out there who I suspect to be as real as I am. Rexie is one of 'em."

"So why are you hurting him?"

Junie looked again at Melba, expecting a response, and Melba sighed.

"This is where the hard part comes in. See—even though I'm still closer to here than to here"—Melba pointed to the bottom of the graph before indicating the middle part, which to her symbolized the passage into the death experience— "until the very first second I'm not, I believe my condition makes me sensitive to *all* of this. I am aware of the laws we have discussed and am tangibly aware of things that—"

Mel licked her dry lips and considered how to say it.

"You know in Egyptian mythology? When there's a whole big thing about judgin' your soul and weighin' it and all, and if you're bad a crocodile gets to eat you forever, but if you're good Anubis will take you on through an eternal life?"

Junie nodded.

"Well, it's like I can hear Anubis now, before I'm dead," said Mel with a final shrug. "Which I reckon makes sense, because if my soul is immortal and he and I are to be together eternally, well, then I am just as immortal now as I will be once I have seemed to die. And because I am aware of him, and because he is omnipresent and omniscient, he tells me the moves to make to achieve my greatest potential to make sure I'm the true me; the me God is watching. One day, he revealed that he was born on this world in the form of Rexie, which is why he talks to me through Rexie."

Junie stared in astonishment while, pushing herself up from the floor with a little grunt and a new appreciation for the bandages Junie had applied to her, Melba put her hands on her hips and regarded her work with a sigh.

"So you see, Junie, when Rexie tells me to jump, I can't even think about sayin' no. He was even the one who gave me permission to tell you all this right now."

"But—how does one become the other? How could a normal man like Rex Virgil become an Egyptian God?"

Melba rolled her eyes. This is why it was so damn hard to explain…folk were so *specific.*

"I made a mistake by bringing up a particular pantheon. He ain't *literally* Anubis, although he *is* Anubis and maybe Hades and a whole lotta other gods like that—but he's also a self-aware part of *the* God. The part of God that guides and protects Himself. He's my angel, Junie. And he told me that he made me shoot him so I'd catch Taylor before he escaped."

June's eyes widened. "You caught Taylor?"

Melba winced, cursing herself and the flow into which

she had fallen during her miniature lecture. "Well, uh—well yes, I did."

"What'd you do with him? Where is he?"

"Well—"

"You didn't hurt him, did you?"

Melba glanced toward their reflections on the other side of all those diagrams. Melba's clone looked equally helpless in her universe; Junie's clone, equally pleading.

"He's in the lake," Mel answered at last.

Junie paled.

"You didn't."

"He's just a clone, Junie, baby. Just a clone. Maybe in another universe, *his* universe, he's a big hero who helps Candy escape…but if that were the case, then, hell—you'd be a clone standin' in front of me right now. We'd both be clones, and I'd be a damn fool."

Inhaling, exhaling, Junie shook her head.

"No," she said softly, "no, Melba, I ain't a clone. I'm real."

"That's what Rex keeps telling me," said Melba, patting her cousin's hand.

It was nice to be listened to—nicer still to finally tell somebody all of that in a way that had seemed, to Mel anyway, pretty coherent. There were still things that were difficult to explain—for instance, the Gray Man picking up the key for her, or the bug problem that followed her around, or the chorus that commanded her into states of heightened paranoia almost every day—but, so far as Mel was concerned, her metaphysical research had placed a satisfactory frame on her relationship with Rexie.

And that relationship justified everything.

This was her destiny: this was her oneness with God. Taylor was a loser, a nothing clone whose death was necessary to shake off the attention of the Gray Man. And these damn clones were everywhere! Just look at Candy and Daisy. Hell… everybody at that fuckin' party down by the lake was probably a clone, too. Maybe even the tattoo artist—or maybe not. He had seemed pretty creative for a clone.

"So basically"—Mel waved across all three panels—"I have to kill some clones to make sure the Gray Man will be satisfied and leave me alone. Gotta feed the crocodile. But—I'm not *really* killing anyone—"

"Oh, Mel, but you are! You are. You're killing real people—people with families, with friends, who love them as much as I love you."

Catching Mel's hand in hers and gazing earnestly into her eyes, Junie let the waterworks flow and said with a little gasp, "I love you, Mel. Don't do this to yourself."

"Junie, honey—Junie…"

"Tell her," Rexie urged. "Just tell her, babydoll. She's gotta learn sometime. Might as well be now."

"If you really are the real Junie—and I do believe you are, because Rexie tells me you are—then you're gonna survive me. As in…I do not expect, from your perspective, that I will live through the night."

Junie recoiled, producing a sad little gasp.

"No, Mel—oh, Mel, please, don't hurt yourself! Don't do anything rash, please, please."

"Now, baby, I'm not doin' anythin' like that. Somethin' *else* is likely to happen. I don't know what, of course, but that's what they talk about when they talk about faith. I do not know the destiny to which I am being led…I only know that I have to let it happen. And so do you, Becky June."

"You can't lie down and let bad things happen to you! You can't keep escalating situations until they're as bad as possible and then give up."

"That is not what I am advisin' by any stretch of the imagination," Mel said with a shake of her head. "We are all participants in a divine plan up to a point—then we have to stop and watch what's been built go into motion. Like a Rube Goldberg machine, baby."

As Junie laughed through her tears at the absurd reference, Melba smiled, set down the deodorant and drew her cousin into her arms. The embrace was a relief; Melba hadn't realized how stressed she was and shut her eyes for a few seconds, just holding Junie there in a tight hug that seemed to release all number of soothing chemicals in her brain and body.

"I know it's gonna be hard for you to think about all this when it's said and done…and I know it's hard for you to go through it now. But—"

Melba set her hands on her cousin's shoulders and leaned back, examining her face with a genuine smile.

"You know I just love the ever livin' shit outta you," Melba extolled while Junie smiled a little wider, "and you know that wherever I am I will continue to love you. And hey, you know what?"

Melba snatched the deodorant back up and extended the braided lines, showing how Junie's would continue straight while hers and Rexie's intersected, curling together—until, at last, Junie's line rejoined the weaving.

"This is only a snag, angel," said Melba with as earnest a tone as she had ever used in all her goddamn days. "Just a run in the stockin'. A little hole that'll be woven back together on the other side. And all the while I'm in here"—Melba circled the area where they were separated—"I'll be missin' you, and lovin' you, and happy as hell for you while me and Rexie are havin' the times of our lives."

Exhaling shakily, Junie managed another, slightly more fleeting smile amid a fresh wave of tears.

"Me, too," she said softly, although Melba knew she didn't wholly mean it. No doubt Junie still meant to intervene in whatever way she could—that Junie still saw everything, no matter how well-diagrammed, (perhaps *because* it was all so well-diagrammed), as the hallmarks of mental illness.

But that was just what the clones all around them wanted her to think, obviously.

She couldn't really blame Becky June for mistaking the clones as real. Of course, in some ways they *were*, which was why Melba was so squeamish at the idea of killing one that didn't really deserve it—even if it meant saving herself from the Gray Man.

Still, desperate times. She had to do whatever it took to reach the pinnacle of what it meant to be Melba Daniels.

When they were back in the bedroom, Candy was thrashing around on the floor and melodramatically complaining she couldn't feel her legs. Melba rolled her eyes and pulled her up to her feet and let her slump against the wall while thinking the situation over. After collecting the gun, she looked around for the bloody knife and handed it to Candy.

"You're gonna hold this, and read these lines here," said Melba, pointing to the script pages Junie had picked up to idly study. "You'll be Trina."

"My name's Candy."

"I think she might be a little too fucked up to read lines, Mel." June frowned at the pages, then frowned more deeply at her own use of profanity.

"She has about twelve of the goddamn things in the section I want us to film! A parrot could say that much."

"Maybe"—Rexie interrupted the argument, turning his face against the pillows—"we should just skip the torture scenes for now. My torture scenes, I mean. All that could be added with special effects."

Melba studied him, his mouth moving in synch with that slick city voice that had once again gained a note of smooth, casual banter.

"But for your idea, capturing her sacrifice on film—that's so great. You're right. We don't want to miss the opportunity. Murder for art's sake. So rare. How about we film the prisoner swap right now, Mel? Cut right to the chase. I'll fix up the rest for you later on."

Melba jumped in place, then regretted it as her bad foot

bled against the bandage. Nonetheless, she clapped her hands in joy.

"Fuck yeah, baby, that sounds like a great plan! Oh—but does it still count if you do it?"

A song by the band Yes started on the radio as soon as Melba finished her sentence. She laughed, cutting Rexie off before he could speak.

"Well damn! Say no more! Here, you—hold this knife"—Melba put it in Candy's hand, then hurried over to check on the camera—"and we'll get rollin'!"

SIXTEEN

IF THERE WAS one thing that Mel had learned while studying the process of movie-making in an attempt to learn more about Rexie, it was that movies took a long, *long* damn time to film. To be frank, their movie-making process that night took a while to get interesting.

For instance, Melba had Junie, her lead actress, run through the liberation scene five separate times—each time, untying and retying one of Rexie's cooperative limbs. The fifth time, Melba got a close-up of Rex's bloodied profile as he said his lines. A glistening drop of sweat picked the perfect time to roll down his red nose and drip upon the bloodied pillow beneath.

"Just let me walk one last time," Rexie begged with his most believable delivery yet, his eyes distant with all number of hopes and dreams and memories through the looking-glass of the pillow. "I promise, I won't scream or try to run away. I'll do anything to get you to believe me. Just please—please. Let me see the sky one last time."

Junie sighed and shook her head, her off-screen response forever recorded by the camera's microphone.

"Can I really trust you to do that, Brett? I'd hate to go to all the trouble of getting half a movie shot…and my client'd hate that, too. Wouldn't he, Trina?"

"Fuck *yeah* he would," was the obviously drunk response.

"I know—I know, and I won't try anything. I swear. I wish there were something I could give you to make you believe me…but, please! Please, I swear I'll do whatever you want. I'm—I'm going to die soon."

Rex's breath hitched, his teeth showing between his lips as he let a few tears escape. "Soon I'm going to be a memory, a dream, a—I don't know what. I don't know what I'll be. I'll be something that will regret not spending more time—awake. Appreciating life. Going outside and breathing the fresh air. So please, God, please—please, just let me walk outside for a few more minutes."

Sighing theatrically, Junie said in her best Melba impression, "Well, that's a mighty pretty speech…I suppose a few minutes' break won't hurt nothin'."

"Okay," Mel said, pausing the recording and setting the camera aside, "let's do his legs and his right wrist, and then we'll do the left wrist on-camera so we can watch him gettin' up. Damn!" Satisfied, Mel untied his ankles. "It's a shame I won't see it edited together. I think this'll actually be one damn good climax to one damn good movie, if it can ever get fully produced."

In no hurry to go anywhere with his leg injury, Rexie remained obediently in place while his ankles were freed. Then, with Melba once again filming, Junie took the small handcuff key and freed Rex Virgil.

This was exactly why Melba wanted to film this moment. Why she knew it would make great cinema. The microscopic gasp of semi-disbelief as the second cuff clicked open; the fluttering shut of Rexie's beautiful blue eyes.

Yes. That was genuine emotion. That was real. "Acting is reacting," Melba had heard more than once. And that was one genuine damn reaction.

Slowly, moving his leg as little as possible, Rexie rotated his hands and then shifted them to push himself up from the bed. Gasping against the pain, he looked around himself in disbelief, then slowly pulled himself to his feet using his bedframe as support.

"Thank you," he whispered to Junie, launching himself from the headboard and stumbling toward her so suddenly that Melba hardly caught it on film. "Thank you," he said again, embracing her with a sob of relief.

While Junie, looking genuinely pained, patted his back and (to Melba's annoyance) flicked more than one obvious glance at the camera, Rexie's sob deepened to something almost frantic. He lifted his head and caught her face in his hands.

"Thank you, thank you."

He kissed her cheek.

"Thank you."

He kissed her mouth. Junie, somehow unready although this had been discussed, inhaled sharply, glanced one more time at the camera, then gave herself up to it all.

The tiniest, hottest little flare-up of jealousy sparked in Melba, but she forced herself to douse it. Rexie kissed all sorts of women in his line of work, and outside of it. He'd might as well kiss somebody Melba cared about instead of some Cali skank whose mouth had given out more than one executive blowjob in exchange for a leading role.

Plus, well—Melba was a professional at the moment. A bona fide director! And, like any director, her eyes were on the uncooperative ditz who stood vaguely watching the scene with a knife in her hand and an obvious lack of awareness.

"Say your line," whispered Melba.

Candy continued staring.

"Your fuckin' line," hissed Melba, "Candy! You bitch—"

"Oh shit"—the moron gasped while the two in front of her continued escalating the kiss into what could have been considered making out—"sorry, uh—'Hey, what the fuck is this?'"

The drunk-ass party animal had the kind of snotty, high-pitched voice possessed by skanks like (legally unconvicted, probable) child-murderer Casey Anthony, although Melba shouldn't have been throwing too many murder stones right then. Damn—Melba was almost falling into one of those catatonic thought tunnels until, per the script, Junie pulled the gun from the back of her shirt and brandished it at Candy. Her hand trembled. Rex, laying a palm along her elbow while he maintained their embrace, helped steady it.

"You already know what it is, you slut! You already—oh, Melba—"

Junie's breath hitched and, trying to repress a surge of anger, Melba paused the recording. "What the fuck is it now, June?"

"I just can't point this *gun* at her, Melba!"

"I *told* you that you don't have to use it."

"I can't, I can't—"

Junie threw it down. It skidded away from them without discharging and Rex looked ready to go after it, even twitching toward it as though with a barely-resisted impulse—but he did resist, which Melba appreciated.

"Okay," said Melba with a sigh, "tell you what—how about we just skip to the part where y'all disarm and tie her up? I only want genuine reactions, anyway…anybody can read a script, after all. They can just edit some other shit in."

Melba lifted the camera and gestured with her free hand toward the bindings on the bed.

"Somebody grab the rope there—"

Melba was interrupted by police sirens from somewhere outside.

She paled. Her eyes whipped toward Rexie, who looked at her in blank anticipation of her next order.

The sirens howled on, drawing nearer.

Her eyes wild, her heart racing, Melba ignored Junie's questioning utterance of her name and rushed past them all to collect the dropped gun. She traded it for the camera, hands trembling, almost dropping both devices in the process.

"Y'all wait here," she said sharply, adding, "don't go anywhere! We're so closeta bein' through—please, Junie, just keep him there—"

Blasting out of the room, the so-called cast and crew left behind her, Melba rushed down the stairs.

THEY'RE ALREADY HERE

THEY'RE BREAKING DOWN THE DOOR

A FEW CAME IN THE BACK

BEHIND YOU!

Melba spun sharply halfway down a flight of stairs and almost slipped down the rest, narrowly avoiding it only thanks to a quick grab of the banister. Gasping, trembling, her other hand waving the gun, Melba scanned the stairs and the foyer above her.

Nothing. Not even the Gray Man.

On the contrary, he was waiting for her at the bottom of the stairs.

He stepped toward her.

Yelping, Melba hurried past him to the front door. She crouched there, listening through the sirens for the shouting of cops.

"Come out with your hands up, Melba! We know you're in there!"

Clenching her teeth, her heart pounding, Melba looked miserably up at the ceiling. No, no! This couldn't be happening! Rexie, Rexie, please—this couldn't be happening, could it?

"It's all part of the plan, baby…just calm down. It'll all be okay."

"But—but how can you and I go away together if I'm trapped in a fuckin' jail cell? Rexie—"

"Don't worry, okay? I'm telling you, Melba, it'll all be fine. Just trust me."

"We know you have a gun," shouted the same officer from before. "If you don't use it to kill yourself immediately, we will have no choice but to enter."

Faltering, Melba looked sharply at the doorknob above her head.

"Told you," said Rex in a soft, sing-song way.

Were those really the cops? Couldn't be. Cops didn't tell people to kill themselves, did they? Seemed like they much preferred having a chance to do it themselves.

So…who was it? Some friend of Taylor's?

Yes—that must have been it. Taylor had survived after all. He had run off to gather some of his friends. The people from the party!

Oh, God.

Melba groaned at her own ignorance and the shame that it brought her. What an idiot! Yes, what an idiot she was. No wonder that party had been going so well for her! No wonder the night had been so pleasant.

They were actors. Every single person there had been an actor hired by Taylor—or, more likely, members of his gang assigned to act for him at various occasions. First, the party. Now—the cops outside.

"Put the gun in your mouth and pull the trigger," commanded another officer. "You're worthless."

"Nice try," Melba shouted through the door. "No way are you gonna trick me into doin' a goddamn thing! I know you ain't really cops."

"If you don't do it, we'll do it," one of them responded. "And we'll shoot Becky June, too."

Melba shut her eyes.

Now *that*, she believed…but thinking it through gave her more confidence.

After all—if these were Taylor's dipshit redneck friends, they probably didn't have their biggest weapons all there with them. A few probably had pistols like what he'd brought, at most. Hard to pack an AR-15 on a trip to the lake. Could be worse, in other words.

Okay. Think.

Her eyes were still a little off after the whole snow globe thing, but since Junie had cleaned them they weren't actively burning anymore. In other words, Melba could probably see well enough to shoot. And how many bullets were still in the gun? She just didn't know…didn't want to end up shooting herself in the head trying to check the clip, neither.

Exhaling, the gun held tight, Melba edged toward the foyer's one window and tried to peer through it without making herself a target. She shut off the foyer light and squinted.

In the darkness, shadows moved.

Shadows, but no red and blue lights.

"Uh-huh," said Mel, murmuring to herself as she sidled toward the door. "Uh-huh, nice fuckin' try…"

The gun held like an action movie cop getting ready to clear a room, Melba threw open the front door.

She was fully ready to shoot at anywhere from three to ten sonsabitches until they turned tail and ran.

Instead, she stood dumbfounded upon the porch.

The gun pointed at nothing.

SEVENTEEN

DAMN! HOW'D THOSE bastards manage to hide so fast? Thunderstruck for only a second or so, Melba retreated into the house and shut the door before any of them could sneak inside unseen.

TOO LATE

Melba whipped around and, seeing nothing, checked the lock on the door five times. She then had to try the windows, front and back. The back door, too.

And all the while, she had to wonder—how the hell was Taylor gettin' the money to finance these idiots who thought they could pull the wool over Melba's eyes?

The more she thought about it, the more disturbing it was. For instance, Taylor must have had access to some advanced medical science to have recovered so quickly from his wounds.

That, or he was some sort of paranormal entity. Some supernatural creature, like a vampire or a werewolf…only, Melba was damn sure nothing like that existed. Maybe some crazies thought they were such things, or that such things were real, but she wasn't one of them.

No, sir. Melba knew of only two actual, verifiable entities that did not appear to fit into the accepted dynamics of the planet's physical structure.

Rexie—and the Gray Man.

Melba's stomach twisted in an awful spell of sickness that quite literally made her feel like she was about to throw up. Her mouth certainly watered like she might; but she panted through it, braced against the stairwell with one hand while her mind sorted the cold truth from the baleful utterances of her choir.

Of course. She should have understood this day was coming. Yes, she should have known it. Before he revealed himself as Rexie, Rexie had been formless. He had not revealed himself in a visible structure except occasionally—a shadow from the corner of her eye, or, when she was being truly rewarded, a fleeting glimpse behind her in a bathroom mirror. This held true even now that he had a definite shape.

But the Gray Man had always had a tangible form. She was accustomed to his visitations; to his gaunt, faceless mask.

Because of this form, she had been tricked.

Tricked into thinking the Gray Man had not, like Rexie, manifested in a human form.

Yes, of course! Of course. No wonder Rexie had told her she needed to spill mortal blood.

Those she had been destined to kill were, in truth, the Gray Man and his cronies. They weren't even clones.

They were nothing—less than nothing. They were slaves to a demon that wanted to consume Melba, and would have if she hadn't made an effort at destroying its mortal vessel. "An effort" here specified because she no longer believed Taylor was dead. There were two kinds of dead among humans, after all—among evil entities like the Gray Man, who knew if death was even possible?

"Death is an impossible illusion for all things," Rexie assured her during the ad break of the music as she passed through the second-floor foyer, where music from the bedroom drifted down to warm her bones. "I cannot die, and when we eliminate the Gray Man, the one thing threatening to kill you will also be dead. But be careful, Melba. Things might still get in our way."

"Like what?"

Nirvana started playing in lieu of a direct answer. "About a Girl." Melba sniffed in annoyance. Nirvana, on a fuckin' classic rock station? No wonder it was time for her to leave this planet!

Upstairs, Melba pushed open the door, expecting to find more bullshit like, oh, a rope of sheets, or some kind of giant booby trap, or a gun in her face—but apparently Rexie was too much of a cushy Hollywood liberal to believe in owning guns even at a property where he preferred to go without security. It was very sweet that he still had so much faith in the kindness of strangers! Melba just couldn't muster it, herself, although she had to admit—Rexie exceeded her expectations when it came to good behavior.

There was Junie, rushing to the door with her hands trembling. "Melba—he—"

"I just thought I'd give you a concrete example of how trustworthy I am," Rex said from the other side of the room, where he stared out the window and into the night.

Melba marveled at the bed.

Candy had been bound spread-eagle in the fashion of Rex's captivity, although for obvious aesthetic reasons the co-ed faced the ceiling. From the looks of it, she had consented. When Melba stood over her, Candy lifted her head enough to blearily say, "Oh, good, you're here. When are we taking our next break? I gotta take a piss soon."

"I'll be sure to let you know," Melba said with a wry look back at Rexie and a high lift of her eyebrows. "You startin' to wake up, baby?"

"I guess so." He lifted a joint Melba now noticed to his mouth, saying idly, "Everything all right downstairs?"

"I don't know if they got in or not," Melba said with a shake of her head, shuddering. "Sounded like they might've, but I gave a look around and didn't see nothin'."

LIAR

YOU BARELY

CHECKED

YOU'RE A LIAR

HE KNOWS

YOU'RE LYING

HE HATES YOU

"I don't hate you," said Rexie, his reflection still in the glass of the window. "'Course I don't hate you, angelbaby! I'd never think a thing like that."

"I don't know what I'd do without you, Rexie…I'm so glad I have you—I'm so glad we're together."

"You know"—his city voice slipped back in as, with a squint, he pressed his face against the glass—"I've wondered all night why nobody called the cops. I mean…look at this window. It's huge. The whole lake has a picture view into my house if the lights are on and they're close enough, or own a pair of binoculars. People walk by all the time. I think I've even heard a car or two go past."

"But then…then it came to me."

Rexie tapped his forehead while turning back to the room, his hand extending in the direction of the camera.

"I thought you were just some crazy little bitch…maybe even stupid. What is she going on about this movie for? If she wants to kill us, why doesn't she just do it?"

As, in the background, Junie begged, "You can't really mean to do that, Melba," Rex continued on.

"Because…as long as there's a camera rolling, you can get away with anything for a little while. They'll think it's just part of the movie…and who wants to be the idiot that interrupts filming?"

"Shit, Rexie, that's right! What a good idea you had. I was wonderin' a little, myself…Junie was bound to figure out where we was headed eventually, after all, even before you let me tell her the truth."

Laughing, pinching his cheek while his brow furrowed in confusion, Melba turned back toward the bed.

Junie now stood conspicuously near the door, her eyes watering with the same terror that kept her complexion pale green.

"Melba," Junie said, "Melba, I think—since Mr. Virgil is—thinking differently, I think I would like to leave. You two can—together— Please, I just want to go."

Sighing heftily, Melba shook her head. "Junie, baby, I'd like to, but you heard them out there. They ain't cops. I know they sound like it, but there's nothin' lawful about them. They're—"

Not knowing the limits of Candy's telepathic communication with the Gray Man, (was she a servant of the Gray Man the way Melba was a servant of Rexie? Food for thought), Melba drew Junie toward Rex. She whispered to them both, her expression and tone intense.

"They're *Taylor's* gang. The Gray Man."

Junie looked all the greener at that, and rightfully so. She had been aware of the Gray Man for most of her life, as Melba had often been frightened that he would bother her cousin the way he bothered her. Luckily, despite being warned of his presence more than once, Junie never seemed to see him; Melba had given up trying to warn her cousin, although she had related details of the demon's harassment campaign many times. Every car breakdown, every late bus, every ticket or illness or nightmare, was in some way coordinated by the Gray Man.

Yes, that hateful sonnabitch had quite the influence. He must have, to have access to so many of the clones, and to be able to influence them so effortlessly.

Melba's face fell.

Where were the clones coming from in the first place?

Oh, Christ. Oh, Rex!

Of course.

Now she understood.

"Melba?"

Junie pulled her from her revelation.

"Sorry, were y'all talkin'?"

"I wanted to know if you're trying to say that Taylor was the Gray Man."

Junie's clarification came at too loud a volume for Melba's liking. She shushed her cousin sharply, glancing over her shoulder to find Candy there, still, pretending to stare at the ceiling.

"Not so fuckin' loud! She's onea them—his clones. No wonder you've kept me in the dark about all this, Rexie." Melba shuddered. "I never woulda gone outside again if I realized the way this conspiracy operates…how deep it goes. So, Junie, I'd love to let you leave, but it ain't safe to go outside right now. All those people—"

"What people?"

"You know!" Waving her hand in agitation, Melba said, "The ones in the front yard, blastin' sirens and tellin' me to come out and all."

"But Melba—Melba, I haven't heard anything *like* that—"

A pit opened below Melba's stomach.

"What the fuck do you mean?"

"I mean that it's been quiet outside all night! I haven't heard a peep—only from inside this house."

Melba glanced up at Rexie, who watched her intensely. She asked, "What about you, baby?"

"Nothing."

Exhaling somewhat raggedly, Melba buried her face in her hands.

"Of course," she murmured. "Of course…I've been a fuckin' idiot."

"It's okay, Melba." Junie's soft hand slid over Mel's shoulder. "It's okay. If you'll just let me leave, I can get some help, and—"

"No, Junie! Don't you fuckin' understand?"

Tears filling her eyes, Mel said in a harsh whisper, "They're usin' *sound weapons*."

All hope vanished from Junie's face. "Oh, Melba, no—"

"I know it's hard to believe—terrifyin'. And you should be terrified. I mean…sound weapons, being tuned to my individual consciousness frequency? That's some *hyper*-advanced technology. This is a *government operation*, Junie—a military operation they've orchestrated against me. Why?"

Looking seriously at Rexie, Melba begged, "Is the government really that afraid of immortality?"

While his eyes trailed toward Junie, that sweet Southern twang allotted, "Why wouldn't it be? If people knew all the things you knew about reality, Melba, there would be no consumerism; no war or famine. There would be no dictators, and ones who tried to become dictators would be easily cut down out of simple moral law. The world would be perfect if everybody were like you, sugar, but the sad truth is they ain't never gonna be. And the *sadder* truth is that the fewer people there are like you in a given universe, the more people the Gray Man gets the pleasure of eating."

Melba shuddered, running her hands over her face and back through her hair. Junie had been saying something in the middle of Rexie's explanation, but Melba hadn't bothered listening because it was rude for June to be talking over anybody in the first place. Now that Rexie had finished, however, she tuned back in to her cousin's pleas.

"…and maybe if you talked to a therapist about these—these 'sound weapons,' they could get you some kind of defense system against it. You know, since they deal so much with the—the mind—"

"Oh, Junie." Sighing, shaking her head, Melba said, "Junie, I wish the world were so simple, baby, but it ain't. Therapists, doctors…they're all controlled by the government these days. I go in and complain about sound weapons, and soon I'm locked in a military prison—or, worse, havin' some van of assholes park down the street to listen into our conversations. Like how it was in the place I was livin' at before I was in prison."

Though Junie looked about to respond, Melba took her hand and held it tightly.

"Look," said Melba carefully, "I can see this is hard for you. But somethin's gotta be done about that fuckin' Gray Man if I'm gonna escape him. Since I can't stand the thought of letting you go try to talk your way through his clones—"

"But I'm sure I could," said Junie eagerly as Melba went on.

"—how 'bout you work the camera, insteada me?"

Rexie, ever the professional, arched a brow. "You're going to act in it now, after she's already filmed a scene?"

Junie's mouth opened in astonishment, her eyes fixed on the actor. "You can't really intend to keep cooperating!"

Rex bleakly returned her look. "I thought we went over this."

"No! I'm not satisfied! How can you cooperate, even if it's to save your own hide? Especially when—"

"I fully accept it might not help me in the end," said Rex, his tone dark and cool beside Junie's highly anxious one. "I know I might still die."

"Then why won't you fight?"

"Because she has a gun," said Rex simply, "and if I'm going to die one way or another, I had might as well spend my last minutes doing what I came here to do: make art."

Slipping out of the whispering triangle, Rexie dragged his bad leg to Candy's bedside and picked up the kitchen knife that had been the cause of so much abuse. He set it aside, beneath the torn organ-meat of the tattered red lampshade.

"I'm ready when you are," he said. "I just wonder what you intend to be done about the changing actress."

"Oh, well…" Tapping her fingertip upon her chin, Mel suggested after a few moments, "Maybe they could just fix it with that deepfake stuff they do now. You know—where one person ends up lookin' like another on accounta AI or whatever. Like when Disney brought Carrie Fisher back from the dead…how was that for some fucked up shit?"

Melba had been laughing at her own commentary even before she finished the thought, but she couldn't help relating the line of thought back to the situation at-hand.

What a fool she had been. Only Rexie was capable of magic; of miracles. Yet, for her whole life, she had thought the Gray Man was some kind of a demon. A specter that haunted her like a poltergeist, harassing her with powers beyond her comprehension.

But there was nothing beyond comprehension about any of it. This was not a demon she was dealing with! After all these years, it was clear.

The Gray Man was an alien. An interdimensional creature that was still a physical being like any other. One that clearly had access to advanced technology—hence the clones.

And the teleporting. That was the Gray Man's most disturbing talent, in her estimate. His ability to simply appear anywhere, and to never move unless it served his purpose of frightening her. It seemed to her that the Gray Man could travel through any amount of space and time in the blink of an eye; less than that.

Now, however, thinking of him in his new and proper context, Melba recognized a very important truth. If the Gray Man could travel through space and time with such ease, was it not possible for him to also transport himself through universes?

"Is it always the same Gray Man?" She looked incredulously at Rexie, who did not immediately respond; as though expecting her to finish a thought that had been half-spoken aloud. "Across all these times and places, is it always the same?"

"It's always the Gray Man," Rexie answered, turning toward Junie, "and it's always me. Even if we don't look like ourselves, it's always us."

While Melba exhaled against her understanding, Rexie told June with a nod, "How about you go grab that camera and we can get the shooting started? The sooner, the better. I'm sure Candy here is getting uncomfortable."

"In a minute," said Melba, shaken. "In a minute. Oh, Rexie—I didn't realize. All these times, all these iterations! I thought—I thought it was *my* prison here. That *I* was the one being punished. But it's *his* prison, isn't it? Why couldn't you tell me?"

"You know why. If I had told you too soon, baby, it would have destroyed you! Can you imagine walkin' around since the age of 9 knowing you were the Nth iteration of yourself? One of an infinite number of helpless fringe victims impacted by the Gray Man's evil? None of y'all would have to suffer like this if it weren't for him…and all the rest are so under his spell that they'd might as well *be* him. See?"

June was saying something while Rexie talked with his mouth closed, which was still rude but more understandable. Maybe Junie thought his voice was part of a commercial or something—whatever the case, Melba didn't listen to her. She was too busy focused on the words of her beloved, who had urged her to look.

But at what?

At the bed.

The Gray Man lay there: not bound as Candy had been but instead gripping the bed as though some reverse gravity threatened to pull him to the ceiling.

She cried out and raised the gun.

"That's it," said Rexie, snatching the knife to slice it down Melba's hand.

Junie cried out at the same time as Mel.

The gun flew away.

EIGHTEEN

EVERYTHING HAPPENED SO dang fast that Melba hadn't even fully copped to her pain before people leapt into action. Rex and Junie both followed the gun. Junie threw the camera—on the bed, praise the Lord!—and dove after the weapon before Rexie, who still clutched the bloodied knife, could make much of a move. He got about a foot before stopping short.

Melba had just enough time to feel panic's pinpricks before the gun's snapping hammer made Rex drop the knife.

"Junie!"

Clutching her bleeding, burning, previously bitten hand, Melba grinned at her cousin. Junie was in no mood to return the expression, the gun pointed poorly but dangerously at Rex.

"I thought you said you *weren't* gonna hurt her," June said.

Rexie stared back at her sternly, his handsome features tensed into a series of sharp, crisp lines. For a few seconds he had no face, much as the Gray Man used to, and Melba saw him only for what he was—the most beautiful shape in the universe, the most perfect shape exhibited as a sentient man, the rays of his divinity shining from his head like a fantastical crown of thorns. Oh, oh Rexie! Her heart screamed with love. She wanted to throw herself upon him, so glad to finally be with him—but that wasn't possible yet.

Not with the Gray Man appearing through his servants.

Candy lay in the Gray Man's place now, no longer a horrific and spidery extension of limbs but a bound young woman slipping in and out of consciousness. In the background of Melba's consciousness, Rexie spoke.

"I had to do what I had to do. She'll be okay—it's no worse than what happened to me. Now, please. Let's get this over with. I think I really need medical attention for this leg."

"No."

Junie stepped toward him with the gun still at the ready.

"No, Mr. Virgil, I'm sorry. We have to talk about what we're gonna do here first."

Rex scoffed. "What do you mean? What the hell do you mean, what is this? This bitch is crazy! She needs medical treatment as much as I do."

"Don't call my cousin a 'bitch,'" Junie shouted, tears in her eyes.

Melba grinned at her man. "Yeah, babe! Not in front of family…"

"Look. I know she has problems, okay? But if we end up callin' the cops and sayin' she had the least thing to do with all this death, there ain't no mental illness that'll make up for it! Even though she's got problems, she's smart as a whip. That's all they'll see! They'll hold her responsible! They'll—Oh, Jesus."

Junie burst into sobs, the gun shaking in her hands, her head shaking with it. "Please, Mr. Virgil, please. I don't have a whole damn lot in my life. What I do have, I just keep losin' and losin'. Please, sir, Mr. Virgil. Don't let them take my cousin from me."

"She's making her own choices, June," Rex said.

With a coo, Melba stepped nearer her kin.

Junie whipped the gun toward her and produced another sob at Melba's inevitable look of shock.

"No, Melba, you stay right there. I don't want you to try and take this gun from me, or talk me into it, or bully me, or nothin' like that. Just stay right there and let me think. Oh, Christ…"

Her free hand pressing to her forehead as she stepped back from both her cousin and the movie star, Junie stared wild-eyed into the abyss. Her mind sorted out options and soon those eyes began to dart around the room. "We need to come up with a story."

"And then let her walk free, unmedicated, ready to do it again?"

"I'll sit in with her therapist appointments if that's what it takes to make sure she's getting treatment—I just need her to be with me. Please, please—"

Rexie's hefty sigh was laden with incredibly convincing anger. "Yeah, because that's been working well so far. Fine… fine, if you want to take care of her so badly, you can. I'll say whatever you want. Just let me the fuck go!"

Rexie took another step toward the door.

The gun's sights aimed at him again, weaving with Junie's untrained grip.

He stopped short.

Melba's heart soared with relief. That Junie should still want to protect Melba after all this was an incredible testament to her loyalty.

And what she said next, even more so.

Junie stared into Rexie's eyes.

"I don't trust you," said June, her voice quivering but firm.

Rex almost laughed, his wet blue eyes sharply rolling toward Melba.

"But you trust *her*?"

"In some ways more than others. You, though, Mr. Virgil—I know you'll tell me anything to get out of this situation. You'll make any promise, do anything at all to save your own hide, and I do not blame you one whit. That is natural. That is human nature; good and wholesome behavior and the Lord inspires in all living things. But I am also trying to survive. I am trying to protect my family. And I need to be absolutely sure that you will not, under any circumstances, go to the police. We need to decide what we're going to say, and then I need to figure out how to make sure—how to make sure."

"Well," Rex said coldly, "what would you suggest?"

"You don't need to go to all this trouble," Mel tried to tell her, but Junie was already making suggestions.

"We can, uh—maybe—oh, oh! Let's tell them everybody came over for the party! Yes, that's exactly right."

Nodding eagerly, lifting her free hand to her brow to wipe her temple before returning it to the gun, Junie said with hope, "You had all these folks over, us and Taylor and his sister and Candy, and…and there was a Manson family-type thing that happened, uh-huh, that's right. Taylor and, uh—Taylor went crazy, and he was here with other people, and—"

"Hell, Junie, sounds like *you* shoulda wrote my script!"

"—and things just—happened the way they happened. But *we* were victims, too. Look at her! She can pass. Poor Mel, oh—we need to check your eyes out, honey."

It was true that there were more shadows dancing in her periphery. Other than that, however, Melba felt just fine. Coulda been the cocktail and beer earlier, or Rexie's proximity, or some combination of adrenaline and endorphins, but Melba felt like she was having some kind of second wind.

"Don't you worry about me, baby," Melba said with a wave. "You just keep workin' this out for your own sake. Seems like a damn good plan, though, if you really want to keep my nose lookin' clean."

"Of course I do, Melba—I love you. Oh—Mel." New tears blazed in Junie's shining eyes. Inhaling sharply, Junie said to Rex, "I'm sorry to ask you to lie like this, and I'm sorry to ask you to prove you won't tell a soul. But…I have to."

Rexie spread his hands in agitation. "How in the hell am I supposed to prove that?"

Junie said nothing.

She let her gaze trail away until her sad eyes fixed on Candy, whose head hung back and mouth was open slack.

"God damn you," whispered Rex after a few seconds of mortal contemplation. "God damn you—you can't ask me to do this."

"It's just so we're all on the same page," June swore, sounding on the other side of a tunnel for as quiet as she was.

Melba puzzled this together like a little kid trying to figure out the unvoiced conflicts of adults.

"You mean you want him—aw, Becky June, you really are on my team! I'm so glad."

Yes, it was nice. Nice to be seen, to be understood. Melba had wanted her whole life for one person on Earth to really understand her—but, then, if that had been the case, she wouldn't have needed Rexie. Even right now, as close as she'd ever been to understanding Melba's reality, Junie didn't quite get everything that was happening. That was okay, though.

For instance, she thought that she was protecting Melba from the police, or the government. In reality, those superficial aspects of mortal existence were just manifestations of the Gray Man. Like Taylor and Candy, the institutions themselves *were* the enemy. So, Junie was right in what she was doing... she just didn't understand why she was right.

That was okay, though. It was enough to have her cousin on her side. Enough that Melba's heart glowed with relief to know she would still be loved after she was gone. Even after all of this.

"I sure do appreciate you, June."

Rexie did not seem to share this perception. He bared his teeth.

"I won't do it."

"I can't let you leave until you do."

"Yeah? And what if I don't, June? Going to hold me here a day, a week? Somebody's going to check on me. That won't work out for you."

"No," said June, her affect grim. "No, sir, I will not do that."

"Then what are you going to do?"

June said nothing. She looked on at Rex, her hands trembling.

Melba and Rex realized what she was implying at the same moment. Palms beginning to sweat, Melba stepped toward her cousin and, when this didn't elicit a renewed aim of the gun, extended her bloodied hand.

"Now, Junie—there's no need to hurt Rex—"

"Not if he proves we can trust him," Junie agreed, her focus trained exclusively on the quieted actor.

That sneering, almost amused expression of his had fallen away; a new quiet overtook him, as though a greater fear possessed him to be held at gunpoint by Junie than by Melba. He looked briefly at the bound woman on the bed.

"Of course, we can trust him," Melba insisted.

Junie's head shook. "No, we can't. We never could. I—ugh. I never wanted to tell you this, Melba…but I don't like Mr. Virgil at all."

Melba's face froze in shock while her cousin went on, looking at Rex.

"I think he's a sneaky, mean, entitled—*prick*, who took advantage of a little girl and helped mess her up for life. He's rotten, Melba. In fact…in fact, I almost think it'd be the best thing for you if he were just to up and—"

"Please."

The demeanor turn that had possessed Rex upon his

freedom disappeared. Now, hands clasped, Rexie stooped in lieu of the painful act of kneeling.

"Please, June, please, don't hurt me. I know I've done bad things—"

"Don't you even have the nerve to tell me that to my face now. If you really felt bad, you would have dropped the damn charges on Melba and been satisfied knowing she was in treatment. What the fuck did she even do, anyway? Talked to a confused desk clerk, got a key to your room, looked in the trash, and then waited for you. And what did you do when all was said and done? *You* filed sexual assault charges against *her*. *You* charged *her*, and accused her of stalking. But she's sick. She's sick, and you took a sick girl and made her feel like a princess for three hours in exchange for the rest of her goddamned life.

"Mr. Virgil, sir, strictly speaking—I have only refrained from shooting you so far because I am a good Christian woman, or used to think I was. But I find you to be a cruel, petty, and mistrustful man. The safest thing for both myself and my cousin is seeing you dead on this here floor…but I am willing to negotiate with you. I suggest you work with me, please."

Rex stared Junie down while Melba stood at the peak of their triangle, floored.

"I ain't never heard you talk that way, Becky June."

"I ain't never *felt* this way," said Junie, gun trembling in her hand. "Never in my life. Oh, I feel sick! *So* sick, like I've been close to pukin' all night but there's too much happening to make myself. Like I'm in too much danger to vomit. Everything is wrong and awful and evil and ugly tonight—but the night'll be over before we know it, and everything can be different! We can sweep it all under the rug. It was Taylor. We overpowered him. You killed him, right, Melba?"

"I thought so, but then he came around with all them cops, remember? Pretend cops, anyway…"

With a piteous look at her cousin, Junie said, "Well, if you can kill all these people tonight…then I have it in me to take one life, if that's what I have to do."

Nodding toward the blade at his feet, Junie said, "If you value your life, Mr. Virgil, sir, you will do it."

Rex's teeth grit, the tears in his eyes glossy but unflowing. His lips trembled.

Slowly, he turned his face toward the knife.

With an equally dragging pace, Rex knelt to pick it up.

He held it in the palms of both open hands, studying it as though it were water in an oasis.

Those wet eyes traced back up to the knife Junie pointed at him.

"Is this it? This is the only way?"

"This is the only way," Junie said, jerking her head toward the bed. "Why don't you pick up the camera, Mel?"

Hurrying to obey her slightly unhinged cousin, Melba picked up the device and trained it on the most beautiful man in the world. Rexie's face and a camera's lens were made for each other, his features striking in the digital preview even with amateur lighting. As he began to slowly nod, those expressionistic shadows deepened into the pits of his eyes.

"If this is what I have to do…then I have to. I have to. You, Becky June—you're no different from your cousin."

With a motion so sudden and animal that Melba jumped a little, Rexie looked Candy in the unconscious face, raised the knife high above his head, and lunged upon the drugged girl to plunge it through her chest.

While the co-ed awoke with a noise more like a yelp than a scream, Rex yanked the knife out. Crimson blood shown newly wet upon it, dripping from the blade even as its tip snarled back into Candy's breast.

Now the true screaming began. Melba glanced gratefully to the wall-mounted speakers as she trained the camera on the scene, thrilled by the way the ruby lampshade enriched the violent hues. They couldn't *not* use this in something someday. It was all too good. What director wouldn't want to be known as the one who had the real murder in his movie?

Besides…Rexie just looked so especially damn good while he was stabbin' the Gray Man's bitch. Every time the knife impacted the girl's chest he had to force it all the way in, through cartilage and sometimes even bone that more often stopped him sort. In those seconds of extra pressure his teeth would bare. His eyes would light in a horrified fire, a tearful anger, that was so becoming Melba's heart raced. The butterflies in her stomach hadn't been this enthusiastic since she met him for the first time. Her lips parted, a gasp escaping as, with the yanking out of the knife, a long line of blood splattered across his unsullied cheekbone.

"Are you happy now?" He stabbed down into the girl's throat. Blood foamed from the wound and her mouth amid fruitless, ever-weakening writhing in her binds. "Are you happy? Are you? Is this what you wanted to see?"

"Yeah," said both women at once, each in a very different tone.

Melba glanced over at her cousin's sorrowful utterance, wiping the proverbial drool from her chin to look a little more professional. Junie had lowered the gun. She now let it hang limply at her side while Rex massacred the final hostage.

Blood covered everything: the knife, Rex's hand, Rex himself, certainly the co-ed and Rex's bed. When, with a cry of agitation for the wet wheezing of the girl whose body wept, Rex threw the knife away and picked up a pillow. It was already so soaked through it might as well have always been the color of violent death.

His arms tensing with the exertion, Rex slammed the pillow down on the girl's moaning face.

He pressed it there until she stopped breathing.

Shoulders rising and falling with his panted breaths, Rex stood with his hands in place for a long time. When he lifted them away, he let the wet pillow remain where it was.

His cold gaze turned toward Junie.

"Now let me go."

Melba rushed through the contents of her mind for a way to keep him there; to find the solution for the third kill that night. As, in his country voice, Rexie secretly intoned, "The second blood has been shed," Junie turned pleading eyes toward Melba.

And, before Melba could even open her mouth, the solution presented itself in the ringing of Rex's doorbell.

NINETEEN

UNDER THE CIRCUMSTANCES, any visitor was an unwelcome visitor. Anyone coming by would not be able to comprehend what was happening. They would most certainly insist on doing something stupid.

However…this was it. They were so close to the end, and all this time Melba had been cold with terror about what would happen when they reached that end. Rexie had told her it would take three lives to shake off the Gray Man—she supposed it was so she, Rexie, and Becky June could all survive this time unscathed before going separate ways.

As though to confirm her thinking was on the right track, the radio played "Separate Ways" by Journey. She laughed, looking up at the speakers, then over at Rexie. Junie whipped her head toward both of them.

"What do we do?"

Rexie's respiration was rapid, his eyes darting from Junie's lowered gun to the bedroom door. Those well-trained actor's lungs expanded his chest with a great breath.

"Hel—"

Almost forgetting the gun, Junie threw herself upon him and added the pistol into the mix but belatedly. With one hand covering his mouth and the other aiming the weapon at his head, Junie hushed Rex in terrible desperation.

These were the two people Melba most wanted to protect in the world—the two people Melba most loved. All this time, she had been sick with the near-certainty that she would have to find a way to kill one—Junie, of course—to make good her safe passage.

But it had all been a test. Oh, yes! Melba's heart soared to think of it. She smiled at the vision before her.

"I get it now," she told Rexie, assuring him as the door downstairs opened, "you're so smart, so damn smart!"

"On the Mount of the Lord it shall be provided," recited Rexie in his true twang. Even through a hand, his voice sounded crisper than Junie's harried whisper.

"Stay quiet, Mr. Virgil, please. We can send her away, I'll go and turn her right around—"

"Too late now. There's all that fuckin' blood in the foyer!" With a deep breath, Melba hollered, "Hey! Party's upstairs!"

Rex's brows worked in a fury, his eyes red with rage while Melba grinned.

"Oh, Junie! You wouldn't believe how worried my ass has been since that sorority sister choked on her vomit. I thought for sure Rexie wanted me to kill *you!* But now I see it was all just a test of faith. That preachera yours is right. The Lord has provided!"

Shocked to hear she had been on the offer, Junie asked, "What do you mean?"

"It's what it takes to survive the Gray Man, like I said. You gotta feed him enough blood that he'll stay here and go bother somebody else."

"Rex?"

The feminine voice calling up the stairs changed Rex's

visible facial features at once. Those dynamically articulating brows collapsed like a bad bridge, knitting deep furrows into his forehead.

"Edie," was his garbled pronouncement, sad and helpless, behind Junie's hand.

Edie? Edie! Edie O'Keefe. That bitch. Damn! Rexie and the starlet had been coworkers and romantic partners for years, or so the Hollywood producers (another institution of the Gray Man, now that Mel thought of it) wanted the world to believe. She must have been the one he was trying to lure over when Melba listened into his call. It would have been funny if Melba were not now all on pins and needles, excited and afraid.

This was it. This was the last chance. If Edie got away, well—shit. If Edie got away, something real bad would have to happen.

So…Edie was not going to get away. Hell no. Not tonight. Edie O'Keefe had enjoyed life handed to her on a silver platter. Rexie had too long pretended like he cared about her when, all the time, he was whispering in Melba's ear.

Another echo from downstairs: "Is everything okay? What's going on? Rex? Your phone's dead, and there's all this stuff on the—"

Junie shrieked and whipped her bitten hand from Rexie's mouth. Edie's calls came to a stunned stop.

"Run, Edie," bellowed Rex. "Call the cops!"

"Is this some kind of joke?"

Junie, nursing her bleeding hand, let Rex get three steps. Mel grabbed him by the collar and pressed the dropped knife to his throat, the inert camera's blind lens staring into nothing from where it had been left on the bed.

"Give me the gun, Junie."

Mel's harsh whisper came as Edie called from downstairs, "Are you okay? Rex?"

A foot on a stair. Mel kept the knife in place but released

Rexie's collar, her hand open at her hip in anticipation of the gun.

"You don't have to do this," he whispered, his small words never small enough to keep his Adam's apple from bobbing along the knife's blade.

"You're so funny, Rexie…June, come on."

"But, Mel, he's—he's right. Please, can't we just—"

"What'd I tell you? It's gotta be done, and I gotta be the one to do it. Easiest with a pistol. Now either give it here or do a better job keepin' Rexie quiet while I go deal with his bitch."

Her breath hitching, Junie deliberated. Rex shut his eyes.

Edie climbed the stairs.

"What on Earth *happened* here— Yes, I'm at Lake of the Woods—"

Oh, Rexie! Mel whipped a sharp glance over her shoulder while Rex gasped wetly to realize 911 had at last been called. Her face crumpling in agony, June looked at the dead body and bloody pillow that represented Candy's demise. Then, at Rex.

Then the gun.

Tears streaming down her cheeks, June put the gun in Mel's empty hand.

"In the eyes of the foolish," Rexie recited to Mel as she lifted the knife from his neck and made him back off, "they seemed to have died, and their departure was thought to be a disaster, and their going from us to be their destruction; but they are at peace. For though in the sight of others they were punished, their hope is full of immortality. Like gold in a furnace he tried them, and like a sacrificial burnt offering he accepted them."

"Oh my God!"

Mel—who had been sucked into Rexie's crooning of some Bible passage so intensely it reminded her of when she used to smoke weed to try to hear him more clearly and would end up staring at his poster for three hours, catatonic amid the sound of his voice and all the sweet promises he made as Junie got more and more worried by the second—snapped out of her daze to see Edie in the doorway.

"Please hurry," begged the starlet into her phone, "oh—oh!"

Mel turned the gun on her without hesitation.

As her finger pulled against the trigger, Rex gave a cry in his city voice. His body appeared in her periphery and, her head barely turning, Melba gasped.

The interfering hand he'd thrown across the gun had redirected it down into his gut.

Rex's eyes widened, his mouth opening with a sound like a gag.

The world's handsomest man fell at her feet, his palm upon the broadening bloodstain of the gut wound that had been meant for his girlfriend.

Becky June said something amid the noise. Melba felt like her insides were about to slump out of her torso.

"Rexie," she gasped, "oh, Rex—"

"Those who trust in him," continued his real voice, tranquil and unharmed, "will understand truth, and the faithful will abide with him in love, because grace and mercy are upon his holy ones, and he watches over his elect."

In other words—in other words.

The third blood had *not* been spilled.

Hands still numb with the panicked thought that she might have killed her sacred ascended master and doomed herself to being eaten by the Gray Man, Melba snapped back to reality.

Doorway empty.

"Stay here," she shouted at Junie, dropping the knife altogether as she lay chase.

The gun still in her hands, Mel burst from the bedroom in time to see Edie's blonde head streaking down the stairs: just out of sight. Her bloodied feet burning as though she walked through fire, Mel rushed after and got a clear shot.

She missed twice.

By the coming of a third opportunity, the gun was empty.

When it clicked in her hand, Melba swore, hurled it after her target, and carried on running after her anyway. Daddy sat masturbating in the little sitting room where the Gray Man had been before; Melba glowered at his nasty fat face.

"You ain't my Daddy—you never was, never was the real man. Just another fuckin' clone. I understand it all now."

As she passed a pillar, the duplicate was replaced by its hateful master. The Gray Man sat, face empty, hands tight around the arms of the chair, it beady pinpoint eyes fixed on her as its head turned with her passage.

Mel rushed on, leaping down three stairs and swearing to land on her bloody heels.

Hard to see through eyes that still sometimes burned and a head that swam and the rising voices that had been agitated into a piercing

YOU BITCH

nasty

YOU'RE NOTHING

chorus

DEATH IS IT

that lied

IT'S ALL THERE IS

and tried

THIS PLACE ISN'T REAL

to keep

YOU'RE NOT REAL

Melba

WHEN YOU'RE DEAD

from getting

YOU WON'T EVEN KNOW IT

the axe

YOU MIGHT AS WELL HAVE NEVER LIVED.

from the garage.

Shit was heavy as hell in her hands.

Hadn't expected that somehow.

Out in front of the house, Edie had managed to drop her keys like one of her own dumbass horror movie characters. She was only barely in the vehicle by the time Melba appeared. Hands shaking, mouth contorted in a cry of terror, Edie started her car.

Melba strode right up and swung the axe down into the hood.

That was one sharp motherfucker. It punctured the metal and jerked roughly at her urging, next shattering windshield glass across Edie's pretty face.

Edie's scream was audible outside the running vehicle. Her foot slammed on the gas and the car reversed wildly out of the driveway. It smashed into a tree with a calamitous crunch of metal and glass and wood.

Shrieking, Edie shoved open the door and clambered out a step.

One high heel sank into the dirt and kept her stuck there.

By the time it was out, Melba was at her right with the axe raised high.

The smell of gasoline suffused the air as fuel leaked from the crippled Jaguar. Blood splattered freshly across Melba's face and hands while the starlet fell twitching upon the grass, the axe buried in a new cleft three inches deep into her skull. Harder to get past all that bone than Melba had expected—funny, considering it'd got through the car and windshield—but, all the same, Edie was not long for the world.

Just to be sure, Melba pushed her into the leaking gasoline and dug around for her lighter.

The howl of the Gray Man rattled far and wide, so shocking and fear-inspiring that Melba almost dropped it.

"The third blood has been spilled," Rexie announced.

Melba's heart seized with joy.

"Is that it?"

"That's it, angelbaby. Now come on back upstairs. Let me give you your reward."

Tears filled Melba's eyes. Her heart stung anew. "Is it really time?"

Rexie's voice was warm and tender; solemn, but consoling.

"Yes, angel. It is."

"Oh, Rex—"

Melba hesitated, her lip bitten and her brow furrowed. She didn't even see the body at her feet anymore.

"Rexie…I'm afraid."

"It's natural to be afraid, Melba…but you know there ain't nothin to really be afraid of. Trust me."

"I do." Gasping sharply, nodding through her tears, Melba looked down at the corpse again.

"Yes, Rex. I do."

She lit the gasoline-soaked foliage around Edie O'Keefe, catching the starlet's blouse to be extra-sure. Then, stepping back and leaving her lighter there with the flames, she listened.

No cops yet. Ain't a surprise. Lake of the Woods was secluded. Going fast as they could, it'd still be at least seven, eight minutes before the cops made it to the resort; probably another five to ten before they figured out exactly which house was Rex Virgil's.

Well…maybe not that long.

The fire crackled behind her as, light and free as she'd ever felt, Melba ascended the stairs to Rex's room.

It did not even occur to her until about halfway up that the voices had fallen silent.

Would they be back? Would they ever be back?

"No, baby. They ain't never gonna be back."

The sitting room was empty. No Gray Man; no clones. Melba paused to admire the empty chair, a hand covering her mouth as it emitted a happy cry. Her fist pressed to her heart.

"Thank you, Rexie. Oh, Jesus, thank you—"

"I always promised I'd cure you, sugar. Come on up, now. Let's heal the rest of you."

A half a skip in her step, Melba hurried up to Rexie's room. She found her cousin weeping with him in her arms.

"Oh, Becky June!"

"I'm scared he ain't gonna make it, Mel."

Junie turned tearful eyes up to Melba, her breath hitching with her little sobs. Mel tutted and hurried over, relieved and sad to see her cousin.

And happy.

So, so happy.

"Sure, he'll make it! Put him down."

While Junie obeyed, Melba stooped beside Rexie to stroke his face.

"Here I am, Rex…just like you wanted. It's all done. When do we go?"

Rex looked at her as though uncomprehending, his mouth opened to allow only the smallest gasps of air he required. Each breath he did take still seemed to pump a surprising amount of blood from the bullet wound in his stomach.

"How about you tell Junie good-bye," Rex suggested kindly, his tone warm and gentle.

The love-pain of parting again. He was right; this was their only chance.

Reluctantly, Mel nodded.

She lowered her lover from her embrace and studied him, unable to face June just yet.

"Okay. Okay, uh—"

Her throat tightened sharply, her breath hitching.

Jesus, hell. This really *was* it, wasn't it? Oh, Christ. Melba had never been so happy and so sad all at the same time. This was how it must have felt running off to Vegas. So exciting but so jarring. So happy but so devastating in all the finality.

"You don't have to come with me, angelbaby," cautioned Rexie, adding, "but—"

"Yes I do," whispered Mel. "Yes I do, Rex. I'm the real me, and I'm comin' with you no matter what it takes. Junie—"

Melba's lips trembled. Tears overflowing her reddened eyes, she stumbled up and wrapped her arms around her shocked cousin. Junie produced a little sob of her own.

"Melba, oh! Melba, it's okay—"

"Yes, June, it is. It *is* okay."

Lips trembling, Melba leaned back and caught her cousin's face in her hands.

"Becky June," she said, "I love you. I love you like Gemini, like Castor and Pollux, love each other. You remember that story, right? I think I told you when I's doin' your horoscope that time."

Junie shook her head: not to indicate that she didn't know but to reject the inevitability.

"We can't always be together," whispered Melba, because the only alternative to a whisper would have been some very unbecoming, very childish sobs. "We can't. And that's—that's just the way it is. But you know what? That ain't so bad. I hold you back, Junie."

"No! Melba—"

"It's true, June. If you can't look around this room and think that, you're lyin' to yourself."

Despite herself, Junie laughed a little.

Melba laughed, too; smiled, at least.

Were those sirens in the distance? Real cops this time, or more clones of the Gray Man? Shit, oh, she was so worried about Junie, but, well—like she'd just said. They couldn't always be together. Junie couldn't always protect Melba, and Melba couldn't always be there to help June.

But…she did look forward to the day they could be together again.

"You'll do just great without me," Mel swore, releasing her cousin. "You'll do just great, whatever it is you end up doin', and you'll have yourself a family. A nice partner, and kids. And you'll be so happy that you'll hardly remember me."

"I'll always think about you, Melba, but—"

"No. Junie—accept it."

June fell silent, her lips pursed. She glanced over her shoulder, toward the great window that displayed only their reflections but also allowed those sirens to grow louder all the time.

"I got to go," Melba said earnestly. "And someday, you'll need to leave, too. And—and when you do, Becky June, you'll see all the things I been tellin' you today. You'll see why I did this. We'll be together. You and me, our family, your kitty cat—everybody's gonna be all together again someday, Becky June."

June's brow had furrowed all the more deeply, her eyes searching.

"But—my kitty ain't dead, Mel. He just ran off."

Ah, hell.

Well…shit.

No point dying with a lie on her soul.

"No, Junie," said Melba with a hefty sigh of genuine shame and a glance from her cousin's face. "No. He's dead."

The sirens grew.

"How do you know that?"

Mel sucked a tooth at her cousin's sheet-white face.

Typical June…always was the sort who could watch a movie where fifty folks died, but would burst into tears as soon as the dog was killed. What a soft heart.

"Because I did it, Junie. I killed your cat. Okay?"

"Wh—wh—why would you—"

"He was al*ready* dyin', June."

Her pupils tiny pinpoints that shimmered with her tears, June searched for any trace of a lie in Melba's face.

"What do you mean?"

"I took him to the vet a couple times when you were at work on accounta he stopped eating. You remember?"

"Yes, but it was just because we ran outta his normal food, and tried that other kind, and—"

"And you remember the way his leg always used to tremble? And how he'd chew up all the paper he could get his little paws on?"

Junie sobbed as she hadn't all night, recoiling from Melba, her hands flying over her mouth.

Sighing in pity, Mel shook her head.

"It was liver failure. All his life he'd had some kinda liver disease and—what the hell, you really gonna make a cat go through dialysis? So"—with a reflexive glance to the window and the growing fire that marked Edie's corpse—"one day, I took him out to the woods in a nice peaceful spot. I made sure it was real quick, and that he had the sun on his face, and that he never knew. He was happy."

"Why didn't you tell me? Why didn't you let me take him to the vet and have him—oh, he needed to be put down! He needed me with him—"

"Look at yourself, Becky June! It would have devastated you. Clearly it *does*. I am sorry to tell you this now but, hell… maybe, with everything else from tonight, it'll get lost in the mix."

"But why didn't *you* just take him to the vet, Melba?"

"Because—because."

Melba's breath hitched. The sirens were in the resort now, albeit on the other side.

"Because," she admitted, "gettin' put down on some metal table with a needle ain't no fuckin' way to go. It ain't right."

Melba looked very seriously at June.

"If I had to choose how I wanted to go, and my choice was

between dyin' on a table or alone in a cell, or dyin' someplace I liked by the handa somebody I loved, I think the choice is pretty damn easy."

June shut her eyes, tears still streaming, her shoulders shaking.

"I love you, Becky June."

"I love you, Melba," Junie hiccupped violently through all her many tears.

Tires skidded before the gate of Rexie's property.

"I'm sorry about your kitty," Melba told her. "And I can't wait to see you again."

At last, she turned from her cousin. While officers outside struggled to open the gate around the property and, given the flames, quickly gave up to await the tailing firefighters, Melba slid her arms around Rex and hummed at his noise of pain.

"That's it, baby," said Melba. "I'm ready for our honeymoon."

"Have I ever told you that you're a crazy bitch," whispered Rexie in his city voice, the words small and wet with blood.

Melba laughed a little, a kind of twinkle in her eye.

Behind her, Becky June picked something up from the floor.

"Once or twice tonight, but rest assured you would not be the first."

There was so much more she wanted to ask—more she wanted to know while the fitter cops, having gotten over the fence, kicked in the front door. She even opened her mouth to speak.

Then June's hand was in her hair, tight against her scalp, jerking her head up and back to ease the slice of the knife.

Blood poured out of Melba's neck, rushing after the blade to splatter across Rex's face.

Shocked, she raised a hand to the hot surge. Panic overwhelmed her body, her heart thudding in her ears as though to hasten her bleeding.

Was this what was supposed to happen? That was what she wanted to ask, but the only sound that came from her lips was the same bubbling hiss that wheezed from the gushing wound.

Melba collapsed atop Rex, fear and sorrow in her heart.

Junie dropped the knife with a sharp cry.

Cops burst into the room.

All the fleeing blood pulled Melba's heavy eyelids down.

Rex's body was so warm.

EPILOGUE

BECKY JUNE DANIELS checked the address of the hotel one last time. There it was, plain as day on her phone; and there it was when she looked up through the taxi, towering at the end of the block.

"Do I know you from somewhere? A movie or something?"

"No," said June to the taxi driver who, with the destination close, could no longer resist his curiosity. "No, I ain't been in a movie. I'm going to do a documentary interview today, though."

"Oh, really! I love documentaries. What is it, true crime?"

June glanced a little quickly at the eyes in the rearview.

"Lucky guess," crowed the driver, grinning in a well-meaning way. The light turned green. He pulled through. "My wife got me hooked on 'em, those true crime documentary shows. Podcasts, too! Are you some kinda expert? A psychologist, maybe?"

"Uh—no."

The eyes, once set upon the road, lifted to her reflection again.

They narrowed.

They widened.

The driver leaned back in his seat a little bit, silent.

June looked out the window and wanted to be home. Tina had been right. This was probably a mistake.

Why had she accepted the invitation to do this? Junie had sat down and done the math only after she agreed. Fifteen years. It had really been fifteen years? Yes; somehow. It had been there in black and white.

Seemed like longer and shorter all at once. Like it was just yesterday. The night, the arrest, the trial that never happened.

Junie had one person to thank for that.

The taxi pulled up along the curb and June swiped her card in the payment processor affixed to the back of the passenger's' seat.

"Hey, uh, Miss—I didn't mean to offend you."

"You didn't," she told him, electing to leave a fifteen-dollar tip for the twenty-minute ride from the airport. "Do you have something I could sign for you and your wife?"

Had to make something good come out of her infamy, after all.

It was a weird kind of fame, but a manageable kind. She couldn't imagine a more all-encompassing kind of fame. The kind of fame Mr. Virgil experienced. That was the kind of fame that made you have to hide.

Not that a fella like him could hide, as such. Even in a pair of sunglasses, she recognized him at the hotel bar and cringed.

This was the possibility that she had most wanted to avoid. Even seeing him in person was too much to endure. She turned her eyes away from the bar as she passed the doorway to it and hurried to the check-in line at the front desk, but only one clerk was working and two people were still ahead of her.

Sighing, June looked at her phone. She sent Tina a text message that she'd made it to the hotel. She asked to send her love to their daughter. She thought about adding something about the cat, but Tina was always complaining that June treated the cat too much like a second child, so she resisted.

She closed the text message app and stared at the generic flower background of her phone. That immense sadness that so often swept down once more veiled her soul.

The air to her right elbow felt so cold and empty that she did not see so much as sense when it was filled by a human body.

"Hey."

Anxiety grabbed hold of her spine and used it to turn her insides upside-down.

After lowering her phone, June looked into Rex Virgil's face, briefly acknowledged the security guard monitoring the scene from the other side of the lobby, then forced herself to address the celebrity.

"Mr. Virgil," she intoned softly, nonetheless drawing a glance from the only person between her and the desk. While that person turned away and whispered something to their partner, June realized Rex offered his hand. She took it.

She didn't say anything else, because she didn't know what to say.

"You're looking well," he told her with genuine warmth, lifting his hand away to remove his sunglasses. When he shifted back, she realized he leaned against an old-fashioned walking cane braced in his other hand. It made her very sad.

"I don't think I've seen you since the motion to dismiss," he continued.

Despite herself, June laughed in a hitching way. She looked down at her shoes. "Well, sir, I do not imagine our paths have all that many opportunities to cross in life. You got a real different existence from me."

"That may be true, but we're bound together forever now, in a way—excuse me—"

The people ahead of her had at last decided who between them was going to approach Rex first. Now Junie had to wait for him to shake hands and take pictures and sign something for a couple that was simply overflowing with excitement. At the very least, it gave her the chance to go ahead of them in line.

Midway through her check-in, right as they were asking her for a card to cover room service or restaurant visits not footed by the documentary producers, Rex appeared with an Amex that charged Junie interest just for looking.

"Let me take care of it for her. Here."

"Oh, Mr. Virgil, please, you don't have to do that—"

"No, it's okay. I want to. Like I was saying…I'm just surprised I haven't seen you at one of these before."

"I've never *done* one of these before. I'm very nervous."

"Ah, no reason to be. It's just questions. I always like talking about myself, personally."

"I don't."

With half a chuckle on his lips, Rex accepted his card back and signed off on a digital pad. "I suppose I can almost understand that. It's not as bad as you're thinking, though. They've got a nice room for it, and they'll make sure to feed you. This company's a good one."

"I suppose that's good to know— Thank you." With a brisk, fading smile for the clerk, Junie accepted her plastic keycard and slid it into her wallet. Her hand dropped to her small rolling suitcase. "And thank *you*, Rex."

"Think nothing of it. Are you talking to them today?"

She shook her head. "Tomorrow."

"Aha, I see." They edged away from the desk, the security officer's eyes on them all the while. "Then you've got a good long night of tossing and turning ahead of you, probably… well, try not to worry about it. I'm sure you'll do great."

When he smiled, she became more aware of the alteration

made to his nose's aquiline shape. His leg, his nose. She'd even heard something about a piece of some internal organ he'd had to have removed in surgery. No wonder he looked so much thinner now, too. Oh—

"Hey! June, hell—"

"I'm sorry."

June threw her hand over her tearful eyes, her lips contorting in an abrupt dissolution to sobs.

Tutting, Rex put a hand on her shoulder and led her blindly to the sitting area in the lobby. He pushed a tissue from the coffee table into her unready hand. More people stared than just the security officer.

"Hey, June—it's really okay."

Her head shook, her voice straining to keep quiet. "No, it's not. Just looking at you, I can't—I can't—I'm so sorry. I'm so sorry. I wish I had done so much different that night."

"If you had, she would have killed you, too."

Nodding, Junie squeezed her eyes shut. "That's what my therapists tell me, too."

"Probably doesn't make it much better," Rex allotted.

She said nothing.

Virgil took her hand in his. The guilt his kindness caused her was palpable; as physical as a tumor, or an open wound. She still did not think he was a very good person, but his capacity for forgiveness was a shining virtue that made her ashamed to be alive.

"We both did what we had to do, June."

Still mute, June nodded. She pressed the ratty tissue against her wet face and, releasing Rex's hand, leaned forward for another one.

"Do you still think about it?"

"Yeah."

His answer was one word that contained multitudes of information. June nodded, slumping back in her armchair with her fist tight against her mouth.

"I think about it all the time. Not as much as I used to but, oh, probably still once or twice a week, at least. On a good week. Sometimes there are still weeks where it comes after me every day. Sometimes— I don't know. I don't know."

Clearing her throat and gasping for a ragged breath of air, June said, "I'm so grateful to you, Mr. Virgil."

"You don't need to call me that."

"Yes, sir, I do. You saved my life. You coulda sent me to the big house as easy as snapping your fingers…but you didn't."

"What difference would it have made?"

"I guess that's true."

"You know, June…"

He leaned forward in his seat, his hands folded between the splayed knees upon which his elbows rested.

"I like to think I'm a different man than I was before Lake of the Woods." His focus fell from her and one hand lifted to rub his jaw. "I *know* I am," he added. "Gray hairs and more movies and the passage of time all aside, when something like that happens, you're always wondering. Always asking yourself, "Who would I be if that hadn't happened to me?" But…I don't have to tell you that. I did a movie about six years ago—I don't know if you saw it—"

"I don't watch a lot of movies these days, sir."

He smiled a little, like he was glad to hear it for some reason, then went on.

"Well, anyway. I had to play a detective. I got an Oscar for it, Best Actor. My first-ever Oscar. And I believe that performance was as raw, as moving as it was to the Academy voters, because of my experience. The trauma. It came *through* me. My detective was traumatized just like me; dedicated to using his trauma to fuel him in his work, just like me. People talk to me about that movie all the time, and I get the sense that it's going to be one of the big roles I'm remembered for— one of the ones they'll put in the clip show when I'm dead. And I think of all the young actors, directors, writers who are experiencing—and *will* experience—that performance in perpetuity, until the movie is so lost it's not even a memory. And I wonder, in that time, how many more pieces of art it will inspire. How many *people* it will inspire. You know? Sometimes—sometimes, I just sit there and I think, "My God. I don't think I would even have gotten that job if I hadn't been through that night, and now look at all that it's given me.""

June had stopped crying somewhere along the line. Now she just listened, and listened so intently that, when he came to a stop, she had not come up with anything to say.

Rex said it for her.

"If there is one thing that night, that senselessly evil night, taught me, it's that God is complicated. Creation, and the way we emulate it with our little creations…it's complicated. There's not just black and white. There's black and white and brown and yellow, and aquamarine. And red.

"I don't know if evil really exists outside a subjective modality, but I do know one thing. It's not an emptiness, June. That night was not empty for me; what I took from it, pain aside, was not empty for me. God was there in the blood and the fear and the death just like He's been in the world for me every day since. And…it's impossible to say if I never would have felt that way without that night, but that's still what it gave to me. And that's more valuable than feeling stable, or safe, or pure, I think."

Now it was his turn to look a little sad. Very sad. His eyes focused far away, off into the annals of time.

Moved, June extended a hand. Rex took it.

Somehow, it was like touching Melba.

He cleared his throat.

"I won't keep you, since I'm sure you're eager to check in…but you should send me an e-mail sometime, when you can." Rex dug a pen out of his pocket and found a small appointment book in the same. "I'd love to hear how you're doing these days."

"All right."

He smiled as he jotted his e-mail. June smiled too, following the bobbing of his pen.

Her eye fell from his pen to the tattoo that adorned his forearm, just visible beneath his jacket.

A circle with a number in it. A planet, an atom, Malkuth on the Tree of Life all together at once.

Branches, orbitals, that disappeared up into his jacket sleeve.

Rex tore the page from the appointment book and passed his e-mail to June with a soft smile.

"You really will write?"

"I promise," she said, meaning it more now. "I'll write when I'm back home."

"That's good! Maybe we could do Christmas or something. It'd be nice to have you over."

Stretching his leg and fetching up his cane as he rose, Rex slid his sunglasses on and reached for June's hand one more time.

"Try to have fun with the documentary, Junie. Don't sweat it. I promise, it'll be easy. They seemed like nice people."

His cane tapping with his steps, Rex released June and made his way to the security guard.

The guard said something into his earpiece.

June looked down at the e-mail address while her phone buzzed with Tina's reply.

MELBA WAS SHOCKED to find herself alive.

The room looked nice. Nobody was around, and it took her a few seconds to realize she was on the bed that should have contained Candy's body. A song was finishing up somewhere: "Smoke Gets in Your Eyes," by the Platters.

"Rexie?"

"In here, angelbaby."

Amazing! Not a stick of furniture was out of place. The blood-soaked sheets had been completely replaced, neat as any she'd ever seen in a hotel. Had they been ironed? Hot damn. And the carpet—no broken glass, no corpses.

No Junie, neither.

Sniffing lightly, Mel stood up and marveled. There was her reflection, red hoodie and short-shorts and the same old Melba she saw all the time.

And she looked just as fine as the room.

Laughing, touching her face and her brow and her head, Melba hurried across the floor only to stop short in the bathroom doorway.

There he was, humming with the song, making one last shaving stroke of the razor along his jaw.

His name was a soft gasp on her lips.

"You ain't gotta be shy, angel, everybody's gone now—oof!"

He laughed, staggered back a step by the force with which she threw her arms around his neck.

All she did was hug him, at first: press herself against him as though she hoped to climb right into him.

When she raised her face from his wonderful-smelling chest, he smiled at her.

He bent to kiss her.

She gasped, opening herself to him fully, his every kiss better than any earthly sex. "Cum On Feel The Noize" started up and she turned her face away only long enough to scream, "I love this song! I love you, Rex Virgil! Oh, Christ!"

"Melba, Melba, Melba Daniels, fuck, angel, oh, hell, I love you so goddamn much—"

They didn't even try to make it to the bedroom. It was too animal, too passionate. He fucked her with an enthusiasm far surpassing that which he'd shown on earth the first time, when she was too young for him and he thought he was just some movie star.

After, they lay in the bathtub just like she'd dreamed, a stew of hot water and semen enveloping their bodies.

"I'm kinda surprised you ain't cried yet, sugar."

"I done enough cryin' while tellin' Juniee good-bye," she said, her throat tensing a little at the memory. "Ain't needta do more here when I'm with you. I want to be happy with you."

"Well, I'm sure happy here with you. This is already workin' out to be one fine honeymoon."

"Are we already married?"

To answer her own question, she looked down at her left hand and laughed.

"Hell! I ain't even noticed." Mel lifted her hand toward

the light. Her new ring gleamed brilliant gold while her heart thudded in her chest. "I feel like I'm in a fairy tale."

"You are, baby. You sure are. And I'm your one and only Prince Charming."

She laughed, her head rocking back against his chest. "That, you are…I just sorta wish you'd helped me get outta there sooner."

"You weren't ready. The Gray Man wanted you too bad. For most real people, there's only a few windows in their lives where I can save 'em. Sometimes, well…sometimes, folks let all those windows close, and I come to understand they were always the Gray Man's. And I gotta accept that. But you, angel!"

He pushed her hair back from her forehead and smiled down into her face, kissing her brow and the temple and the cheekbone down beneath.

"I knew you would do it. I knew you would trust me."

"Ain't like I ever had a choice to the contrary. Oh, Rex!"

Mel's brow furrowed. Shit, damn, he was right. She was fixinta cry.

"What's the matter, Melba?"

"Just—hell."

She laughed and wiped her thumb along the lid of her eye.

"I guess I just wish my life hadn't been so, uh, 'fraught,' as Junie says when she ain't wanna say the word 'depressin'.' I mean, you and she were the best parts of it…and only *she* consciously knew that at the time."

"Well, now, I had my own journey. A man's gotta go through a hell of a lot to get to where I am…and not all my lives have been all that happy, neither."

"Lives other than Rex Virgil?"

"Yes, ma'am."

Melba sniffed sort of pathetically and rinsed her nose with a pinch of her watery hand.

"What's your real name, Rexie?"

"Logos."

"Your *real* real name," I mean.

He laughed a little. His smiling mouth pressed to her ear and he said it there, the universe expanding from his mouth in a vast breath that contained all time before Melba was born and everything after her departure from the earth and all the stuff that had happened in between, on her side of the world and the other side and the top and the bottom, through the eyes of every conscious man, woman, and child. Her body rippled out of this orgasm of real-ization and she moaned, leaning back against his chest.

"That's some name, baby."

"Don't try to pronounce it all at once, now."

Melba laughed a little, grinning to herself, then turned her pondering eyes up at him.

"Is your real face as handsome as this one?"

"Oh, it's beautiful."

"Can I see?"

Still smiling, Rex lifted his head to gaze into her eyes.

"How about," he said, "we enjoy our honeymoon awhiles, first?

Fine by her. It was everything she dreamed about. Indulgent and wonderful and rich. They made love in every room of the house and got high on every dug you could name—and even at her absolute highest, Melba never (not once!) ever saw the Gray Man. She never even really thought about Daddy, either, except once or twice, and through a new lens of pity. No voices assailed her to say she was worthless and ought to kill herself (though maybe that was only because she was already dead). No cursed text messages came in. No centipedes appeared in her purse. She never had the least compulsion to check a doorknob or mess around with lights.

She was free.

It was better than she had ever dreamed. The peace! The absolute thrill of having her mind under her own control, and *only* under her own control. Not even Rexie was in it now, although she assumed he still knew her every thought and impression. Still, he respected her boundaries enough that he never brought it up, and never got jealous when they'd watch a movie together and she'd think to herself that, say, a certain actor was cute. She would notice, though, that the next time they went to the store, the clerk had a way of looking an awful lot like that former co-star of Rexie's.

It was the ultimate vacation. Every care slipped up and away, and the structure of her mind changed in a way she could feel. Mel had read about things like neural pathways. They could be ground into the mind in such a rut that it was physically hard to change a way of thinking, a lifestyle habit, after a certain point of practice.

But, in that wonderful honeymoon with Rex, she was liberated. She was not served by any rigidity of thinking. She let all her beliefs go.

Eventually they left Lake of the Woods, because he knew she wanted to see some places in the world like France and Japan and Israel. Everywhere they went, he showed her a good time. Nobody ever recognized him, but everyone was always very friendly and polite, and Melba frequently noticed when they paid the bill that the waiter had forgotten to include an item or two. Always gave her a little kick to feel like she got something for free, whether or not she deserved or needed it.

These travels continued awhile. How long precisely, Melba did not know. Time was a funny thing when you were in Eternity. All she knew was that, when they went back to the States, Junie had settled into a house just down the path from Rexie's. Lake of the Woods held a new life and oh, Junie sure did cry. Melba too, maybe. She couldn't remember because Junie's crying stole the show. It was so funny, so ridiculous to cry in that place.

There were other people she'd missed, too. Their grandmother, for one, and lots of Melba's nicer teachers, and the tattoo artist, and even her parole officer. Not Daddy, thankfully; though it made Melba glad to know that, somewhere, even he had a happy spot if he earned it in some iteration that was truly his own.

And life was good for everyone. It climbed to a height of goodness that made Melba's body feel like it was going to burst when she thought about it—until, one morning, Rexie put down his newspaper and looked out the window.

"Shoosh! What a glorious day outside. You wanna go out on the lake with me, baby?"

Hell yeah, she did. Rexie got out the rowboat and, while Mel leaned back in comfort, he worked the oars in perfect sync.

Slowly, the shore drew away from them.

"You know, Melba…I sure am glad I married you."

"Shucks, baby, I'll blush."

"I mean it! You're a great woman. Carefree, funny, creative—and you love *me*, which, if I may say so, is among your highest virtues."

Laughing, Melba splashed him. He laughed and splashed her back, then quit rowing.

Hands folding, Rex looked at her with a kind of mystified fondness. His eye twinkled as if with a tear.

"Are you happy?"

"Happier than I ever been."

"I'm so glad."

"Except—"

He waited. She ground her teeth into her underlip before sitting up.

"Can I see it, please? Your real face. I—I love you so much, Rex. I know that you're as beautiful as you say you are under there, but…I want to see it for myself. To experience you. All of you."

Her hand slid into his. He tightened his grip on her, their rings connecting.

"You sure you want to?"

She nodded.

"You know what it means, right, sugar?"

"Ain't like I'll mind."

He laughed a little and glanced down at himself.

"I reckon that's true…ah, Mel. Melba—I really love you, you know."

He looked back up at her. His smile remained, but his eyes grew a little sad.

"I'm sorry, too. About your life not bein' as gilded a path as, say, mine. But…I hope this all made up for it, even just a little."

Shaking her head, Melba shifted along the boat to sit properly beside Rex.

"You ain't got nothin' to make up for, and you know it. Everythin's the way it hasta be. I know that."

Smiling slightly, Rex turned.

His hand pressed to her cheek as he kissed her.

When he lifted his head away, it was different.

SHE SAW HIM.
ECSTASY FILLED
MELBA'S SOUL,
THE ECSTASY FELT BY
THE IGNITED WICK
OF A CANDLE MADE TO BURN.
THE BOAT ROCKED BENEATH THEM.
MELBA THREW HER ARMS AROUND HIM
AND KISSED HIS REAL FACE.
TEARS STREAMED DOWN HER CHEEKS.
THE SUN ABOVE
BURNED BLACK
AND THEY ALL LIVED
HAPPILY EVER AFTER.
AND THEY ALL LIVED HAPPILY
AND THEY ALL LIVED
AND THEY ALL
AND THEY
AND THE
AND
THE
END

ABOUT THE AUTHOR

Regina Watts is the penname of M. F. Sullivan, founder and flagship author of Painted Blind Publishing. From her cozy home a few universes away from this one, Watts transmits Sullivan stories that are then transcribed and published. Her available titles range from transgressive erotica to psychedelic fiction to horror to romance. Be sure to sign up for her mailing list at hrhdegenetrix.com!

ABOUT THE PUBLISHER

Painted Blind Publishing and its erotic imprint, Painted Blue Publishing, are the brainchild of author and devoted editor to Regina Watts, M. F. Sullivan. Founded in 2015 while Sullivan resided in Tucson, PBP is a house dedicated to bringing readers the finest in consciousness-expanding fiction. Be sure to check out the wide variety of essays available for free at paintedblindpublishing.com to learn more about the company, Watts, and Sullivan.